The Eviction of Hope

a 509 Crime Anthology

Edited by Colin Conway

The Eviction of Hope: a 509 Crime Anthology

Cover Design by Zach McCain

ISBN: 978-1-7368543-2-7

Original Ink Press, an imprint of High Speed Creative, LLC
1521 N. Argonne Road, #C-205
Spokane Valley, WA 99212

Table of Contents

What is the 509?

Separated by the Cascade Range, Washington State is divided into two distinctly different climates and cultures.

The western side of the Cascades is home to Seattle, its 34 inches of annual rainfall, and the incredibly weird and smelly Gum Wall. Most of the state's wealth and political power are concentrated in and around this enormous city. The residents of this area know the prosperity that has come from being the home of Microsoft, Amazon, Boeing, and Starbucks.

To the east of the Cascade Mountains lies nearly two-thirds of the entire state, a lot of which is used for agriculture. Washington State leads the nation in producing apples, it is the second-largest potato grower, and it's the fourth for providing wheat.

This eastern part of the state can enjoy more than 170 days of sunshine each year, which is important when there are more than 200 lakes nearby. However, the beautiful summers are offset by harsh winters, with average snowfall reaching 47 inches and the average high hovering around 37°.

While five telephone area codes provide service to the westside, only 509 covers everything east of the Cascades, a staggering twenty-one counties.

Of these, Spokane County is the largest with an estimated population of 506,000.

You will never find
a more wretched hive
of scum and villainy.

- Obi-Wan Kenobi

Introduction

Most readers of crime fiction anthologies skip over the introduction to get to the good stuff. Who can blame them? Not when there is mystery, mayhem, and murder in the pages that follow. Heck, even if it were only general mopery that followed, most would still gleefully jump over the introduction.

But not you.

You, my friend, are a smart one. And for that, I'm about to reward you with an insider's tale that will make reading this anthology even more enjoyable.

But first, I need to tell you about the Hope.

The Hope

Years ago, I wrote a short story titled "Foolproof" that appeared in a local anthology, *A Dead Night in Spokane*. As part of my tale's tapestry, my protagonist faced eviction from his apartment building due to a planned redevelopment. That building was the Hope Apartments.

I liked that story but loved the idea of the Hope as a hotbed of criminal activity. It was based on the Otis, a single-room-occupancy hotel built in the early twentieth century converted to low-income, non-subsidized housing. Only a few rooms on each floor had private bathrooms. The rest shared a restroom down the hallway.

As a police officer, I visited the Otis several times. It was not a pleasant place to go, and it seemed a tough place to live. When the building was sold shortly before the Great Recession, it was primed for redevelopment. Unfortunately, it sat vacant for more than a decade. I once toured the building in that empty and dilapidated state. It was an odd (and slightly scary) feeling to prowl those once-bustling corridors with nothing more protective than a flashlight. At that moment, I missed my gun and police radio.

The 509 Crime Stories is set in Eastern Washington. As that series has grown, I've kept coming back to the idea of the Hope. I wanted to do something meaningful with it. An occasional passing reference in one of my novels or short stories never felt enough.

The Hope was bigger than that. It wanted to stand by itself.

Then an idea hit me.

The Invitation

My perspective is skewed. That doesn't take much introspection to understand since we all have biased viewpoints. It makes us individuals, and that's okay. We need to embrace who we are so we can accept the differences of others.

I've spent most of my adult life in Eastern Washington. I try hard to see the world through the eyes of others, but it's still a view I can only see through my own lens.

The proximity of so many together in the Hope made me think of people coming from outside the region. There had to be some living there who viewed the world radically different than their next-door neighbor. For a fleeting moment, I considered writing a book of short stories all told from various viewpoints. Then I realized there would be a better, more fun way to accomplish that goal. I would ask other authors to tell the stories of Hope residents.

Of course, the whole thing seemed an excellent excuse to have some of my friends come and visit my fictional playground of the 509. I invited several, and they jumped immediately. Many had participated in themed anthologies before and got what I was after. When these friends introduced me to other friends, I suddenly had a full slate of contributors.

However, there was one author who was a bit mercenary with his demands.

The Insider Tale I Promised

There was an author I desperately wanted to be part of this anthology—I won't name names.

I'd met him at a writer conference, and we enjoyed a beer together. The guy is one of the best storytellers I've had the pleasure to meet. He also had a unique life history that would bring a certain validity to the Hope.

However, he also carried a strange appreciation for Taylor Swift.

This author—I mentioned him being a mercenary type, didn't I? Well, he listened to my anthology pitch then said he would participate if I did one thing.

"What's the thing?" I asked.

"Say Taylor is better than Britney."

You see, somewhere along the line, I made the ill-advised comment that I liked Ms. Spears better than his favorite and he wouldn't let me live it down.

Did I *want* to say the Holy Spearit was less than Tay-Tay? No. Not at all. But an editor must occasionally do an awful thing to appease the artists he works with. So, I said, "Taylor Swift is better than Britney Spears."

Now, I'm not going to name names, but I'm glad I did it. You see, this unnamed author brought along his writing partner, Tom Pitts, and contributed one heck of a great story.

Am I sorry I threw Britney under the bus for the greater good of the anthology? Yes, for sure. But in her defense, I offer this vital insight—while those two might be the peanut butter and jelly of crime fiction, I got to write the final story in this anthology.

And that's your reward for reading this introduction. You're an insider now.

Enjoy the book!

Colin Conway
May 2021
Spokane, Washington

The Eviction of Hope

a 509 Crime Anthology

Just to Watch Him Die

Holly West

I didn't kill my husband. That's what I keep telling myself, anyway. Despite everything, I still loved him.

Mind you, I'm not a suspect. The official cause of death, according to the Spokane County Medical Examiner, was drowning, a probable suicide. David Severance jumped—or fell—into the Spokane River.

Assuming he jumped, he didn't leave a note, so the precise reasons for his choice were known only to him. Some people probably believe our breakup had something to do with it, but I can't—I won't—let myself go there. If I'd had any indication he was suicidal, I would've done something to stop him. I was clueless about this and so many other things.

A week after I learned about his death, I arrived at the Hope Apartments, where he'd been living since I kicked him out of my house. Stepping into the building's lobby, I was reminded of an old fleabag hotel, the sort that charged by the hour and cost two dollars extra for a set of sheets. As I waited for the elevator, I read a notice posted nearby: The property was being redeveloped into a hotel, and all residents had to move out by October 31, less than thirty days from now. Gentrification, it seemed, had managed to find its way to the Hope.

I was surprised David hadn't mentioned his impending eviction. It would've been a convenient excuse to snake his way back into my life. Another reminder that I'd never really known the man and another clue as to why David killed himself, if, in fact, he did. I didn't quite believe he'd done it, even if the prospect of homelessness would make anybody desperate.

The elevator was too slow, so I opted for the stairs instead. The morgue attendant had given me a bag of David's belongings after I identified his water-logged body, which included a ring of several keys. I cycled through a few before I found the one that opened the apartment door. Flipping the light switch, I got my first glimpse at David's living conditions these last three months.

The building might be called the Hope, but this room, stinking of stale cigarettes and mildew, was closer to hopelessness than I'd imagined. To the right of the door was a small kitchen consisting of a shelf, a cabinet with a sink, a two-burner stove, and a mini-fridge. There were two empty liter-sized bottles of vodka in the sink, which puzzled me. David did like his booze, but this seemed excessive, even for him. The rest of the room was furnished with items that looked like they'd been found curbside next to trash bins, and the bed was made with linen I recognized from my own closet.

I went to the window at the far end of the room and pulled the cord on the vertical blinds to let in more light. Opening the door to what I assumed was the bathroom, I found a closet. The apartment didn't seem to have a bathroom at all.

David was a sharp dresser, and the tiny closet was stuffed full. I ran my hand along his suits, sending a whiff of his cologne into the air. It made me dizzy with memories.

We met at a bar two years ago, shortly after he relocated from Seattle to Spokane, where he told me he was temporarily staying with a friend. He was mid-forties and handsome, with charm to spare. I was fifty-five, but I take good care of myself and wear my age well. We were instantly drawn to each other. A few hours of conversation and a few too many drinks later, I invited him back to my place, and he never left. A few weeks later, I married him on a cloudy afternoon at the courthouse. Last June, I asked him to move out after a year-and-a-half of marriage.

The recollection of our first meeting brought tears to my eyes. I caught sight of myself in the full-length mirror and wiped them away. Even dead, David didn't deserve my tears—he'd hurt me too much. He'd had affairs with at least three women during the time we were together. Meanwhile, I paid off thousands of dollars of his debt, hoping to set a solid foundation for our future. Stupid, thou hast a name, and it is Cheri.

I stood on my tiptoes to reach a suitcase on the top shelf and began to take his clothes off the hangers, working like a robot to empty the closet. I retrieved a couple of garbage bags from the kitchen to hold what remained, then went to work on his bureau. Halfway through the first drawer, I discovered a framed photograph of a somewhat younger David with a frail older woman sitting in a wheelchair, along with a man and woman who appeared to be in their twenties. In the photo, David stood behind the woman's chair with his hands on her shoulders. She'd raised her left hand to meet his, lightly touching it.

Who were these people?

I'd seen a photograph of David's parents—this wasn't his mother. But what stood out the most was her left hand. I could clearly see the ring on her third finger.

It was the same one David had given to me when he proposed.

***

David took the ring with him when he moved out. I had hoped to find it amongst his things, but now, seeing the way he was living, that seemed unlikely. Chances were, he sold it.

I took the picture out of its frame and examined it more closely. Turning it over, I saw that *David, Alice, Shane, Kathy, December 2016* was written on the back. It was taken nearly four years ago.

I opened the browser on my phone and typed in their names: David Severance, Alice, Shane, Kathy. It wasn't much to go on, but the first link that came up was a brief obituary in the *Tacoma News Tribune.* Alice Grundy Severance, age 63, died after a long illness on April 21, 2017. Survivors included her devoted husband, David, her son, Shane Grundy, and his wife, Melissa, and Alice's daughter, Kathleen Grundy Chapin, and her husband, Michael. Three grandchildren were mentioned but not named.

David told me he'd never been married. Watching his parents' marriage deteriorate convinced him he never wanted to walk down the aisle himself. Until he met me, of course.

There'd been men in my life—plenty of them—but I'd never married, either. A male friend once told me he could sense the desperation coming off single women over the age of forty—it was like a smell. I was in my early thirties then, and I laughed, thinking I'd be married long before that. Forty came, then fifty. I was pretty enough, had financial independence, and a lot of friends, but finding a life partner was something that eluded me. When David got down on one knee and held up the ring, a ruby surrounded in diamonds set in white gold, and asked me to marry him, it felt like a miracle.

But apparently, David had a whole other family, including grandchildren. Why had he kept them a secret from me? And had he been in touch with his stepchildren after Alice's death?

I considered knocking on his neighbors' doors, asking if he'd had any visitors while he'd lived in the building, on the offhand chance that one of them might be part of this family. But it was nearing one o'clock, and I had to get to the salon for an appointment. In the lobby, I stopped by the manager's window, where a stick-thin older woman with faded red-blonde hair sat, busy with paperwork. I introduced myself, and she told me her name was Dorothy Givens, the onsite manager.

"We're all so sorry about Mr. Severance's death," she said. She had a slight accent I couldn't identify, comforting and down-home sounding. "And such a terrible way to—" she stopped herself. "Well, that can't be helped now, can it?"

"I saw the eviction notice," I said. "I'll have David's things moved out by next week."

"That's probably for the best. You have until the thirty-first, but I expect there will be a lot of last-minute scrambling by our tenants to get out. The evictions are quite a disruption for most of them, even though they've been given ample notice."

"Did David know about the evictions when he moved in?"

"Yes, ma'am. That's why we required him to sign a month-to-month lease."

Knowing David, he probably expected to find someone else to take advantage of before he was forced to move. "While I've got you, did you happen to notice David with any visitors while he was living here?"

"The police asked me the same question. I'll tell you what I told them: we don't monitor the lobby twenty-four hours a day, and our security cameras are recorded over every two days. I can't possibly keep track of everybody's comings and goings. But I did see Mr. Severance with a woman a few weeks ago, the only visitor I ever noticed."

I took the picture out of my purse and showed it to her. "Is this her?" I said, pointing to the woman I believed to be David's stepdaughter, Kathleen.

Dorothy shook her head. "She was heavier and blonde. About the same age, though."

That old feeling I used to get when I found evidence of David's infidelity rose in my throat. It didn't matter that we were separated or that he was dead. It still hurt.

***

I arrived at my salon, Coiffures by Cheri, a half an hour late for my best friend Renee's appointment. I expected her to be testy about it, but instead, she hugged me. "How are you doing?"

I leaned into her embrace. "I'm okay. Sorry I'm late—I was cleaning out David's apartment."

Renee made a face. The Hope had a reputation. "What's it like in there?"

"Grim. I almost can't believe that's where he ended up."

"Any news?"

I set her up in the chair and caught her up while I applied brown dye to her roots. "He was seeing someone. Some young blonde."

Renee made a face. "And you're the one cleaning out his apartment? Let his new girlfriend do it."

"I'm still his wife. And some of that stuff is mine. He stole my sheets; can you believe it?"

"Oh, I believe it."

"That's not everything. He had a family he never told me about. At least, I think he did. A wife and two stepchildren."

Renee turned so quickly in the chair that my brush slipped, marking her cheek with dye. "You're joking."

Rubbing her skin clean with a towel, I told her about finding the photograph. "Alice died in 2017. Six months before I met David."

"And he never mentioned her?"

"Never," I said. "His stepchildren have children. He was a grandpa. I'm trying to decide if I should let them know he died."

"You know how vain he was about his appearance. He probably didn't want you to know he was old enough to be a grandpa." She got serious. "Honey, I know you loved him, but he was a dirtbag, plain and simple. I don't care if he is dead." She took out her phone. "I'm gonna look them up. What did you say their names were?"

I hesitated. This was probably a mistake. But I was curious about them, too. "The son is named Shane Grundy," I finally said. "He'd be in his late twenties or early thirties, and he's married."

"Here's a phone number. Should I call?"

It was scary how much you could find out about a person in just a few moments on the internet. I set the empty dye bowl on the tray beside me and fiddled with the brush, giving myself a second to think. "All right."

She pressed the numbers and put the phone to her ear. My heart beat faster as I heard the faint ringing sound, then a trio of beeps. She held the phone out and put it on speaker, letting me listen to the end of the message. "… this number is out of service."

"I guess you can't find everything on the internet," I said, mildly relieved.

"There's another number listed for him. Should I try it?"

"No. Maybe this is a sign I should let this be."

"Nonsense. What's the daughter's name?"

"Kathy… no, Kathleen." I re-checked the obituary on my phone. "Her married name is Chapin."

"Got it," Renee said. She ran her index finger along the screen. "Here's one. Kathleen Chapin in Seattle." She dialed the number before I could protest then quickly handed the phone to me.

I had no idea what to say, so I was relieved it went to voicemail. "I don't know if this is the correct number, but I'm looking for Kathleen Chapin. My name is Cheri Severance. David Severance is—was—my husband." I recited my number and asked her to call me.

"What now?" Renee said.

"We wait for her to call back, I guess."

***

The next morning, I stopped by the police station to speak with Andrew Parker, one of the detectives who worked David's case. He led me to his cubicle and invited me to sit in the chair next to his desk. "What did you want to see me about, Mrs. Severance?"

Being in the station made me nervous. And Detective Parker, with his over-confident swagger and watermelon-sized biceps, reminded me of a guy I'd dated once, a bodybuilder with a walnut-sized brain and a penis to match.

"The manager at David's apartment building told me she'd seen him with a woman in the weeks before he died. I was curious if you'd spoken to her."

Detective Parker folded his hands in front of him. "I can assure you we interviewed all pertinent witnesses and examined all the available evidence."

"It just… it came as a surprise to me. Not that he had a girlfriend, but I told you before that David wasn't the type who would kill himself. When the manager told me about the woman, I thought that maybe there was some connection."

"Mrs. Severance, I know it's upsetting to find out your husband had a girlfriend you didn't know about. But you *were* separated—he wasn't exactly cheating. As for his suicide, he was facing the breakup of his marriage, eviction from his apartment, alcoholism—"

"David wasn't an alcoholic."

The detective's voice was gentle. "We found evidence of abuse. Whether it was chronic is difficult to know."

We were getting off track. "Did you speak to this woman?" I asked.

At this, his face showed the first sign of annoyance. "We couldn't locate her."

I felt vindicated. "And did you know he'd been married before? He had a whole other family he never told me about. If he lied about that, who knows what else he lied about? The man had secrets."

"What are you suggesting, Mrs. Severance?"

"I don't know. I just wanted to make sure you were aware of all the factors surrounding his death."

"It's always difficult to accept a loved one's suicide. As painful as it might be, my advice to you is to close this chapter of your life and move on."

I left the police station feeling surly and dissatisfied. Detective Parker clearly hadn't taken my concerns seriously. In his mind, the matter was settled. David had committed suicide.

***

I was halfway to the salon, stopped at a light when my cell phone buzzed. I pressed the hands-free button. "Hello?"

"Cheri Severance?"

"Yes?"

"This is Kathleen Chapin, returning your call."

I pulled my car to the curb at the first available space. "Thank you for getting back to me," I said.

"I wasn't going to call you back. I didn't see the point—my family's relationship with David ended on bad terms, and I haven't heard from him since my mom died."

"I wanted to tell you that David passed away." The silence on Kathleen's end felt interminable. "I'm really sorry," I continued. "I wasn't sure if you'd want to know."

"I'm shocked, is all. He was young—how did it happen?"

"He drowned in the Spokane River. The police suspect suicide."

“Jesus.” She paused. “You’re his wife, right? I’m sorry for your loss.”

“We were separated.” I paused. “Here’s the thing. David never told me about his marriage to your mother. I just found out—there was a photo in his apartment. Until yesterday, I didn’t know you all existed.”

“To him, we probably didn’t. As soon as he got the inheritance money, we never saw him again.”

My stomach twisted at the mention of an inheritance. “How did your mother die?”

“Cancer. David was her home healthcare worker. She married him two months after we hired him, saying she couldn’t afford to wait.”

“How long were they married?”

“Long enough for David to get himself written into her will. Mom’s cancer was in remission when they married. Shortly after the ceremony, she took a downturn and died, which seemed fishy. My brother, Shane, told us he’d checked David’s references, but he didn’t—he assumed everything was above-board. So when we learned David had forged the paperwork, Shane blamed himself. By then, it was too late. Mom was dead, and David walked off with her savings.”

“How much money are we talking?”

Kathleen’s tone turned sour. “I should’ve guessed that’s what you were after. Don’t start buying diamonds yet. It was only about ten thousand, and knowing David, he pissed it away within a couple of months.”

Remembering David’s spending habits, I knew Kathleen was right. “Didn’t you have any legal recourse?”

“The cops wouldn’t touch it. There was nothing suspicious about my mother’s death, I mean, she had cancer. We had no money to cover the legal cost of suing him over the false documents. I was just glad to be free of him, but Shane couldn't let it go."

"Do you think Shane would speak with me? I tried to call him yesterday, but the number I found was disconnected."

"Shane died shortly after my mother did. He shot himself."

The revelation felt like a gut punch. "My God, I'm so sorry."

"Yeah. He left behind a wife and two children. Listen, you sound like a nice woman; you probably didn't deserve any of the crap David laid on you, whatever it might've been. Move on—he was bad news. The world is better off without him."

***

I parked in my usual spot behind the salon and killed the engine, still thinking about my conversation with Kathleen. Her story rang true. David told me he'd worked in healthcare before we met, but he'd injured his back and was waiting for his disability checks to kick in. As far as I knew, he didn't receive any while we were living together, and the one time I asked about it, he said it was delayed due to some kind of mix-up.

Both Kathleen and Detective Parker advised me to forget about David and get on with my life. But I couldn't. Not with so many questions about his death left unanswered.

Maybe I was subconsciously trying to postpone my grief by chasing a crazy theory that some unknown woman had killed my husband or that his dead wife's family wanted to avenge their mother and brother's deaths, but

David was a con man. And he wasn't suicidal. I was more certain of that than ever. He wasn't one to sit around licking his wounds, especially since there were plenty of women—in this case, a curvy young blonde—standing in line to do it for him.

Beyond the lies David told me, the money he'd taken, the women he'd slept with, I now had evidence he'd committed fraud at least once in his life. It was entirely possible he'd swindled others who might want to see him dead.

***

After work, I went home and logged into Facebook on my laptop. David wasn't on social media, but I searched for his name anyway, thinking he might've signed up after we broke up. With no luck there, I typed Kathleen's name in and found her profile. Her security settings prevented me from seeing much, but I was able to access her friends' list. This led me to her brother Shane's page.

The latest visible posts were written in December 2017 by family, friends, and colleagues who eulogized Shane and offered condolences to his wife, Melissa, and his children after his death. He'd killed himself in the days leading up to Christmas, which struck me as a particularly cruel thing to do to his kids. But if the Facebook memorials were to be believed, Shane had been a funny, sweet, well-loved guy and a good father.

Oddly, Melissa Grundy's page was filled with pictures of her posing in different outfits. The clothing was colorful and flattering to her figure, which was rather voluptuous. I realized she was an independent consultant for a multilevel-marketing clothing company. A few of my clients at the salon were sellers for the same company.

Fascinated, I watched a video of Melissa, posted two days earlier, modeling the clothes in different sizes and offering styling tips for each item. As a hairdresser, I couldn't help noticing her hair, which was bleached and heavily damaged. She wasn't unattractive, but she was somewhat unkempt, overblown. Frowzy, my mom would've called her.

I was too busy evaluating her appearance to take note of her jewelry until she reached up to tie a scarf around her neck. "Holy shit," I whispered, hitting pause. It was on her right-hand pinky finger, but there was no mistaking it: Melissa was wearing my engagement ring. The same ring that Alice had worn in the photo.

My racing heart made it difficult to think, but eventually, something clicked. Blonde. Curvy. Melissa was the woman Dorothy, the Hope's manager, saw with David.

***

The drive to Tacoma, where Melissa lived, took less than five hours. After watching her video a few more times, I joined a group dedicated to her business, knowing she wouldn't recognize my last name because I'd never changed it on Facebook. She accepted my request, giving me access to all the group posts, and I saw she was hosting a pop-up sales event at her home the following weekend. With her address now in hand, I got a few hours of restless sleep, packed a bag, and started driving.

The journey gave me plenty of time to contemplate what I'd say when I arrived, but when I pulled up to the curb in front of her neighbor's house at eight o'clock that morning, I was flooded with doubt. What was I doing here? I wasn't ready to believe Melissa had killed David, but I was certain she'd been to the Hope in the days before his death. It was the only way she could've gotten the ring. Whether David had given it to her or she'd stolen it, I couldn't say. But I wanted to know what had transpired between them.

Melissa's door opened, and two middle-school-aged children ran out, apparently late for the school bus. Melissa herself came out, shouting something at them as they raced down the sidewalk. I watched as the bus stopped at the corner and picked them up.

I locked my car and walked toward the house, my pounding heart offering a rhythm for each step. I rang the bell and held my breath. Melissa, wearing a fuzzy pink robe and slippers, opened the door.

"Yes?"

"Melissa?"

"Yes." She blinked rapidly. "How can I help you?"

"I'm Cheri Severance, David's wife. I came because—"

She looked at me with disdain. "I have nothing to say to you."

I said the first thing that entered my mind. "I came because I wanted to tell you that David is dead. He committed suicide. I thought—I thought maybe it would give you some peace."

It wasn't entirely true, but it seemed to soften her up. "Come in," she said.

I sat down on her living room sofa and accepted her offer of coffee. While she was in the kitchen preparing it, I gazed around the room. It was a bland place, filled with matching furniture and cookie-cutter art purchased from a low-priced showroom. The coffee table was cluttered with the evidence of somebody's meal in front of the television set: fork, knife, dirty plate, empty glass.

Melissa returned with two mugs. "It's a mess, I know," she said. "It's always a mess. Being a single mom with two kids doesn't leave much time for cleaning."

"I'm sorry for intruding. I tried to call, but the number I had was disconnected."

"But you found my address?"

"On the internet," I said sheepishly. "Nothing's private anymore."

She nodded, seemingly satisfied, though if it were me, I'd be alarmed that a stranger could find me so easily. She lifted her mug to her lips, and I caught a glimpse of the ring. "That's a beautiful ring."

"It was my mother-in-law's. My husband inherited it when she died."

"I'm sorry for your family's losses. David told me a little bit about Alice and what happened after her death."

Melissa raised an eyebrow. "Did he also tell you that he murdered her then ran away with all of her money? My husband killed himself over that, you know. Shane hired David thinking he'd take care of Alice but instead, he killed her and took everything."

She spoke quietly, but the set of her jaw made her rage obvious. I put my hand over my mouth and shook my head. "I shouldn't have come here."

She slipped a hand into her pocket and pulled out a small gun.

"Jesus," I said, jumping up. "What the—"

"Sit down, Cheri." she said, rising to her feet. I did as I was told. "You're right. You shouldn't have come here."

"Please, I'm no threat to you. Let me leave, and I'll never bother you or your family again."

"It's too late for that. I got a visit from the cops yesterday, asking when I last talked to David. Seems like someone informed them about a few details from his past life, and I'm guessing that someone was you. I didn't kill David if that's what you think."

"I don't think anything. Truly, I don't know why I came here—I saw the ring and—"

"David stole this ring," Melissa said. "I'm not giving it back."

"I don't want it, I swear. I just want to go home and pretend none of this ever happened." It was the truest thing I'd said since I arrived.

The doorbell rang, catching both of us off guard. I recovered more quickly than she did, and I grabbed the knife off the table while she was distracted.

Melissa returned her attention to me, re-aiming the gun. "Don't say a word."

The bell rang again. We held still while we waited for whoever it was to leave. I pressed the knife under my thigh, using the time to calculate my best chance to get away. It was a steak knife and sharp, but no match for a gun-wielding crazy person.

Finally, Melissa said, "Get up."

"Please," I said, slowly standing. I held the knife against my body. "I mean you no harm."

"The harm is already done."

"It's not too late. I'll go to the police and—" I sprang at her, mid-sentence, plunging the knife into her arm as deeply as I could. She screamed, dropping the gun, and by some miracle, I caught it, jumbled it right way around, and pointed it at her forehead.

***

I didn't kill Melissa Grundy. Thankfully, I didn't have to. The threat of the gun was enough to keep her in check while I called 911. The cops who arrived weren't surprised to see who they were dealing with since they'd visited Melissa the day before.

When I returned to Spokane, I learned that my visit with Detective Parker prompted him to do a little more digging on the Grundy family. He sent some Tacoma officers to her home, and she freaked out, thinking she'd be arrested for David's murder, but at that point, they only wanted to ask some questions.

If she'd kept her head and not panicked, Melissa might have gotten away with it. But in the end, she confessed, saying she'd gone to Spokane with every intention of killing David after he'd recently called her to ask for a loan. She plied him with drinks and the promise of cash and sex, then led him to the riverbank and pulled the same gun on him that she'd tried to use on me. During their tussle, he fell into the river and drowned.

Melissa Grundy didn't kill David. She only watched him die.

Dead Beats Calling

Joe Clifford & Tom Pitts

"You're out of your fucking mind," Tom said.

"I'm telling you." Joe hopped up from his chair. "Dude fits the profile."

"What profile? Ain't no profile for something like that. It was a one-time thing."

"Say what you will, I saw it on TV."

"Oh, well, my goodness, you should've said so. A television? Then it must be true."

"You don't have to be a dick about it." Joe lit a cigarette, walked to the window, and knocked it up. The sounds of the street—the traffic, the sirens, the yelling—all kicked up a notch.

Tom rolled his eyes. You weren't supposed to smoke at the Hope. Not like it mattered. They were already evicting everybody in the whole building.

"When was the last time you had a job?" Joe asked.

"Fuck you."

"Seriously."

"Seriously, fuck you," Tom said. "I work."

"I have *never* seen you with a paycheck."

"I worked all last spring."

"Driving Candy back 'n' forth to that shithole isn't work."

"You don't know Candy."

"Yeah, well, neither do you. Not anymore."

A thick second ticked by. The weight of Joe's comment sat stuck in the middle of the tiny room like a cloud of noxious gas. Candy's fate was a flashpoint between them, an easy wedge Joe used only when he really needed to swing Tom's vote. Only in the most extreme circumstances. Emergencies. In other words, every damn day.

"That's not cool," Tom said.

"Look, I'm not the one wallowing in the past. I'm trying to face our future, you know? They're knockin' this shithole to the ground next Tuesday in the name of gentri-fucking-cation, and we will be among its many... casualties."

Tom said, "They ain't tearing shit down. They're redeveloping."

"Same thing." Joe cleared his throat and spit out the open window. He did this whenever he was building a bluster of bullshit. He was stalling, trying to figure out how to make the words in his head make sense when they flew out of his mouth. "My point is, we ain't getting no rent-controlled place passed down from our mamas this time. We'll be stuck. Just like last year. Out in the street. Nowhere to go." Joe pointed out the window into the low wispy fog. "You know how cold this place gets in the winter."

"No." Tom deadpanned. "No idea. While you're up, put out that fucking smoke and shut the window. It's freezing in here."

"You don't like my idea? Fine. Go apply for a job. Explain your twenty-year gap in employment, and why you'll need a lot of 'sick' time." Joe shook his head, dismissive and smug like Joe did, but he had his interest. At least enough for Tom to hear the plan through.

Tom reached for the cigarettes and lit one up. "Go ahead then," Tom said. "Enlighten me."

"So you know Sierra?"

"No."

"Yes, you do. She lives in one-oh-four with her mom. She's the one who did the two guys for the half a bag."

"It was a full bag."

"Oh, so you do know her."

"Just fuckin' tell me your big plan already."

"So her mom, Janice—she's been here since seventy-one."

"Oh fuck." Tom shook his head.

"What?"

"Those oxy you had last week. You and Sierra stole 'em from that old woman. That was her cancer medication."

"Like you wouldn't have, fuck you. And you're missing the point. She says he moved in, and I quote, 'Around Thanksgiving… 1971.'"

"Who moved in?"

"Don! Pay attention."

"I'm sure a lot of people moved into this dump in 1971."

"Yeah," Joe said. "But how many are named that?"

"Don? It's pretty common name."

"Did you know his middle name is 'Bertrand.'"

"No," Tom said. "And how do you?"

"Larry knows. It's on his mail. Larry goes through everybody's mail right when it gets here. Looking for checks 'n' shit."

"Larry? Larry is so high. Dude, I saw him having a full-on conversation with a falafel once."

"Don't mean he didn't see it."

Tom stubbed out his cigarette, shaking his head. "So Don Bertrand... Crawford... jumps, walks into town—practically moves into the same town he's supposed to be running from—doesn't bother to change his initials, and has been living here, in the wide-open, as one of the most wanted men in history?"

"It's kinda brilliant if you think about it."

"No," Tom said, "It's kinda stupid."

Joe started nodding his head. He had that goofy glaze in his eyes like he was trying to hold back a dirty secret. "Two words," he said. "Rent control."

"Huh?"

"If Don's been living here since seventy-one, think about it. Same reason they're demolishing the whole complex. He's probably paying eighty-five dollars a month or some shit to live here. Dude *never* leaves his room except to get take-out. Watches TV up there like a goddamn king. Hear it all goddamn day. Never has to worry about money in his life."

"How much longer would that even be? Dude, even if Don *was* him, he'd have to be a hundred years old now. I seen Don. He's old. He ain't that old."

"Ninety," Joe said.

"Ninety what?"

"That's how old he'd be."

Might as well be nine hundred.

"You see that ol' fucker move? Don could be ninety. For sure."

"I'd put him closer to seventy, seventy-five."

"Because dude don't have no stresses, man. Not like us. He's got money, food, security. A roof over his head."

"Not much longer," Tom said.

"That's what I'm trying to say. Listen, any dude who's lived that long, that alone—is that old—he don't have no one to leave the money to. He walks out of the Hope on D-Day, with a big ol' briefcase of cash—"

"Briefcase. Because the papers said he had a briefcase when he jumped ten thousand miles fifty years ago?"

"Rule number one: no major changes in lifestyle."

"Oh, there's rules?"

"Yeah, don't flash. Keep a low profile. No big purchases. You know."

"Whatever."

"Yeah, whatever." Joe scoffed. "Whatever is sitting upstairs with a suitcase full of cash, he'll make it about two blocks before someone mugs him." Joe threw up his arms. "We'd be doing him a favor."

"By robbing him first."

"Well, we won't hurt him."

"How we gonna get the money—which, by the way, if you think somebody is keeping—what he get away with? A quarter of a million?"

"Around that."

"You think he's keeping a quarter mil in his fucking room?"

"It's worth more now, too," Joe said.

"How you figure?"

"Economics, bruh. It's just fact. Two hundred thousand in seventy-one is worth, like, I don't know. Two million?"

"Not if it's cash sitting in a closet."

"You think he's got it in his closet?"

"No, I don't think he's got shit."

"Fuck, Tom. Did you even pay attention in school? If you had, like, one hundred dollars in 1850, it's worth, I don't know the exact number, but, like, a million."

"Jesus, listen to yourself."

Joe shook him off. "Doesn't matter. Two hundred thousand dollars would last us the rest of our lives."

"You're giving me a headache, man." Tom started listing items on his fingers. "First, he would've spent some of the money. A lot of the money. Maybe *all* the money. Because he's had to stay alive for *fifty fucking years*. I don't care how cheap rent is. Living is expensive. Doesn't matter what fucking decade you do it in. Two, ain't no one keeping cash in their closet at this dump. Because if you had a closet full of cash, you wouldn't be living at this dump. And three…" Tom stopped, his lips pulling back against his teeth, something he found himself doing whenever Joe wouldn't listen to logic. "Y'know what? I don't need a three. This is one of the dumbest conversations I've ever had. And it's been hours since I had any dope. I'm getting sick."

"Exactly!" Joe said. "Me too. That's why I'm telling you this. Listen, man, just come with me upstairs to his room, okay? We just go say hi all neighborly. Feel it out? We can say goodbye, sorry the place is closing down. Ask how we can help? You need a hand with the boxes, shit like that. Like we're good guys."

"And if I see maybe, what, a giant wet parachute for a bedspread, then we know we're onto something."

"Don't be an asshole." Joe waited, thinking. "But maybe we see *something*." He shrugged.

Tom felt the greasy nausea waves begin their assault. In another couple hours, it would be the cold flashes and then the runs, and then he'd be done, curled up in a ball, praying for a miracle. No, he didn't believe Joe, who was, at best, a fucking idiot, and robbing an old man was as low as low goes. But Tom had done worse.

***

When the old man answered the door, he smiled and seemed genuinely pleased to have company. For the entire time Tom and Joe had been living at the Hope, the old man, Don, had been in the apartment directly above theirs. Tom never saw much of the old man, but when he did, he didn't recall Don smiling so much. Not that he was rude or gruff. He was quiet and kept to himself. Remarkable how utterly unremarkable the old man was.

"How can I help you, boys?"

"Wanted to get our goodbyes in." Joe poked his head in, peering around the small apartment.

Tom went to pull him back but couldn't help taking a look around too. Like the old man himself, the apartment was ancient, all its décor rooted firmly in the '70s. Some of it looked in okay shape. Lamps, end tables, and an old stereo would buy a fix at the pawn shop.

"Because the Hope is going away," Tom added, catching the old man's beaming grin, which made him feel horrible for what he was considering doing.

"You boys like to come in?" Don asked, stepping aside. "I was just about to put on some soup for lunch. There's plenty. It's from a can, but it'll stick to your ribs."

Joe smirked, slipping past the old man. Tom winced a grin. He couldn't turn back now.

Inside, Tom surveyed the rest of the furnishings, which were, admittedly, better than he and Joe had. Granted, that was a low-hanging fruit.

The old man pointed the two to the table and told them to have a seat.

With his back turned, Tom pantomimed they should go, Joe shaking his head. "Easy money," he mouthed.

The smell of tomato and Italian seasonings floated through the tiny kitchen. Even if it was out of a can, the soup would be the first thing Tom had to eat all day. When your life is heroin, eating is a luxury you can't always afford.

"So," Joe said. "How long you been living here?"

"In Spokane?"

"No, here at the Hope." Joe's eyes darted around the room with no idea where to land.

"Let's see…" Don's back remained turned, and Tom could hear him scraping hard cheese into the soup. "Got here end of seventy-one, I think."

"What you do for work?" Joe asked as Tom shook his head, shooing him to shut up.

"Oh," the old man said, turning around. "I'm retired. Been retired for a while." He coughed a weak laugh.

"What did you used to do?" Joe asked.

"Used to work for the airlines," Don said.

Joe's eyes grew wide as if to say, "Told you so."

The old man placed the soup in front of each of them, reaching back for his own bowl on the counter. "Eat up," he said.

Tom saw the can of soup in the trash. A cheap, dented can. Don didn't look like he had much. It was a meager apartment with few luxuries, and, sure, these things would fetch some money. But how low do you have to be to eat an old man's soup and then rob him? Tom had enough. He started to get up when the cramp seized up his gut like his intestines had been tied in a knot. Fuckin' dope sickness closing in on him. Like Satan himself urging him to take out this old fucker.

"You okay, son?"

Across the room, Joe slurped his soup, flecks of red tomato flying from wet lips. Tom knew Joe wasn't going anywhere, not now with the prize in sight. Tom reached for his spoon.

"I'm fine," Tom said. "Just not feeling well."

"It's a hard life you boys have," Don said. "Little soup'll make you feel better. Old fashioned medicine."

Tom wondered if Don knew they were junkies. Of course, he does. *We look like shit.*

The old man smiled. "Thin walls in this place."

Joe stopped machining the spoon into his mouth long enough to say, "This fuckin' soup is grubbin'," before plowing back into his bowl.

Tom lifted the spoon to his mouth. It wasn't half bad. A bit salty. He took a few more spoonfuls.

"We've been neighbors so long," the old man said. "It's a shame we never got to talk."

Tom nodded. The soup was actually pretty tasty.

"In this day and age, it's good to get to know your neighbor. Learn a little about who they are, you know?"

Was Joe even listening? No way was this ordinary guy hiding a secret identity. But he could see in Joe's eyes that his running partner—he'd never call him a friend—was going to carry this plan out, with or without his help. This was all going to shit. All Tom had was the truth.

"Want to hear something funny?" Tom said.

"Like a joke?" Don asked, slowly walking to the other room.

"Sorta," Tom said, glowering at Joe, who shook his head, a message for Tom to keep his mouth shut. Tom wasn't letting Joe do this. "This guy here," he pointed at Joe, "thinks you're a celebrity."

The old man poked his head back in the room. “A celebrity?”

“Kinda. More infamous than famous.”

“Shut up, Tom,” Joe mouthed, opening up enough so a rivulet of tomato broth rolled down his scruffy chin. He tried to whisper, but the desperation and dope sickness made it come out louder than he intended. “Shuff it,” Joe slurred.

Tom looked over at Joe. His eyes drooped; his face was slack. For someone cryin’ about being dope sick, Joe sure looked comfortable. Tom continued, “He thinks you might not be who we all thought you were.” When it came time to say it, Tom realized he was scared to say the name aloud, now that he was looking the old man in the face. “He thinks you hijack—” Tom stopped talking when he heard a splash.

Joe’s head had dropped directly into his bowl of soup. It lay there motionless. Then there was a gurgle, and Joe turned his head to the side, pulling in a long, wet snort of air, the bowl of hot soup cradling his head like a pillow, a gentle crescent smile on his sleeping face.

“What the fuck?” Tom said. But he wasn’t sure if he said it out loud. His ears were tingling a little. Tom’s chin tugged toward his chest. He felt warm and good.

“You’re not the only one stealing Janice’s pills.”

When Tom opened his eyes and looked up at the old man, he was wearing sunglasses and a toupee, just like in the infamous “wanted” photo. He had to admit the resemblance was uncanny. In his hand, he held an old, tattered brown briefcase.

“The walls are paper thin,” the old man said. “Floors too.”

Don brought the briefcase to the table, flipping it on its back and opening up. He took out a stack of bandied twenty-dollar bills and slipped out two, passing them along to Tom.

With blurred vision, Tom tried to study the bills. They were the old-style twenties, with the tiny head of Andrew Jackson, each one from 1963.

"Hope that helps you feel better," the old man said. "I'd tell you be careful where you spend it, but we both know where that money is going. And by then, I'll be long gone."

The old man clasped Tom on the shoulder.

Tom looked up, then back at the soup, then back up, unsure if he should be grateful, angry, or relieved.

"Can I give you some advice, boy?"

Tom nodded.

The old man didn't say anything for a moment, and Tom wondered if he was going to tell him to clean up his act like everyone else did or how life is a gift, that's why it's called "the present." *No, not the old man.*

He pointed at Joe, slumped over the soup, blissfully snoring. "You can get away with just about anything if you can keep your mouth shut."

"But wait..." Tom's tongue was thick and his mouth full of cotton. "It's just money. I don't know what... Who is? Are you... really...?" Tom blinked. The old man was at the door now, the daylight behind him in the hall masking his features, making them hard to see.

"Maybe if you eat that soup slow, you won't have to think about robbing another old man 'til Tuesday." With that, the old man picked up his briefcase, turned, and headed down the musty hall of the Hope and out into the cold Northwestern afternoon.

The Gravity of Hope

Mark Bergin

"You know, for somebody who didn't want to be found, Turner sure made a lot of noise with his bottles," Henry Becker said.

"His bottles? How do you mean?" Detective Marci Burkett asked.

Henry looked at the interview room glass, mirrored on this side as if it were the window through which he had first seen James Turner draped on the fire escape above.

"He'd sit up there, right above my rooms. Doing a six-pack. Drop each bottle down into the dumpster. He'd prop open the lid before he went up, before he even came in the building 'cause you can't even get on the fire escape from the ground, it's got that ladder on runners with counterweights so you can ride it down and when you get off it goes back up and—"

"Bottles?" Burkett was a patient interviewer and only interrupted to get the older man back on track.

"Bottles. Every night, well, most nights, unless it was raining hard. Some lighter rains, he'd be out there. Had a big black raincoat that covered most of him, orange inside like yours are. Wore a hat. Told me the rain just ran down around him, and he didn't mind." Henry looked at his own reflection. And through it. "Bottle from five floors up makes a big sound in an empty dumpster."

"He told you about the rain? So you two talked? Like friends."

"Sure. Some." *Not enough.*

Henry Becker first noticed James Turner in late spring, just a week after Turner had moved into the building, a foolish move in that the Hope Apartments were slated to close only five months later. But they were cheap, had openings as the less optimistic or more realistic occupants read the writing on their soon-to-be renovated walls, and moved out to places unknown, at least, unknown to Henry. Nobody from the Hope kept in touch when they left. Most didn't even reach out while still there. But Henry had or had tried when he recognized the pattern of the bottles.

Henry was sitting in his kitchen-cum-living room at the window, watching the sunset. Always beautiful here in Spokane, in eastern Washington ("the state, not the DC one," he used to tell ignorant people back when he still cared about them). He saw a reflected flash next to the fire escape, a sunshine spark, followed by a crash below. He realized he'd heard the same sound twenty minutes before and had, in fact, been hearing the same booms for days, if not weeks. But they hadn't registered at first, lost in the constant cacophony of the busy neighborhood around the Hope.

That night was finally warm enough Henry could lift open the perennially sticky window. It let in actual air and clear enough sound that he could identify the source of the boom—glass in the dumpster—and let him look up to locate its source, a man reclined near the top of the black metal fire escape structure on the west side of the five-story apartment.

After that, he began to notice him elsewhere. Walking through the high-ceilinged lobby but never checking his mailbox, or around the neighborhood, in the bodega down the block, carrying a bag home most nights. Skinny guy with big hands, nowhere near the beer belly he should have for slamming a six every night out there. Henry figured the guy just walked it off. Spokane was good for that, some hills, some pretty parks. But Henry rarely took his wheelchair out of the building himself so he could only vouch for what he saw from his fourth-floor window, west side, almost sunset-view save for the high buildings across the street. Maybe when the Hope closed, he'd move somewhere with a better view. Maybe he'd better start making some plans for that. But he knew God would provide.

"So, you became friends. What did you talk about?" Burkett asked with a smile. Forced, Henry thought. *Friends like you'd like us to be, Detective.* He'd think she was pretty if he were still young. She seemed smart and tried to be tough. Intimidating in that way cops had to be, more so than Nash, Henry's first detective today, the one who'd brought him down here to Headquarters to "talk" about a missing person, Nash said, someone in the building. Burkett took over from him because of some change, some new thing she'd leaned in and whispered to Nash after she entered the interview room. Something about "negative on the cameras" was all Henry could hear.

Nash got up. "Will Delaney be here too? I'll tell him where you are."

"No, he knows. He's right next door," Burkett said, jacking a thumb at the adjacent interview room. She sat down across from him. Two pairs of steel chairs were riveted to the floor facing each other across a similarly bolted-down table. Henry was parked at one end in his wheelchair, and the lady detective sat across the corner of the scarred metal table from him and crossed her legs. She wore higher heels than Henry thought cops would wear. That was an hour ago.

"Lot going on at the Hope," she said. And waited, staring flatly out from under her black bangs.

After a minute, Henry gave in. "Not really. Mostly just waiting for the building to close. Developers. Sterling Management makin' it into a hotel. Really didn't think it would come to this. Cheap place, but it was kept up, and we figured all our rents were nothin' but profit for the owners after all these years. I been there twenty myself. Never thought to move. Doors're big enough for my chair, and the elevators worked most of the time. I can still stand up, can walk a bit when I have to, so I could get out and meet up with James on the escape."

"How often was that?"

"Not often at first. More later. He didn't want company. I figured he was hiding out. Never said that, but it was clear. Later, I came to think he did want it, or at least he needed it. He didn't have nobody wanted him."

"He told you that?"

"After a while."

"What did he say?"

"Said his wife was dead, and his kids were pretty much gone."

"Pretty much? Odd way to put it." Detective Burkett opened one of her files and dropped sheets of paper into her lap, where Henry could not see it. "What did he mean by that?"

"Said she died. One time, the way he said it was, she was killed. Never went beyond that."

"And you never asked him, *beyond that*?"

"Not my business. Figured he'd talk about it if he wanted to. He talked more later. And even more, the more bottles he drank. I think maybe if he was to drink more than a six, he'd'a opened up. But he never did. Controlled. Never lost his aim either. All six, always right in the dumpster, every night. Sometimes five, 'cause sometimes he'd give me one, but not every night. I don't need getting up the middle of the night to pee."

"What else did you talk about?"

"Sometimes we'd talk about trains." And a bad man in the building, and danger, and how Henry had stayed down and let James Turner handle it.

"The train sets in your apartment, you mean?"

"How you know about that?"

"I'm sorry, Mr. Becker, I thought that Detective Nash had told you." She pulled up the pages from her lap, several sheets stapled together. Upside down, he saw his name typed on the top sheet. "We searched your apartment this morning. This is a search warrant, a copy. Your copy is on your kitchen table… Where do you think you're going?"

Henry rolled backward till the handles of his wheelchair bumped against the wall. He looked at her in the glass reflection, not directly, and at the image of his own wild eyes. "What call do you have to search my home? You think I did something."

"Well, we know you did something with James Turner. We don't fully know what yet. But we want to find out." She reached into her pile of files again and pulled out something more with his name on it. A stiff yellow envelope with blocks for writing and EVIDENCE printed in bold letters on both sides. Inside was another smaller envelope, empty now but once puffy with the girl's panties, that had *Henry Becker* written in ink across the tape seal. Written by Henry himself.

At Turner's direction.

Burkett held it up and said, "I think this means we have to read you your rights now. Are you ready for that?"

***

At the start of the summer, Henry Becker hadn't been ready for any of it.

He had watched as others, James Turner among them, had moved into the Hope, foolish actions in the face of its imminent closure but understandable for folks poor in bank and spirit willing to take any shelter in the face of Spokane's housing shortage. Henry was a long-timer at the Hope, not an original occupant but one of its senior tenants, in more ways than one.

When the management company notified them last year that the building was being sold and turned into a hotel and they all had to vacate, there was the expected anger and disbelief. And resistance, such as resistance could be to an inevitable, inexorable force. Like cursing the rain. Some, *many*, moved away soon after the notices appeared, yellow form letters taped on doors, in mailboxes, and slipped into the inspection certificate frames of the elevators, under the sometimes-functional security cameras.

Unfortunately, those who moved early made room for trouble, in the form of Ki Sun Minh. Small from a distance, like a kid but in his twenties. A family of six kids with Ki the oldest. And most aggressive. Several Vietnamese families had moved into the Hope near the end, and some Korean and Laotian and Cambodian. Each ethnicity pulling in more of their own subgroup.

But Ki circulated among them all. Not always welcomed. Sometimes sailing in on force or aggression or personality like he did with Henry. Or tried to. Until Turner.

"You talk with that kid a lot," James Turner said one night, an hour and three beers before sunset. Henry knew James timed his consumption to the setting of the sun, guzzling and bombardiering four bottles in the runup to darkness and two thereafter, each taking about twenty minutes, each punctuated by the bonging as the bottle dropped into the steel dumpster. Never missing once.

"He's gonna help me with my trains." It had seemed such an innocuous activity, but it had started so much.

One day Ki intercepted Henry as he rolled in the front door and across the Hope's high-ceilinged lobby, the spacious room grand in its bones but worn down, paint chipping and worn carpets bumpy under his wheels. Ki had been at the mailboxes. He spent a lot of time there watching, Henry had noticed. As he stretched for the call button, Ki swept up and snatched the grocery bags off Henry's lap.

"I'll help you, old folks," he said. Henry was surprised and sputtered his resistance, but Ki persisted.

"You old. I'll help you get these into your apartment. It's nothing. I can help you. Whatever you need, I can do. You need things?" Ki was well dressed in black t-shirt and jeans, and white sneakers. Short black hair looking shiny but not greasy, though his manner was. Henry told him he did not need help, but Ki did not give back the bags. In broad daylight, in his home building, with a young man whose name he knew and whose family he had spoken with, Henry was uncomfortable but did not fear. Maybe he should have.

Ki and Henry rode in the elevator to the fourth floor. Ki lived on the third in a double with his family. When Henry took out his keys, Ki reached for them, but this time Henry was ready and rebuffed the grab. But as the knob unlocked, Ki took control of Henry's chair and pushed him inside faster than Henry liked. Ki left the door open and gazed around at the racks, rail sets, and shelves full of trains. Dozens of electric trains, scale models of modern diesel engines, and vintage steam locomotives. Rolling stock, tank cars and box cars and passenger cars and Pullman coaches. All in O scale, larger pieces, not toys. Ki gazed in fascination at all of them like most visitors did, though most visitors did not ask the questions Ki did.

"These worth a lot, right? These toy trains, you bought a long time ago. You sell them now and get a lot, right?"

The breach in his loneliness broke through his suspicions, and Henry responded to Ki's interest. Though he had not evaluated his childhood hobby in decades, the collection had continued to grow even after he and Maddie had moved to the Hope, after the war and his first two jobs and before her cancer. A pension, an inheritance, and her small insurance policy sustained Henry as he hid here in the Hope, childless and motionless and hidden from change. But his hiding place was about to fall out from under him. And Ki seemed to sense this.

"I help you get rid all this. Get you good prices. We not share, you can get it all the money." He picked up a black steam engine replica, looked at the wheel carriages and the shiny electric motor housing visible underneath. "I'll show you. Let me sell this one, you will see I can take care of it." Ki's eyes glinted, not with friendship.

When Henry finally said no, Ki's eyes flashed further into the dark. "I sell this one. I will take it; you will let me. I will show you." Now Ki loomed over Henry, his small frame still bigger and tougher than Henry's chairbound body could match. Henry felt fear though Ki was never overtly threatening. Certainly, nothing actionable as a threat, as Henry told James Turner that night.

Turner's eyes narrowed at the story. He straightened up from his recline on the fire escape and leaned forward. "How much was that train worth, Henry?"

"I don't know, James. I'm not really sure which one he took. Probably a Norfolk Southern F9. Those go anywhere from three hundred to a grand. I don't want to make a big deal about it and, really, I got to let some of them go. Maybe all of them. Maybe I'll see if he comes through."

"Got another engine like it?"

"Lots of them."

"Can I see one?"

"You want to come into my apartment?" Turner never had, despite several invitations at the start of their acquaintanceship. Henry would have two visitors in a day!

And a third visit came the next afternoon when Turner knocked on Henry's door and was let inside. Just like normal people, not fire escape denizens. Turner had news.

"I went to the library and checked it out, the engine you showed me. Did you know there are magazines and clubs dedicated to these things? I guess you did." Turner was happier than Henry had ever heard him. "Do you know how much it's worth? Just that one engine. Yeah, that one," and accepted it when Henry plucked it gently from a track diorama set up on a plywood platform that filled his living room. He took out a small notebook. "I looked this one up. Good condition, Lionel Union Pacific Legacy Big Boy locomotive. It'll go for around two thousand dollars. Just this one.

"See, they got serial numbers, under here, did you know that?" He smiled at Henry, the first time ever. Henry knew they did but let Turner keep going, riding his wave.

"There's whole catalogues you can look them up. And page after page of ones for sale and places you can go to sell them. I can probably show you on the web. You have a computer?"

"No. Never got around to one."

"Smart phone then?"

"Nope."

"Me neither, now. So maybe we can go to the library together." Henry looked around at the dozens of train pieces on the diorama and shelves and in boxes

"And I could get Ki to sell them for me?" Henry asked. And James Turner's smile went out.

***

"So, he got mad at you?" Detective Marci Burkett asked. She'd had Henry read and initial each line on the Spokane Police Department's Rights Waiver Form, then sign the bottom. She surreptitiously compared Henry's form signature with that on the envelope in evidence, and her eyes remained flat.

Henry caught her, a lifetime of his dark skin making cops mistrust him. He tried to let it go but code-switched a little to tell her he knew. "Well, not mad. Disappointed, I'd say. I's being a fool thinking I could trust this kid I ain't ever even talked to before. But it be a way for me to get ready to move. I knows I can't take them all with me when we have to move out of the Hope. I just wasn't thinking. But I never thought the way James did."

He stopped when she squinted at him, like she knew, too.

***

Turner held the Union Pacific locomotive and said, "Henry, that kid is never gonna pay you what these are worth. You think he might 'cause you're a good man. But the world is not full of good men. It's full of criminals, bad men who would not lose a minute's sleep stealing all you're worth. Ki's one of them." He stood over Henry in the wheelchair.

Henry looked up at him forthrightly.

"You want to trust him. I get it. But do this. He'll come in here with a story about selling the one you gave him for, I don't know, two hundred dollars. We know it was worth more than that, but we don't know for certain 'cause you don't know exactly which one he took.

"But we know this one." Turner held the locomotive aloft, big as two bricks. His spirit returned with a sneakier smile. "You give him *this* one to sell. He'll come back with a price, it'll be ridiculously low, then we know what he is. And we go from there."

***

Henry paused in his telling. Burkett stopped swinging her foot, crossed it over her other knee. "And where *did* you go?" Like she had all the time in the world for Henry's story, but she couldn't keep her feet still, and they gave her away. *How does she run in those shoes?* Impatience sharpened Henry's words.

"Smart lady cop, you know. Ki came in that night and told me he had sold it for big money. He said he got four hundred dollars for it. But he didn't have the money, he said it was coming in a check, and I had to give him twenty to mail the locomotive to the buyer. In for a penny, so I did. I wanted to play James's game, it was worth a few more bucks. And I gave Ki the Big Boy to sell next." He paused long and gave her back the stare.

This time, it was Marci Burkett who charged into the silence. "So?"

"So what? What did I do? And what did James do?" Henry was playing sharp now for an old man, trying to be in control of the game and surprised at himself for it. But his eyes clouded as he thought forward, formulating his answer, and remembering where that night had taken him. His imploring look was lost on the veteran detective. He stepped off the cliff.

***

"So you think you'll trust him," Turner said. "Even after what I told you might happen, actually happened? You've lost one train already."

Henry shrugged. "Got too many now. More than I can lay out and for sure more than I can take somewhere else when I gotta go."

It was a *yeah-I'll-have-one-of-your-beers* night. They were inside Henry's kitchen, James Turner drinking indoors for the first time Henry had seen. Wind gusts blew heavy rain at the window in sheets that hid the fire escape. Inside, bottles fell gently into Henry's trash can. A change in the natural order.

"Where will you go?" Three beers in, but Turner didn't slur. He stared through the closed window at the sheeting rain, flooding over the sounds of Spokane street life filtering up from below. Cool in October, just days until the Hope closed.

"Don't rightly know. Haven't been told."

"Told?"

"I wait for the word."

"What word? *The Word*, like with a capital W word? The Lord's word. God's gonna tell you what to do?" Turner gaped at him, though Henry didn't feel contempt from his new friend.

"I have hope. I have faith in God, that he'll tell me what to do. Where to go. I'm old. Got a little in the bank, prolly not enough for a down on a good place. But an okay place? I can find that. Hope will pull me there."

Turner faced him now. "So you're just gonna fall into the flood and let it take you somewhere? Carry you to the better shore? You hope that will work? You just gonna trust The Word?"

"Worked so far. Always has. Look what it did for you and me and Ki."

"Huh?" Now Turner looked at Henry like a specimen, a new species, an inexplicable sound.

"I'm old, but I'm alive. You're here to talk with me. I have hope. Ki's helping me. He's getting me something. Maybe not what I could get if I had time to sell properly."

"Ki's ripping you off, Henry. He gave you two hundred dollars for a train that's worth a grand."

"It's easier, James. I get something."

"You get so little, and there's no reason for it."

"I can't take them with me."

"How do you know? You don't even know where you're going? Look," and Turner got up and walked to a wall with several tight shelves displaying rows of train cars. His voice got loud.

"These'll fit in a box. This whole wall could fit in four or five boxes. You can take them with you anywhere, they won't take up that much space. Don't dump them this way."

Henry rolled closer and waved at his chair. "How you think I'ma gonna carry all these boxes, James? What am I gonna do with them when I get there, wherever? You gonna help me?"

"Sure, I can help you. I can, I can help."

"I don't need your help. I don't want your help. You can't help. You can't do nothing, you sitting out there every night looking at the sunset. What are you, that that's all you do?"

"I can help. I want to help." His voice soft again, Turner looked out the window. "I could."

"Forget it, James. The sun's down. Go home."

"No. No, we're gonna go talk with Ki Sun Minh. This is not right. He's been pushing around people in this building. I am not gonna let him continue it." Turner seemed to stand straighter, taller, looming over Henry but not in a bad way.

Turner led Henry out the door and to the elevator, where they went down to the third floor and Ki's apartment. Henry was torn between exerting himself to stop this and allowing himself to be borne along on the current of Turner's will. A woman answered Turner's fist to the apartment door. Her English and Turner's lack of Vietnamese did not allow clarity beyond "Mother, yes." But her body language was clear, and Turner followed her troubled glance to the stairwell entrance across the hall. He turned away, pushed open the stairway door, and it struck Ki right on his bare thigh as he pistoned over a girl supine on the hard corners of the stair treads. Ki jumped up as Turner grabbed him by the shirt and threw him across the landing, exposing himself and her bare groin. He yanked his jeans and yelled at Turner first in an unintelligible volley of what were probably curses, subsiding into accented but clear English and finally settling on, "What the fuck you want, fuck. You get out of here. We're not done."

"Free stairwell, punk. How old is she?" Turner pointed at her, and she turned away in her obvious shame, sitting forward and pulling her dress down over her thighs. She looked mid-teens, but it was hard to tell for sure beneath the delicate hands that now shielded her eyes.

"She not your business. She girlfriend. You get away from here." Ki looked around and saw Henry behind Turner. "Why he here? Why you here? You got more trains?" Ki finally pulled up his pants, heavy pockets clunking against the stair rail, affixed his belt and stepped into the doorway but kept it open and his hand on the girl's chest.

"You treat her as well as you treated Henry. You're not selling any more of his trains. You owe him money for the one you took already. And how old is this girl?"

Pants and dignity back on, anger rising, Ki spat and said, "You don't matter this girl how old. She with me. She whore. She get paid. She like it so I don't pay. She mine." Gibberish with fierce eyes.

"I'm not so sure of any of that," Turner said, his voice flat. He stepped close to Ki, who stepped back and pulled a small pistol from his pocket. He waved it wildly at

Turner and at Henry behind him, reverting to Vietnamese for a time.

And Henry, behind and slightly to the right, watched Turner pass through a series of tiny moves. Turner glanced down at the gun but locked his eyes back onto Ki's face. As the gun swung away, Turner brought his hands slightly upward but froze as the gun returned to point at him and at Henry. Turner's body turned to counter the swing of the barrel, and with each swing, he tensed, coiled and ready, a grab away from safety or loud, horrible failure. Choosing.

Ki stepped to his right, and Turner shuffled to his left, shielding Henry. Both shifted again, with Turner keeping up the block. Maybe six seconds passed in what felt to Henry like an hour, and as Ki's jabber slowed and toned down, Turner's readiness dropped from spring-loaded to ready to calm. Ki stepped back out of range, and Turner relaxed.

"She mine, you fuck. You nothing." Now Ki, the gun still pointed out of grabbing range, reached under the girl's thin dress. His arm clinched as he clawed her panties and pulled. She collapsed back hard against the steps as he yanked the undergarments down her legs and over her bare feet. Pulling the gun in tight to his hip, Ki held the panties out, stepped close to Turner, and pushed them against his chest to force him against the hallway wall. He stuffed them into Turner's shirt pocket.

"She whore, you see. She was ready for me. I give it to her. You can tell. I give you this."

To his side, Henry watched Turner's fury flame out to cold calculation. His eyes flickered between Ki's spitting mouth, and the small gun tucked against Ki's side.

"You do what I say," Ki said.

"Sure, Ki," Turner said, with a barely visible softening of shoulders and jaw, just enough that Henry saw, and Ki reacted. The gun came up higher.

"Can we leave?" Turner's voice was low and even.

Ki grinned and stepped back. "You go. You go now. But I come at you later." Ki faced off to Turner with the propped façade of power a gun gives weak men. Turner wore no expression, but his eyes hardened when Ki stepped around him and went on. "You, old man. I talk with you. Yeah. Talk. Ha. Ha. Ha. Ha." Each word emphasized with a narrow wave of the gun barrel panning over Henry's chest.

Turner and Henry backed down the hall, passing Ki's open apartment door where his mother watched silently. After a few more feet, Turner spun Henry's chair, and they continued to the elevator. When they got back to Henry's apartment, Turner left him there, quietly walking back down the hall toward the stairwell.

***

"And you didn't call the cops?" Marci Burkett asked. Henry shrugged. Burkett uncrossed her leg and stomped her heel. *Maybe she takes them off like that blonde actress on* Cagney and Lacey.

"Henry? A gun's pulled on you, he's raping a child, he stole from you, you don't call police?" Burkett shook her head, for the first time showing emotion that Henry knew wasn't feigned.

"We didn't get shot. And maybe we started it. James grabbed him. I don't know from rape, she didn't try to get away from him, we didn't know what was going on there other than what was obviously going on there. Stole from me? That's hard, I gave him the trains to sell. Besides, James said he'd handle it."

"Handle it? What do you… James Turner's handling it is why we're here. Do you know why we're here, Henry?"

"The other guy, Detective Nash, when he brought me down here, said it was for a missing person. Thought it was Ki. Is it that girl?" Henry sat up.

"No, it's not the girl, though she's fifteen, by the way. So you did see a rape, at least statutorily, even if no force was used. But an adult has sex with a child while carrying a gun, that's rape a number of ways. And you should have called us. But no, she's not missing. She's home with her family, but not talking with us yet. Maybe never.

"No, it's Ki Sun Minh who's missing. Near as we can tell since the night he raped her. And you were among the last to see him, to talk with him. To fight with him, Henry." She picked up the envelope with his signature. "And you had her panties in your apartment. In this. With a note from James Turner. Can you dig why you're here now?"

Henry breathed deep, looked at Burkett but tried not to, looked at his reflection and noticed the shiny box with the red light above the mirror. Oh.

"Here's what we know. Ki was a thug, a member of a Vietnamese street gang called, well, it doesn't exactly translate. He'd been shaking down people in the building, getting into their apartments, stealing and defrauding them. He'd help them cash their checks and take a cut, he'd lift their jewelry. He even stole your toy trains."

"Scale collectible models."

"Whatever. But his mom called us, says he didn't come home Tuesday night. Which is the night of your little dance party in the stairwell. Mom says you and Turner had a run-in with him. So we searched your house. And what did we find?" She flapped the envelope.

As if on cue, the interview room door opened, and a lanky man entered. He took the chair next to Burkett at the table, away from Henry. As he sat, his sport jacket rode up over an empty holster on his belt. Burkett waved the envelope at him like a game show host and said, "My partner, Quinn Delaney. He can show you his badge, but why waste time. I think you get who we are—"

"So there's no question we get to ask you questions, Mr. Becker," Delaney jumped right in. "And tell you things about yourself and your life and where your life is going now." Delaney leaned forward to place a clear baggie on the table close to Henry. A pair of panties was visible inside, pale green and lightly discolored. Delaney waited until Henry looked back up at him, then spoke.

"I know you know what these are, but I'll tell you anyway. They're the panties from the envelope you sealed and hid in your apartment. With the note from James Turner and, by the way, that's not his name." Marci Burkett's mouth twitched, and she slowly turned to looked at Delaney.

"That's right, Marci, you don't know this part yet. This is good. But Henry, first, tell us about these panties and the note in the envelope, which we found in your bedside table. In your apartment. With your fingerprints and your very own name on the outside. And a note signed by James Turner saying 'Ki handed us these. Henry Becker witnessed.' Now, Henry, tell me again."

Henry talked for an hour, taking Delaney, and Burkett for a second time, through the bottles, the shared time on the fire escape, the model trains, the confrontation with Ki, and the sealed envelope. "James told me to hold on to it until it was needed but never said when that would be."

"Well, it's needed now. She's fifteen, sex between a minor and an adult is statutory rape, a felony even if he didn't use the gun to get it. She's not talking, shy, but juvenile court is closed to the public. And we can make the case without her testimony. With you, Henry. Turner set that up. When we get labs on the fluids and hairs to match him and her, we got Ki."

Delaney stopped, and Burkett went on, but to Delaney, not Henry.

"A paper evidence envelope for the panties, right? Wet evidence." Her eyebrow cocked.

"Yep, partner. So that cloth with fluids can dry out in storage and not rot. Packaged just like we do." Both cops nodded, and Delaney peered at her. "You don't know the half of it. Yet."

Burkett pushed past her puzzlement and turned to Henry. "What we don't get is the real James Turner. What do you know about him?"

Henry, dazzled and adrift, sat silently for a minute. "Nothing," he said.

"You knew the guy since, what did you say, May? Six months. You had to talk about something."

"Nothing. Beer. Sunsets. Dropping bottles down the building into the dumpster. He never missed. Not much else."

Burkett stared at Henry, then said, "You said the bottles usually made a lot of noise, and you finally noticed them and so noticed Turner up on the fire escape above your apartment."

"That's right. Every night, around sunset. I'm on the west side of the building. Sunset side. You can see the sunrise from the other side fire escape. He didn't go there."

"But you didn't hear the bottles every night, so that's why it took a while to figure out what the sound was?"

"Yeah, well, sometimes the dumpster is full. Trash and cardboard and orange peels and stuff. You wouldn't hear them hit if it was full."

"When's it emptied?"

"Wednesdays." Burkett frowned, and Delaney wrote a word on her notepad and underlined it. They shared a look, and Delaney got up and left. Henry read it upside down. DUMP. When Delaney came back, he glared off into space for a few seconds and said to Burkett, "They're taking a crew out now to search." He turned to Henry.

"What do you know about Turner? Henry, you don't know nothing. Here's the tale. James Turner is not James Turner. He's a cop, ex-cop, named Martin Schaller. From Virginia. He left the force there two years ago; we think he drifted west and stayed out of trouble till he got here.

"Trouble?" Henry asked.

"He killed his wife. Not really, but that's what he thinks and what he thinks his kids think. Anyway, he got in a shootout there two years ago, and she got killed. He got wounded, and the force out there dumped him. His kids yelled at him at the funeral, told him he got her killed, that it's his fault. Apparently, he just left town. And came here. Henry, you thought he was hiding? You were right."

"Hiding? How do you know *hiding*? Wait, how do you know who he is, and all this stuff about his wife and all?" Henry looked agape at Delaney.

Delaney pulled out his own file folder. "There were fingerprints on the baggie with the panties. Yours were on it. His too. We ran them. They match Detective Martin A. Schaller, formerly of the Alexandria, Virginia Police Department. All cops are fingerprinted and entered in NCIC. Checking takes a few seconds.

"Just got off the phone with a commander in their personnel section. Seems Turner, or Schaller, spotted a guy while he and his wife were out to dinner. The guy was a scumbag Schaller'd been after for a while. Not a big scumbag, basically a thief. But Schaller decides he's gonna be a big shot and take him, all by himself. No worries, just a thief. But the guy's got a gun and starts blasting. Kills Schaller's wife right there. She was a teacher. Shoots Schaller in the chest. Damages his heart, and they can't fix it right, so they throw him off the force. And, the commander tells me, his kids blew up at him 'cause he got their mom killed being a cowboy.

"So." Delaney looked more at Burkett than Henry as he said, "Great cop, all the moves, commendations out the whazzoo, and he fucks up. And they dump him. Wife's dead, kids are dead to him, department throws him out. And he ends up here. Hiding, basically. He's got a pension, not big but enough. The fake name?" Delaney paused and looked at his partner. "My guess is so the kids couldn't find him. Not easily. The commander out there said he thought Schaller blamed himself for his wife, too.

"It's easy enough to change your name. Find a baby died the same year you want to be born, apply for a birth certificate, get a driver's license, and off you go. Could the kids find him through his bank, he got his pension name changed and forwarded? Yeah, maybe, probably. Not if they don't want to. Guess he figured they wouldn't want to. Fuckin' tragedy."

"Yeah, we're the tragedy squad," Burkett said to Delaney. Not Henry.

"But you know what?" Delaney perked up. "The commander called me back. He made some calls out there, called his kids. They want to talk with him. They do. Commander gave me their numbers."

"They do? That's great! What a drama. Shakespeare's got nothin' on the Spokane PD." Burkett and Delaney looked at each other until Henry coughed, startling them both.

"D'jou forget me? Old black man in a wheelchair, I get that a lot. But I gotta ask, does James, er, Martin, I guess, does he know?"

"He does."

"Where is he?"

"In the room right next door to us here. Been talking with him for a while. Tough guy. But when I told him his real name, he talked. All this razzle-dazzle with the panties and your signature? Was so you could testify if he wasn't around. Had it all figured out. He even starts asking me questions, like I'm gonna answer him."

"Like what?"

"Like, do we know if the cameras worked all the time, or they go out so somebody could come and go without getting videoed? So, Ki could have walked out of the Hope sometime all healthy and nothing for us to worry about here. Always possible, but not here, the videos are all solid. Ki dropped out of sight some way we haven't seen, 'cause he sure ain't in the building now, and he doesn't show up anywhere leaving. And Turner's asking me do we have an officers' group, like a fraternal or a service association, does things for the community. What's that all about?" The two detectives locked eyes.

"He's making the case for his defense," Burkett said.
"Fairly well, I have to say." Delaney said.
"Case?" Henry said. "What case?"
"Well, Henry. We're charging him with murdering Ki Sun Minh. What did you really think this was all about?"

***

In the end, Burkett and Delaney let Martin Schaller/James Turner go. A search of the dump by evidence technicians and cadaver dogs proved negative. "For now," Delaney said when Schaller walked out of headquarters nine hours later.

Schaller showed up at Henry's door at four a.m. Henry let him in and offered a beer, one of his own from the last time he'd been there, which he declined.

"So James, or do I call you Martin, are you on bond or what?"

"No, free as a bird. Or at least a bird with a chain on. I can't leave the state while they're investigating. But they don't have enough to bring charges. And they can't find Ki Sun Minh so they don't know what to do."

"They told me they were charging you with murder."

"Well, cops lie. They're allowed to, to fool a suspect or an accomplice—and by the way, they think you're my accomplice—but they can't charge without some evidence. Like a body, or a witness, or a confession. They apparently spent all night searching the dump where our dumpsters go. Came up negative.

"Absent a body, I'm free. Sort of. For now. I have to tell them where I am and, after tomorrow, I don't know where that is. We all gotta be out of here, with the building's closing. There's folks in the service elevator right now moving stuff out. Me, all I have is some clothes and books. All the furniture stays.

"But you, Henry. What are you going to do? It's tomorrow. Did you figure something out?"

Henry smiled and shook his head. "Yup. There's an apartment building nearby with openings, and I have one locked in. Two, actually, I get to choose. I made some calls."

Schaller waggled his head. "How can that be? There's a major shortage, and you made calls. Just like that. You wait till the last minute, the last second, and just make some calls. That's faith."

"That's hope. Hope has power. It pulls us," Henry said.

"Oh, yeah? You know how you're gonna move your trains and stuff?"

"That I don't know, yet. Something will happen."

Schaller smiled for a moment. "Yes, it will, Henry. Listen, gimme your phone number, I can reach you when you're settled."

"You have a phone? I didn't think you had a cell phone."

"Burkett and Delaney took me out and made me get one at a store. Part of my conditions of release. I haven't had one in a while."

"Not since Alexandria?" Schaller jerked, startled. "Yes. They told me."

"They got big mouths, don't they? Fuckin' cops are all the same." And he smiled to blunt the words and share the joke.

And, right or wrong, Henry decided his friend wasn't a killer.

When Martin Schaller left Henry's apartment, he didn't go up to his own or to the westside fire escape. He instead went to the east side, climbed the escape to the last flight of stairs just below the roof, and took out the cell phone. He called Detective Delaney, who confirmed what they'd talked about in the interview room.

"They should be showing up around now," Delaney said.

"Good. That's a good thing. You're doing a mitzvah, know what that is?"

"Yeah, a Jewish good deed. I'm not the one's doing it; the youngsters out there are. You can thank them yourself."

"Nah, I'm not going near them. I'm still a murder suspect to them."

"To me too, Schaller. Don't forget that. I know you dropped him down the fire escape into the dumpster. I just can't prove it. Yet." Schaller thought Delaney would bite the phone when he went on. "I'm only letting you walk around 'cause I got to. I'm not just doing a cop a favor."

"Ex-cop."

"No such thing. But don't get me wrong, I'll nail you."

"Maybe. I'll see you around, Delaney."

"Not if…"

Martin Schaller hung up. Down below in the parking lot, several newer-looking performance cars and pickup trucks had pulled up, with young men and women getting out and meeting at the door, some carrying empty cardboard boxes. Off-duty cops pulled together by Delaney. Schaller knew in a few minutes, at dawn, one of them would call Henry Becker and tell him his movers had arrived. As ordained?

He looked further east toward a faint orange line beginning to glow across the horizon. Far beyond his sight, Schaller knew, his kids were waking up in Virginia, three hours ahead. He took out his new phone and a piece of Delaney's notebook paper with their numbers. He would call when the sun rose.

He needed a drink for that, but he wouldn't take one.

Infinite Penance

Travis Richardson

Yet another day. Chad wakes up, sun streaming through a dirty window with white moted rays penetrating his skull like diamond tip drills. Wincing, he lifts his body, puts his feet on the ground, and starts to stand… but not yet. A surge of acid shoots up from his stomach, burning his throat, but he swallows it back down.

Standing on the second try, he shuffles over to the in-room sink, scoops some water to drink, and then rinses his face. He would like an ibuprofen. Ten of them. Everything aches. He looks at the bottle on the counter, offering momentary relief from the pain. He closes his eyes and shakes his head. No, that would be cowardice. Suppressing his deserved suffering is for weaker men.

***

Half an hour later, he showered in the bathroom down the hall. Dressed in ratty but washed jeans and a faded blue T-shirt, he passes the unmissable yellow signs announcing the upcoming Halloween eviction taped on every door. Refreshed and somewhat alive, he makes his way downstairs, four flights. His eye catches a new graffiti tag. *Skinny* written in a Sharpie. The inked letters drawn too exact as if tracing from template. Not a confident, loose signature. Definitely the work of a novice. Probably a junior high kid just learning to tag. Unfortunately, the script has elements of the Trouble Kings gang style. Not a good sign. He hopes the tagger isn't Esther's son, Emanuel. The kid has intelligence but also mistrust and burning anger. He, like the boy's mother and other residents, has learned to mad-dog Chad. To give him a look of brutal scorn. And that is as it should be.

Penance should never be an easy cross to bear.

Walking into the lobby, he sees Dorothy, the Hope Apartments' elderly manager. An angel in human form.

"Hello, Mr. Graham."

He nods and whispers, "Hello, ma'am."

"You've heard about the closing, right?"

Another nod. "Kind of hard to miss the signs around here."

Anita, the assistant manager, looks up from her desk and narrows her eyes, giving him an unmistakable look of contempt. Seven years of residency and the same withering look. Chad drops his head in shame and shuffles to the front door.

"I really wish you'd lighten up on him. He looks like hell and then some," Dorothy says, her voice carrying across the lobby.

"Lightenin' up won't bring DeShawn Matheson back. What he does with his life is his own choosing. It don't change what he done." Anita's voice is loud enough to make sure Chad won't miss a word as he lets the door close behind him.

Stepping outside, Chad glances at the Lamplighter Inn attached to the apartment building, longing to walk inside and obliterate the rest of the day in booze. Unfortunately, there are at least two more hours before Les might consider opening the door. Besides, Chad has things to do. A check is coming his way today or tomorrow. He'll pay off his tabs and send out the remainder. But now, he needs to do something to occupy his time. Litter on the street catches his eye. A McDonald's take-out bag, a broken Modelo beer bottle, countless random junk mail, and flyers. Cleaning the environment was something that had been important to his sister. In her honor, he collects the take-out bag and drops the broken glass bottle inside. Grabs some of the loose paper, too.

"You think you can do a better job than me, copper?"

Chad turns to see Earl, the wiry little maintenance man. Broom in hand and cocky smile under his mustache, Chad sees him for what he is. An insecure man trying to feel strong by preying on those he considers weak. He's seen worse. Men who wore badges to terrorize others. Degenerates who beat children and women. Weaselly predators. A previous version of himself might have given Earl a witty comeback along the lines of looking in the mirror if you want to find a pitiful person to pick on. But not today's Chad Graham.

"Just tryin' to make your life easier, Earl."

"Uh-huh. Just like you did with DeShawn's family."

Chad holds Earl's stare for a moment and then shuffles on. He no doubt heard Anita's criticism and felt the need to pile on. While Anita had the right to hate Chad—her righteous outrage came from their shared history—Earl did not.

Dropping the bag in a nearby trash can, Chad decides to clean litter around the streets and bus stops. But there isn't as much garbage as one would think. Downtown Spokane has cleaned up considerably from where it had been in the '90s when he used to patrol.

Hip restaurants and tattoo shops that catered to the upper class took up storefronts, displacing the adult video stores and five and dimes. Fancy nightclubs for professional twenty and thirty-somethings to sip over-priced drinks and abandoned factories that had been renovated into expensive lofts for them to screw and sleep.

And now the Hope Apartments is the current target of downtown's gentrification on steroids movement. Hope would be gutted and remodeled into an uber-modern sleek boutique hotel absent a soul. Where Chad would go after the eviction was anybody's guess. Same for many of his neighbors. He wished the best for them, hoping against history that they would find better places to live. As for himself, living under a bridge in a sleeping bag seems adequate enough. Maybe too nice. Plus, if there is a bonus flash flood under a low bridge, he could drown his misery away forever.

Fifteen minutes later, he is looking at the Spokane River that cuts through the heart of the city. A pleasant way to kill time. He walks along a gravel path beside the river, reminiscing about his days of innocence. Before the tragedy. Back when he was an affluent kid growing up in the North Indian Trail area of Spokane. He had a high three-point average in high school, lettering in football and baseball. His future had an unstoppable upward trajectory. Visiting the falls was something he always enjoyed, inciting pride of being fortunate enough to be a resident of such a beautiful city.

As Chad walks up to the lower Spokane Falls, he laments on how his view of the river and city has changed. The awe of his youth is gone. Thirty hard years since he was a teenager. This is not Niagara Falls by any stretch of the imagination. If he were to jump in a barrel and float down the river, his survival rate would hinge more on his ability to get out of the contraption or the toxicity of the water than surviving the drop.

In the distance, Chad spots a transaction going down under a red pedestrian bridge. Two men talk. Shake hands twice. Then the man dressed in shabby clothes walks away with a bounce in his step. No doubt jonesing bad and eagerly anticipating flying sky high within the next few minutes. The dealer glares at Chad.

He nods with a half-smile and moseys along. No sense in earning the wrath of a street pusher.

Chad continues his journey along the path toward Canada Island when he sees a tall, angular kid with a backpack coming his way. He walks with a quick but hesitant step. His eyes wide, looking around for a bogeyman. It's Emanuel from 316—Esther's kid. Shouldn't he be in school? He spots Chad and narrows his eyes. Turning, he runs up a hill. Chad doesn't know for sure, but he's guessing that the boy is heading to the dealer under the stairs with a re-up of heroin or whatever the pusher is selling.

A few steps later, there's a fresh Sharpie tag on a railing. *Skinny*. Yep, he's the tagger working with the Trouble Kings crew. A bunch of retrograde gangsters pushing, pimping and extorting. When Chad had been a cop, they had been an independent crew terrorizing Spokane until the SPD tore the majority of the organization down. Last he had heard, the crew had reformed and were answering to a Mexican mafia with a lot more firepower. It's hard to get away from those gangs like that once you're in. They own you for forever… or until breathing is no longer possible.

Guilt can own you, too.

Chad circles around the park and back to Hope. The mail should be arriving shortly. He enters the lobby. From behind the front desk, Anita gives him a scowl. He ducks his head and shuffles to the bank of mailboxes, inserting his key.

Bingo. He reaches into the box and pulls out an envelope from the City of Spokane among the junk mail. He walks up the stairs, feeling Anita's stare burning into his back.

Inside his room, he rips open the envelope and looks at the check. A smile crosses his lips. He grabs his own checkbook and writes out a check to Hope's management company and puts it in an envelope.

Back down the stairs, he stops at the front desk and slides the envelope across the table, keeping his eyes averted.

"You're the only one who pays rent before it's due," Anita says. "Havin' a monthly paycheck for the rest of your life must be nice."

Chad takes two steps away and stops.

"Nothing in my life is nice," he says without turning. But he watches Anita's reflection in the pane glass window as her face scrunches. What is she feeling toward him? Anger? Pity? Who knows? Only one thing is certain, she will never give him a chance. She snatches up the envelope and tosses it into a drawer.

Chad hesitates for a moment longer and then exits. Walking by the Lamplighter, he fights the urge to stop inside. His brain cells will need to wait a little while longer. He needs to attend to a few responsibilities first. If he steps inside the bar, he might not leave until closing time.

***

He walks to a liquor/convenience store three blocks away, bypassing the busy 7-11. Mr. Quan has been running this store since the '80s, and since then, nothing has really changed. No doubt there are decades-old Twinkies that have never moved off the shelf.

A bell jingles on the front door as Chad enters.

"Hello, Officer Graham."

"Hello, Mr. Quan."

"Is it payday?"

"It is. How much do I owe?"

The store owner pulls out a spiral-bound notebook. He studies the list.

"One hundred and twenty-two dollars and seventy-one cents. That includes a ham sandwich you're going to buy in a minute," he says with a chuckle.

A half-smile creeps on Chad's face. "What if I get a tuna sandwich?"

Mr. Quan shakes his head. "No, I wouldn't recommend it. Made it yesterday. The bread is probably too moist now."

Chad writes the check and hands it to the owner.

"This won't bounce, eh?" he says with another chuckle.

"Has it ever? I just gotta deposit my check at the bank."

"You should do direct deposit. Life would be easier."

"Nah. I'd have to get a computer… or a phone. And I don't want either."

A few minutes later, Chad is eating the ham sandwich as he walks to the bank. More of those *Skinny* tags are written on walls. Stupid kid. He's just looking to get busted by the SPD. There's a task force that records all the tags they can find. There's probably CCTV of him in several places defacing property. All that evidence will be compounded if he gets busted for doing something stupid for the Trouble Kings. That kid needs to break free from them before it is too late.

Inside the bank, he goes up to Monica, his favorite teller.

"Hello, Mr. Graham."

"Hello, Monica."

He slides the endorsed check over to the pretty Latinx teller. He's probably five years older than her, although he looks closer to fifteen. In another world, maybe he'd ask her on a date. She hasn't worn a wedding ring in two years. But he'd never bring another person into his bleak reality.

"The usual?" she asks, not unlike a bartender.

"Yes. Add an extra one-twenty-five to the deposit and five hundred in cash. Twenties, please. You know what to do with the rest."

She nods. Working behind the computer, Monica deposits enough to cover rent and Mr. Quan's bill. She slides a cashier's check to him with the remaining amount on it. The payee is Belinda Matheson.

"Let me get you an envelope and stamp," Monica says. A sad smile crosses her lips.

***

Dropping the envelope into the postal box, he walks over to the Lamplighter, a literal cornerstone of Hope. Stepping inside, the low light and scratchy vinyl '70s-era funk envelops Chad in an oasis of comfort. On autopilot, he drifts over to his usual stool at the end of the bar.

Les, polishing glass tumblers as if his customers really cared, works on two more before tossing the rag over his shoulder and walking to the far end of the bar.

"What are you havin' today, Chad?"

"My tab, first of all."

The bartender's eyes light up. "Shit, if you'd told me that was the reason you came in, I wouldn't have been wasting my time over there. Speak up, man."

"I don't want to interrupt a man who is busy working on his passion."

Les makes a "*pssh*" sound through his lips and reaches under the bar with a stained sheet of paper. He strains to read the chicken scratch he's written.

"Let's see. It's a new month now. October. So, in September, you had one, two—"

He counts the hash marks. Each representing a Rainier beer. Each draft cost four dollars. Although Chad started his open-eyed slide into oblivion with hard alcohol, beer kept him from going blotto before six p.m. and getting rolled by the less than reputable folks in the neighborhood. Plus, his money lasted longer, and somehow he was getting a diet of barley and hops along with occasional sandwiches, chips, and other snacks.

"It's four hundred and sixteen dollars and a quarter."

Chad's certain the number is a little inflated but paying with a tab and not keeping a ledger on his side put him in a losing position every month. Screw it. He tossed five hundred dollars in bills on the counter.

"Change, please."

"I can always subtract this against future—"

"Change, please. I've still gotta do laundry."

"Okay, okay," Les says with his hands up. "Don't bite my head off. I'm getting' it."

Eighty-three dollars and change eventually make its way to Chad. He leaves a five out and pockets the rest.

"Rainier, please."

Les grabs the bill and pours a draft from the tap.

Eight hours later, Chad stumbles back to his room. Going up the first floor, he sees a tall kid with a hoodie coming down the stairs.

He knows he shouldn't say anything. He lost his moral authority decades ago.

"Emmanuel," he says.

The kid, trying to grow a tough guy mustache, stops and glares at him. "You speakin' to me, drunk-ass loser cop?"

Chad cringes. He's too wasted to censor himself. Something a cautious man would do. "If you need help getting out of the Kings, let me know. I can help."

"What the fuck you talkin' about, old man? I ain't leavin' shit."

He shoves Chad. Even though the scrawny teen is barely over a hundred pounds, Chad takes a step back on the stairs and loses his footing. He falls on his ass and slides four stairs down.

The kid shakes his head as he walks past. "Chuh, you're pathetic, man. Pah-thetic."

Chad wants to get up and tackle him. Show the kid a little taste of authority. Respect for elders. But he sits immobile, feeling exactly like Emmanuel's insult, *pah-thetic.*

***

Six or seven days pass. Maybe eight. Everything blends together on super benders. Sleep, shower, stroll, booze, repeat. Maybe a sandwich if he remembers.

The days have gotten shorter, and the early October winds cut like a jagged dagger. He'll need to get a good sleeping bag and tent to deal with the upcoming eviction. Sure there's a few shelters he could crash at and fend off other stinking dudes over a cot, which he may or may not do. Inevitably cops would get called out to stop a skirmish. Maybe an old colleague on the force might show up to restore order. Nobody he'd want to see. He didn't want to endure their pity.

The way Chad became a cop was a life-changing fluke. Sixteen and already tracked by major league scouts, baseball was a sure thing. Then high school career day happened. Riding along with a Spokane police officer seemed more interesting than watching somebody work on an actuary table or deliver mail. The day exceeded expectations, including an official visit to the shooting range with an unofficial weapons firing, stepping inside the jail cell, and witnessing an actual arrest of a drunk driver. He was sold. If baseball didn't work out, he knew what he would do with the rest of his life. That cocksure confidence of youth had evaporated into dust.

***

Chad walks out of the Lamplighter minutes after last call and onto the desolate street. The world tilts a little more than it should. The sodium-vapor city lights glow soft like they are covered in pale yellow gauze. The cold chills his bones, but in a good way. The air removes a small portion of the cotton candy that coats his brain. Just enough clarity that will help him make the wobbly trip up the steps before passing out on the bed.

Then he hears something. Soft and small in the wind.

"Help."

He looks around, trying to find the source.

"Help."

There are noises too. Crashing sounds. Groans and curses. He follows the sounds up the block. His fuzzy instincts sharpen. In an alley, three men stand over a body, kicking him. The man on the ground pleads and whimpers.

The men above use words like "disrespectin'" and "teachin' a lesson."

Three against one—a coward's fight. He looks around for a weapon of some kind. Fighting instruments might be inside the dumpsters, but for a smelly alley, this location is surprisingly spotless.

So he takes out his keys and jingles them.

The attackers stop their assault and look over at him.

"What-chu lookin' at? Move on now," the biggest of the three says.

In that brief pause, Chad sees Emmanuel look up from the ground. An eye is swollen, and blood streams from his nose. He then notices spray paint can on the ground. Skin written in an orange spray before a line slants to the ground. Tackled mid-spray, no doubt.

Chad continues to jangle the keys, sorting things out as fast as his addled brain can.

"Shit, that drunk fool's still standing there," the smallest of the bunch said. "Let's stomp his ass."

"Take care of him, Romeo."

A hefty kid, no more than twenty stomps toward Chad. Sausage fingers balled into fists. His malevolent eyes bore into him.

Chad waits. *Jingle. Jingle. Jingle.*

The kid rushes him, head down, in the final few feet. Chad darts to the right, leaving his left leg out. The kid bellyflops on the ground with a loud "oomph."

Chad jingles the keys again. "Let the kid go."

"What do you care, old man?" the leader says, giving him his full attention.

The heavy dude slowly picks himself up while muttering curses. Chad realizes he is trapped in the alley. Emanuel, his body quivering, slowly stands. The two attackers in front of him don't notice. His eyes connect with Chad's. Fear and appreciation mix together.

Chad balls a fist around the keys.

"Run, kid."

The tallest man peers over his shoulder. Chad springs, rushing toward him and throwing an arching haymaker that lands on his temple. The big man falls. Chad throws an uppercut to the smallest one's chin. Emanuel runs, dodging past the stocky kid who slams into Chad a second later. Crashing into the concrete, Chad's breath escapes from his lungs. Oxygen is completely gone. The tallest one stands, holding the side of his head. He took a hard hit, just not hard enough to keep him on the ground. Looking down at Chad, a snarl rides up his lip.

"You're goin' to get the beatin' of your life."

The big guy raises his foot and stomps.

***

Baseball worked for Chad until it didn't.

He earned a scholarship at Clark College in Vancouver, Washington, where he majored in Law Enforcement and worked the summers as an intern with Spokane PD. He was the starting right fielder his junior and senior year. He was good but not spectacular. When the Cincinnati Reds drafted him low—their last pick—he considered not playing at all. His parents, however, encouraged him to give it a shot, and his contacts at SPD encouraged him to join the force after baseball was over.

He went out to Billings, Montana, to play for the Reds' rookie league for a contract not much more than minimum wage. The competition was surprisingly cutthroat. Guys his age and younger were desperately chasing an almost impossible dream. The math didn't add up for Chad. There were only a few major league spots that opened each year versus the vast minor league system. And they suited up every game at the bottom of the pyramid. Many of his teammates didn't have a net to catch them if things didn't work out. They were entirely committed to baseball—major leagues or bust.

He sprained his ankle stealing second on the third week of the season and then pulled his hamstring two weeks later running to first. Then his parents got into a severe car accident driving through Montana when their car collided with a migrating elk. His father broke his back, and his mother needed cosmetic surgery for all the glass that was embedded in her face.

He wanted to quit that night, but his parents, from their hospital beds, begged him to continue. He went after the ball like a demon. Swinging hard like his parents' recovery depended on it. Diving for balls that shouldn't be caught. It looked like he was headed for Double AA. Then his sister, a sophomore at Washington State, had a seizure on campus. When she received a brain cancer diagnosis, Chad didn't care to play baseball ever again. While he didn't believe playing ball had caused any of these tragedies, he felt it was a frivolous career that didn't really matter much.

Not when he could have boots on the ground, protecting the citizens of Spokane instead of cleats on the turf, extending his childhood.

***

"Who is Angie?" Chad hears a female voice ask.

His body is immobile, and everything radiates pain.

"What are you talking about?" a male voice responds.

"He keeps mumbling that name."

That's my sister, he tries to shout, but nothing comes out.

"You heard he was that cop from several years ago who shot that black man."

"Oh yeah. I remember that. In that crappy hotel, right? Weren't there a bunch of protests?"

"Yeah, especially after the jury said he wasn't guilty."

Chad didn't want to hear this. Where was he? He wanted to get away.

"Uh-oh," the male voice says. "He's waking up from his coma."

"He's not ready for that."

"Get me a dose of ketamine."

Coma? What are they are talking about? Chad tries to move, thrashing like a fish, although the pain is overwhelming.

He hears feet shuffling. Voices. Digital beeping. A body comes close to him.

"Easy there, bronco," the man's voice says.

Chad tries to shout, *get away*, but somewhere between forming the words and delivering them to his lips, a heavy, dark blanket wraps around his entirety, and the world became cottony quiet again.

***

Chad had been a cop with the Spokane PD for six years when he was assigned to a DEA task force. The work was long but invigorating when they made big busts. One night, he was monitoring a drug buy from a nearby van. An undercover agent would purchase two baggies of heroin. A simple transaction. The team had accumulated a pattern of buys that would be used to take down the 13th Street gang.

As money exchanged hands, two men appeared from the shadows, and one shot the agent in the head. Chad and his partner burst out of their van, not radioing for back-up. His partner shot the dealer but caught a bullet from the assassin. Chad cut the murderer down with three tight body shots. After checking on his partner—saved by a bulletproof vest—Chad took off in pursuit of the third man.

The long-legged criminal ran fast, but Chad could still circle the bases in sixteens seconds. He gained on the hooded man, shouting at him to stop. The man ran into the Hope Apartments instead.

Chad had been inside the apartments before and knew that if the accessory to murder got too far ahead, he could hide in any of the hundred-plus rooms, and SPD might never find him. Charging through the lobby, Chad held his pistol out in front, sweeping the area. Anita stood behind the counter. She screamed when he pointed the gun at her.

"Did a man run inside here?" Chad asked.

She nodded.

"Which way?"

She pointed to the staircase, her finger unsteady.

"Do you know who he is?"

She quickly shook her head. "N-never seen him before."

Chad rushed to the staircase.

When he made it up to the first landing, he saw a shadow and ducked. Three bullets smashed into the wall next to him. Plaster peppered the side of his face. He returned fire, splintering sections of a banister. The man ran up the stairs. Although Chad's ears rang, he was certain that the footsteps continued past the second floor and up to the third. He rounded each corner cautiously, his pistol leading the way. No doubt the gunman didn't go further than the third floor.

There were two long hallways on either side of the staircase. Which way did the shooter go? Chad went right. That is when he noticed fresh specks of blood on the soiled carpet. He walked forward, his heart thumping wildly, trying to discern ancient stains from current blood droplets. He thought he lost the trail when a door swung open behind him. Chad swiveled and saw a tall black man walk into the hallway with a black object in his hand. He fired four times. The man fell backward, blood bursting from his chest. Chad ran up to him and couldn't comprehend what he saw. The dying man, gasping for breath, had on a black robe and a leather shaving kit. Where was the gun?

"Daddy!" a young voice screamed from inside the room.

A young girl with two buns on top of her head stood in the doorway, her mouth hinged open and eyes wild with disbelief and horror.

Gravity became heavier than it had ever been. Chad leaned against the wall, his legs giving way.

Oh no, God. Please, no.

***

Sitting up in a hospital bed, Chad stares back at the Spokane PD officer. The detective's tight lips show her exasperation. She desperately wants to help.

"You're certain you don't remember a single thing about the men who beat the living daylights out of you? I know you've got that steel plate in your head now, but can you remember anything at all? It would help us tremendously."

Chad would have shaken his head, but it's too painful.

"No."

He scratches the cast on his arm but stops. He might be showing a tell. All three of those thugs' faces are etched into his brain in spite of the damage they did. But this incident is about Emanuel, not him. It is the kid's call. Hopefully, he will see this second chance as an opportunity and not blow it.

"Is there anything you remember at all about that night?"

"Just leaving the bar. I must have taken a wrong turn. I have a history of blacking out." He shrugs and raises his eyebrows, trying to give his best embarrassed expression.

She doesn't look convinced, but Chad doesn't need to convince her. She will have to give up on him and move on to the next crime if nobody else comes forward. Cops have too many cases to work and cannot wait out the truth.

***

Chad leaves the hospital early against the doctor's recommendations. He is supposed to remain in the hospital for another three days for continued evaluations, but he has to escape. The constant questions, the never-ending concern. It's too much for a man trying to serve his penance.

Awkwardly changing into his street clothes with his broken arm, he studies the wilting bouquet of flowers Dorothy had sent over. Money wasted. He had not bothered to open the card. No reason to.

Entering the lobby of Hope, Anita glances at him from her desk. The hard glare no longer burns in her eyes but something softer. Chad's stomach churns uneasily. This isn't right. He shuffles over to the staircase, staring at his feet.

"You need any help, Mr. Graham?"

"No, thank you," he says, taking the first of several painful upward steps.

"Remember, there's eight more days until we're all evicted."

October 31st—the day after his cast comes off. A perfect way to celebrate.

Entering his bedroom door, he steps on a folded piece of paper. His healing ribs scream in pain as he bends over. The spiral-torn college-ruled paper has the word "Thanks" with an E scrawled in black Sharpie ink. He stares at the word of gratitude, transfixed.

Maybe, just maybe, he had made a difference.

La Chingona

Hector Acosta

The church stood across the street and flipped God off.

Peering out of her bedroom window, Veronica noticed the old building, its crumbling brick spire poking through the fog like a middle finger directed at the deity throwing down the barrage of rain they had been experiencing in Spokane all week. Inspired by the sight, Veronica joined in flipping God, or at least her upstairs neighbors, off. Rain hammered her bedroom window just as a crack of thunder sent the lights in her room flickering. Upstairs, her neighbors started arguing again, their voices and plodding footsteps crashing down atop Veronica. She'd never met the couple, didn't even know if they really were a couple, just assumed so based on how much they fought. It's something she always meant to ask Dorothy, the Hope's onsite manager, but had never gotten around to. Now, with everyone getting evicted, Veronica figured it didn't really matter.

The memory of the eviction notice she found tacked on the door jumped at her like a wolf at the throat of a felled deer. Developers had been buying entire city blocks all around Spokane, signs around the city advertising redeveloped complexes with names like The Cooper George, The Madison and The West End Lofts. For the longest time, she believed a developer's fingers would never reach the Hope Apartments. The building was almost a hundred years old, an institution Dorothy called it once, and the city would never tear down an institution, right?

Turns out they would, likely swayed not only by whatever money the developers were offering but also by the Hope's reputation as a place which drew criminals and violence to it.

Waves of panic crashed against her, threatening to pull her under to the place filled with empty bottles, fast food wrappers, and slipping time. Gripping the mask lying on her lap, the world went dark as she slipped it over her head, the familiar smell of the sweat-stained cloth becoming a pier to stand on. Split vertically into green, white, and red sections, the colors of the mask invoked the Mexican flag, the design having caught her eyes when she came across it online. The price was more than she usually paid, but she clicked the order button anyway.

Picking up a plastic bottle from the floor, she gave it a couple of shakes and took a sip. The orange and vodka skewed more toward the OJ side of things, but Veronica didn't feel like getting up to refill it. Screwing the cap back on, she threw the bottle on her bed and scooted closer to the desk which took up most of one side of the bedroom. She reached up to the webcam perched atop her computer monitor like a gawking bird and ensured it embraced her in the center of its lens while hiding most of her small and messy bedroom from sight.

Disappointment stabbed her gut when she logged into her online account and saw only a dozen viewers waiting for her. Not for the first time, Veronica wondered how much easier all of this would be if rather than the brown-skinned, slightly chubby, masked woman her webcam captured, she could display a thinner, whiter, and blonder version of herself, features all the top female streamers, the ones with hundreds of thousands of followers and millions of views, had in common.

She had started streaming six months ago, right after she lost her grocery job, and came across an online article about how much money people—especially women—were making by putting themselves in front of a camera. You didn't even have to take your clothes off. All you had to do was play some videogames and maybe talk about your day. And seeing how she was already doing the videogames part, Veronica decided to go for it. If nothing else, it had to beat being constantly rejected for minimum wage jobs because she didn't have a bachelor's degree. Purchasing a web camera with her one and only credit card, Veronica sprung for the best internet package her cable company offered and signed up with the website almost everyone used to stream out of, telling herself she would recoup the costs in a couple of weeks. A month max.

Clicking through her inbox, Veronica scrolled through her messages, responding to the ones which included money—or *donations*—as the website encouraged her to call them. The funds would already be making their way to her bank account, minus the percentage the site took. The donations never amounted to much, barely enough to cover a night at the value menu, but she responded to everyone who sent her money, having learned early on the men (she always assumed they were men) liked to be acknowledged.

She'd finished typing up her last reply just as a digital timer popped up in the middle of her screen, a reminder her stream started soon. Veronica's finger rolled the click wheel on her mouse, as above her the neighbors continued to argue. Wishing she'd gotten up to refill her drink,

Veronica shifted in her seat and watched the numbers on the timer bleed away. When it reached zero, she hit the blue LIVE button on the corner of the screen.

"*¡Que tal cabrones!* How you all doin' over *en el cyber-spacio*?" she asked, looking directly at the camera. Her words were drenched in a loud, over-stylized accent, and she was thankful for the mask as her cheeks reddened, the heat spreading all over her face. "La Chingona sees we got Goku Did It 35 Minutes Ago on here already. How you doing, *esé*?" She waited for Goku to reply in the chat window before moving on to greet some of the other viewers.

Early on, Veronica had tried to stream san masks, but those shows had been disasters. She fumbled with her words, got flustered easily, and had a hard time splitting her attention between the videogame she was supposed to be playing and the viewers she needed to interact with. Worst of all, she never knew what to talk about, leading to long moments of silence. Determined to improve, Veronica spent time watching the more popular streamers on the site, and it didn't take long for her to discover something they all shared in common. Whether it be the girl wearing cat ears who was *really* into Japanese animation, the guy who wore a fake mustache and made dad jokes, or an entire subsection of female streamers who pushed the no-nudity rules on the site by wearing tight, almost painted on clothing, the best streamers all had defined personas. And as 'woman with a non-existent saving account, crippling debt, and no real options' wasn't a character which viewers were flocking to, Veronica set out to find something new to present to the camera.

La Chingona came to her one Sunday afternoon as she was curled up in bed, eating Hot Cheetos, drinking a beer, and stewing over yet another poorly attended streaming session. She was flipping through the television channels and wishing she hadn't canceled the cable when she came across a movie playing on the local Spanish network. It featured a masked wrestler so famous even Veronica, who never had any interest in wrestling, knew about him. Watching the man strut around the screen in his silver mask and impeccable suit sparked an idea, and before long, she was online searching for a mask to buy and watching videos of wrestlers talking directly to the camera—cutting promos—she learned they called it. She spent days in front of the mirror attempting to emulate their speech pattern, the way confidence hung from their words like icicles from a roof.

"*Órale pues*, let's get started, *sí*? You guys requested I play some Call of Duty, which *no sé porqué*—I don't know why—La Chingona sucks at first-person shooters. But a deal's a deal." The character of La Chingona would have never worked without the mask. It shielded her from her fears and worries, allowing her to be someone else.

Though she did wish she hadn't gone so broad with the accent.

She was in the middle of answering a question about what her favorite movie was when shouting from upstairs cut through her explanation as to why the much-maligned Ben Affleck superhero movie was better than people thought.

"*¡Qué relajo!*" she said in La Chingona's voice. "My neighbors, they make all the noise. That's why La Chingona is trying to move." She'd mentioned an upcoming move before in hopes it would garner more donations from people, but she always left the reason as to why out. It felt too pathetic, even with her behind a mask. Today though, she found she was too tired to lie.

"*Saben que?* That's not the only reason why La Chingona is moving." Veronica said, pausing the game mid-level. "The real reason, *la verdad verdad*, is that La Chingona is getting evicted. *Pinche* city is tearing my building down. That's why I need your ayuda. Anything you can do or give to La Chingona will mean a lot."

Her chat window filled with well wishes and emoji prayer hands, and she was notified by a pinging noise of people sending her money, but when she checked her account, she found the amounts to be only a couple of dollars. Nothing which would make a difference. Veronica wanted to cry, wanted to scream about how hard she worked, and how she just needed a hand to pull her from this sink hole. But she'd seen those types of public freak-outs, how they got spread through social media, the women getting labeled Karens, and the men pussies. They got made fun of, abused, and then forgotten.

She wouldn't let that be her.

Taking a deep breath, Veronica was about to get back into the game when a message popped into the corner of the screen. It was a direct message, meaning only she could see it, and it came from an account she didn't recognize.

I CAN HELP.

***

The building wasn't all glass, Veronica decided, stepping inside the elevator. *Only about eighty percent glass*, the stainless-steel (because of course, they would be stainless-steel) doors closing the moment her finger pushed the silver button with its inlaid black number.

Veronica's stomach tightened as the elevators started its ascent to the 27th floor, a sour taste clawing its way up her throat.

She'd spent hours going through her closet, trying to pick an outfit which wouldn't give people the wrong impression. In the end, she decided none of her outfits would hide the fact she was several neighborhoods and tax brackets away from belonging in the type of building she was walking into. So she went with a pair of faded blue jeans and a long sleeve shirt for the cold weather. Her black hair she tied back in a ponytail, and she applied just enough makeup to look presentable. With the elevator pinging the 20th floor, she turned to look at herself in one of the mirrored walls and not for the first time, wondered if she should put on the mask currently bulging in her front right jean pocket.

The message told her to bring the mask but hadn't been specific on whether she needed to show up wearing it or not. In fact, it hadn't been specific about much. Just that he'd been watching the stream for a while now, liked what he saw, and if she were open to it, he might be able to help her situation. The message was signed ZERO_MIERDA.

He liked what he saw, Veronica thought, checking one of the multitudes of reflections the elevator's mirrored walls surrounded her with and running a hand through her hair. She wasn't dumb, she knew the possible implications of an internet stranger asking to meet in his apartment and had been ready to decline the invitation—especially once Zero shot down her suggestion of meeting somewhere public—when she received a notification that one thousand dollars had been deposited into her account.

To show I'm serious, read Zero's second message.

She tried googling his username but found very little information and nothing concrete about the person she was on her way up to meet. Same with checking his account on the streaming site. All that told her was the account had been created recently and that, per the brief analytics the site gave Veronica, hers was the only stream he'd watched in the last few weeks.

I'm only here to listen, she told herself, the doors to the elevator opening and revealing a long, white hallway with a black door at the end of it. Veronica thought of the Hope's own hallways, of the crumbling art deco style no one bothered to ever update, of the broken tiles and scrawled graffiti adorning almost every inch of the walls. If there were any arguing couples on the 27th floor, Veronica was positive the walls would block out their arguments. The urge to slip on the mask rose with every step she took, and by the time Veronica reached the end of the hallway, a piece of it was between her fingers. Rubbing the cloth helped to steady her beating heart as Veronica studied the door in front of her.

I'll be fine, she thought. *I'm La Chingona, remember?*

Stuffing the mask back in her pocket, she took a breath and knocked on the door, the sound dull and weak. She waited.

***

The faces stared at Veronica from the wall, empty eye sockets and slacked mouths reminding her of the painting of sad clowns which people with little taste bought at art fairs.

"Which one is your favorite?" Zero—Trevor, Veronica corrected herself—asked, handing her a can of Coke.

Veronica glanced down to it and confirmed he hadn't opened it for her. Then she looked back to the wall and its countless pinned faces.

Well, not actually faces. Wrestling masks.

They lined the wall of Trevor's living room, a sea of colored and stitched fabric extending from the floor all the way up to the ceiling, the masks all arranged ten to a row. Some featured simple, one-color designs, while others included multiple layers of fabric in all sorts of colors and shapes to make them stand out from each other. Somewhere in the mix, she thought she saw the mask of the wrestler which inspired La Chingona, and because it was one of the few masks she recognized, pointed to it.

"See, that's why I wanted to meet you," said Trevor, apparently pleased with her answer. "You're old school, I dig that. You have no idea how many people come here and immediately splooge over my Jushin Liger one," he pointed to a red and white mask with multiple horns coming from its side which hung on the corner of the wall, before continuing, "I mean, yeah, it's the one he wore for the Tokyo Dome show, and was a bitch to verify, but there's history, and then there's history, history, right?"

Veronica nodded, though in reality, she understood almost nothing of what Trevor said. Which, from the short time they'd been speaking, was becoming a worrying trend.

The man who opened the door had held a game controller in one hand and looked to be in his early twenties. He wore a plain black shirt, cargo shorts, and flip-flops. Pushing away the shaggy, uncut hair from his face, he grinned when he saw Veronica and said, "La Chingona in the flesh." With an awkward flourish, he stepped to the side and invited her in, introducing himself as 'Zero Mierda, but you can call me Trevor' in the same breath. He didn't ask for her name.

"I need to pee," she told him once inside the apartment.

Leading her to a bathroom the size of her own bedroom, Veronica locked the door behind her and did her business. Afterward, as she washed her hands, she looked in the mirror and told herself she would give this guy five minutes and then leave. Five minutes, that's it, she thought, rummaging through the medicine cabinet and finding a medication for asthma which confirmed Trevor's identity. When she came out of it, she found he'd disappeared, leaving her to walk around his apartment and stumble upon the wall of masks on her own.

"I wasn't sure if you were going to show up," Trevor told her, plopping down on the leather couch facing the masks. Opening his own can of soda, he took a large gulp and said, "Also, I didn't know what you would want to drink. I have other stuff if you prefer."

"This is fine," Veronica muttered, placing the can of Coke on the glass coffee table. She sat down on the couch, making sure to keep a couple of cushion lengths away.

"I don't have a lot of food in the house, but if you're hungry, I can order us something. There's a place a couple of blocks away which makes a kick-ass pizza. Or, shit, if you got, like, a taco place you want me to get you something from, go for it. I bet you know the best ones."

"I'm okay," Veronica said, looking around. "I like your place," she lied.

The apartment was gigantic, with a large open living room, a kitchen most chefs would envy, and a view of downtown Spokane. When she received the address of this place, she googled the building and spent a few minutes clicking through pictures of the apartments inside, all mocked up to look their absolute best, with understated artwork and furniture, mood lighting, and classic style. Trevor's apartment was nothing like that. To Veronica, it looked more like a frat house, beer and soda cans spread everywhere, an obscenely big television sitting on the floor, wires running from it to multiple consoles, and a large desktop computer. Clothes were flung everywhere, and if Trevor cleaned up for her, Veronica couldn't tell. The masks weren't the only memorabilia on the wall, as Veronica spotted a signed Cowboys jersey, framed baseball cards, and a gold, oversized Championship belt. Taking it all in, Veronica was one hundred percent certain that somewhere in the apartment, there was a Scarface poster.

"This isn't all my collection," Trevor said, noticing her looking at the wall, "just what I managed to move from my old house in Texas. Cool, right?"

"You're new to Washington?" Veronica asked and reached for her Coke. She wished she could add some Jack to it, but even though Trevor seemed harmless so far, she wasn't about to ask for him to pour her anything.

Nodding, Trevor spent the next few minutes explaining how he moved from Texas to Washington not too long ago, 'right after the Bitcoin market exploded', which is how he'd made all his money. Once again, Veronica understood almost nothing from Trevor's rapid talk and wasn't even sure if anything he said was true. The whole mining for a coin which wasn't really a coin, seemed like a fantasy story. But fantasy or not, she was currently in an apartment with a monthly rent which likely was more than what she paid the Hope in a year. And the man in front of her had given her one thousand dollars yesterday, just to prove he could.

“Thank you for the do—money,” she told Trevor, having to stop herself from calling it a donation. Stupid website.

Trevor finished his soda and crushed the can. “Nothing to it. Your story really touched me, you know?”

Veronica fought not to cringe at the words ‘touched me.’ Setting her still unopened Coke can down, she remembered her promise—*five minutes, that’s it*—and while she didn’t have a watch, she imagined those minutes were ticking down. “You, uh, you said you could help me.”

“Totally,” Trevor said, moving closer to Veronica. “But I gotta ask, did you bring it?”

For a second, Veronica was unsure what he meant, and it wasn’t until she caught his eyes darting to the walls of masks, and then to her, that she understood. Reaching into her pocket, she pulled out the mask. *If he asks me to put it on, I’m out of here.*

“Can… can I see it?”

The tone of the question was all pleading reverence, and Veronica tried not to cringe at the words. Looking at Trevor, she found his own eyes locked not on her but on the mask held in her hands. He remained two cushions away, far enough for Veronica to react if he suddenly tried anything. Still, the question and the way he was acting set off a set of alarms in her head, and she almost stood up and left. But where would she go? Back to Hope and an apartment which would be yanked away from her at the end of the month?

Still keeping an eye on Trevor, she laid the mask down on one of the cushions between them. For a second, neither spoke, both looking down at the tri-colored mask.

"Where did you get it?" whispered Trevor, picking up the mask in both hands, like a priest cradling a baby during baptism.

"Online."

Trevor laughed, a giggling, nervous thing which went for too long and showed Veronica a chipped front tooth. "Online. That's insane." Turning the mask over, he ran his fingers across the laces and asked her if she'd changed them out. "Shame," he said when she told him she did. "Still, I guess it's not a big deal," he added, though his voice said that yes, it was indeed a very big deal. Flipping the mask back around, he brought it closer to his face, stretching the fabric in his fingers and wrinkling his nose as if he and only he could detect an aroma emanating from it. "Some of the stitching is off, but that's to be expected," he said, glancing up to Veronica, who'd been watching this whole time and said, "You said you got it online."

"Off eBay."

"How much you paid for it?"

Alarms rang in Veronica's head again, but this time they were different. Tilting her head, she gave him what she hoped was a warm smile and said, "Oh, I can't remember."

Trevor laughed. "I bet you can't." Placing the mask back down on the cushion between them, he stood and stretched. Walking over to a bar cart by the kitchen, he poured himself a drink and spoke, "I love your gimmick, by the way. The whole Spanglish, the mask, the third person. Reminds me of El Generico in lots of way, but you know, less problematic seeing as you're umm," he turned and motioned up and down, "you know. You. No one is going to accuse you of appropriating a culture."

"Thanks, I think," Veronica said, the can of Coke he'd given her remaining untouched and gathering condensation on the table.

"Oh, it's a compliment. Seriously, you pull the whole thing off awesomely. When someone clued me into your channel, I wasn't expecting much, no offense, but the whole act is really well put together."

"Someone told you about my channel?"

"I got a couple of people who sometimes let me know when they find something they think I'll be interested in," Trevor said and shrugged. "And there's always message boards, and Twitter too. When they started telling me about you and sharing videos, I knew I had to meet you."

"Lucky you and I live in the same city then."

Trevor turned from the bar cart and grinned. "Weren't you listening? I told you I moved here from Texas."

It took a beat for Veronica to register what Trevor was saying, and even then, she found herself repeating the words out loud just to be sure. "You moved here just for me?"

"No!" Trevor giggled again, a sound which tightened the smile on Veronica's face and tensed her body. "That'd be creepy. I was bored of Texas. It's hot down there, did you know that? Plus full of dumb-ass yee-haw cowboys who don't get what I do. I needed a change. So I moved."

So I moved. He said it so simply, as if it wasn't anything to him. And looking at the man in front of her, Veronica imagined that it wasn't, not for him and his kind.

Walking back to the couch, he threw himself on his side and motioned to the mask, "and of course, there's this. You know what you got here, don't you?"

"I think I have something you want," Veronica said. A few minutes ago, she would have been worried Trevor might get the wrong idea at those words, but after watching the way he treated her mask and finding out about his move, Veronica thought she had a good idea of why Trevor asked her over.

"Maybe, maybe," he said, though the way his eyes kept returning to the mask betrayed him.

"You do." Leaning forward, Veronica's hand grazed the mask. "Tell me why, though."

Trevor frowned. "You know whose mask this is, don't you?"

Veronica shook her head.

"That's umm, okay. Wow. I thought you did." Pushing the hair out of his face, Trevor looked up at Veronica and studied her, and she got the feeling it was as if he was seeing Veronica for the first time, and not La Chingona, or the idea of La Chingona he had in his mind. "This," he pointed to the mask, "belongs, or belonged to Gladiador Sagrado." He paused and looked at her expectantly as if the information he just dropped had some weight to it. After a second, he continued, "He's a luchador—" he coughed and added, 'wrestler', which was kind of insulting to Veronica as she got his meaning the first time around, "who came up in the late seventies, early eighties. Never made it big, I think he maybe had a couple of tag matches with El Hijo del Santo, but that's about it, which is a shame because he was ahead of his time in terms of what he could do in the ring." Trevor's voice sped up as he talked about Gladiador Sagrado, his hands gesturing as well. "But the thing which makes him special, at least to folks like me, is that the dude disappeared after a couple of years of going from promotion to promotion. There was no big send-off, no retirement announcement, and no comeback tour years later. That's frickin' rare. *Everyone comes back.*"

"What happened to him?"

Trevor shrugged. "Who knows. Some say he just switched masks, but none of the wrestlers of that era match up to what he could do. Others say, you know," Trevor motioned to his throat with a finger, "offed himself. Couldn't handle the pressure or was sad about his status, but I don't believe it."

"Why?'

Another shrug. "Just a feeling. You watch his old matches, and like, you can tell the guy was having a blast. The love of wrestling just shined through, and I don't see anyone who has that to be throwing themselves off a bridge or eating a gun."

Veronica could have told him differently. Could have told him how sometimes a job was a job, and no matter how much you might enjoy it, at some point, it beats you down. That when your options begin to trickle down, you start to wonder what the bottom is and whether you want to wait to reach it.

"Truth is, I was kinda hoping you were, like, related to him. That you'd come here and tell me he was your *abuelito* or something."

Veronica laughed. She'd only ever met her grandfather on her mother's side, but she couldn't imagine the frail, old man whose faculties were already leaving him by the time she was born to ever have been inside a ring.

"What's so funny?"

"Nothing, nothing," Veronica said and reached for her coke can. She played with the tab on its top, not quite opening but pulling it enough to feel the tension in it. "I'm sorry Trevor, but no, I'm not related to any luchadores. Like I said, I saw this mask online and bought it 'cause I liked the design."

Trevor's shoulders slumped, his pose resembling one of the drooping masks on the wall. "That sucks."

"I'm sorry, but I can still sell you the mask."

"Why would I want to buy the mask?" Trevor asked.

Veronica blinked. "The way you were handling it a few minutes ago like it was a sacred work of art, I—"

"That's when I thought it belonged to GS, that he'd handed it down to his granddaughter."

"I told you I bought it online."

"I figured that was a line you were feeding me, 'cause you didn't want to reveal all your cards. But if you're not related to him, then I guess you did buy it online. And that means this thing is worthless to me." As if to prove his point, Trevor swept his hand on the couch, knocking the mask to the floor. "I get you're not a real fan—which by the way, is super shitty that you lied to everyone that—so I'll explain it to you. Those masks over there? Those aren't cheap replicas. Each of those have been worn by the actual *luchadores*." He rolled the r in the same over exaggerated manner La Chingona did. "That one you pointed to when you got here? That one alone is worth ten thousand dollars. Because. It is. Real. Not something bought online." With a sigh, he reached over and picked up a game controller off the floor and turned on the television.

"You told me you could help me," Veronica said, bending down to pick up the mask. Her mask.

"Huh?" Trevor said, already starting up a game. Without looking away from the television, he said, "Why would I help a liar?"

"I never lied," Veronica said. Something cold lapped at her ankles, but when she looked down, she found they were dry.

“Lie by omission is still a big old lie. You’re out there in your webcam, showing off your tits and pretending like you’re actually a wrestling fan.” Pausing the game, Trevor said, “Tell you what, if you can name three wrestlers off that wall,” he pointed to the masks again, “I’ll transfer ten thousand dollars into your account right now.”

“Fuck you,” Veronica said and rose off the couch.

“No, really, ten thousand right into your bank account.” Digging into his pocket, Trevor pulled out his phone and, after a couple of swipes, showed her his screen. He was logged into the streaming account phone app, and he’d already typed in the amount in the proper section, along with her account in the ‘to’ section.

“Tell you what, *Chingona*, I’ll make it easier. Just give me the name of who wore that mask over there, and the money is yours,” Trevor said, pointing to the mask she told him was her favorite when she first arrived. The mask belonging to the wrestler who she’d seen on television not so long ago, who had inspired her to start wearing her own mask.

“I’ll give you ten seconds.”

Stepping closer to the wall, Veronica focused on the silver mask. Her heart raced as the two empty sockets stared back at her. That cold feeling she’d felt a second ago was back again, and this time it reached all the way up to her knees. She gripped the mask in her hand and searched for her memories. The name was there, she knew it. She just had to retrieve it.

“Four seconds.”

Fragments of the movie replayed in her head as she waded deeper into her mind, the cold waves of panic surrounding her. She resisted drowning in them, focusing instead on the wrestling movie, on the announcer who kept mentioning the title every time they cut to commercials.

"Two seconds."

She almost had it. It was there. The Priest? No. But something like that. Closing her eyes, Veronica gripped the mask tighter, pulled and twisted it in both hands, the laces becoming entangled in her fingers. The name came to her just as a ripping sound filled her ears, her hand tearing the laces and some of the fabric of the mask.

"Santo!" She shouted and turned around to look at Trevor, "his name is Santo."

The two stared at each other, Veronica holding the two halves of the mask in each hand, Trevor holding his phone in one hand, the television controller in the other.

"Oooh, it's *El* Santo. So close, but I'm sorry, the judges won't accept your answer."

"I got the name right."

Trevor shook his head. "You *almost* got the name right. If you were a true wrestling fan, you would have gotten it right. And it wouldn't have taken you ten whole seconds."

"I got the name right," Veronica said again. In her mind, the waves of panic had become still, stiller than they'd ever been even when she put on the mask. "You said if I got the name right, you'd give me the money."

"I say a lot of things. Now, if you'll excuse me, I gotta beat this level. You can either show yourself out, or I can call security, and they'll show you out." Throwing his phone on the couch next to him, he picked up his game controller and sat down.

The masks were all looking at her. She felt their weight against her back, the way they judged her for being here, for having been so dumb to hope someone like Trevor could help her. They laughed at her with the black voids they had for mouths, at the fact she couldn't even name the mask which inspired La Chingona, at the accent she used whenever she slipped her own mask on, at the persona she draped on herself for what? For a couple of dollars and nothing more. Glancing down to her hands, she watched as her fingers loosened and the torn mask dropped to the floor. Looking up, she focused on two things, on the phone next to Trevor, the way it landed face up, and showed he was still logged into his streaming account. The second thing she focused on was the unopened can of coke still sitting on the coffee table.

The ocean inside her mind was perfectly still as she approached Trevor and picked up the can. Trevor didn't even glance at her, his attention still on the television. La Chingona smiled and swung.

Hodge's Lament

Gary Phillips

Earl Ricci groaned as he got up after being on a knee. He'd been tightening a worn elbow joint where it connected with a water inlet pipe to one of the boilers. Before he'd assembled the parts again, he'd made sure to remove any vestiges of the Teflon tape from the threads and had swabbed on sealant. Really the pipe and joint should be replaced, he knew, but at this stage of events, it wasn't going to matter. He stored the pipe wrench in his toolbox and started across the basement to leave, his knee protesting as he did so.

"Christ," he muttered.

Was he always an old man?

There was wetness in the morning air in this town, the moisture trapped in the brick and plaster and lathe of old buildings like this one as if lost ghosts. His joints were forever plaguing him because of that. Now what with pushing seventy, getting up and down the stairs of the Hope was more and more a chore added to the usual crap he had to see to in this crumbling mausoleum of malcontents and the misbegotten. It was a wonder the decades-old boilers kept functioning and that the wiring, last upgraded in the eighties, hadn't shorted out, sparking a fire to burn this place down past the studs.

He looked at the door to the storage room. Mostly it was junk in there. Among the contents, though, was an old-fashioned steamer trunk Ricci was sure he'd be clearing out soon. He was going to miss the hundred each month he'd been paid to pretend it wasn't there. And if anybody came around asking about its owner, to let the owner of the trunk know.

Nothing lasts forever, he reminded himself.

Up he went. Rounding the turn, a figure stood at the top of the stairs. She was backlit there in the doorway, a silhouette familiar to him. This woman had some sort of psychic radar that alerted her to when he was onsite. Wearily, he had a good idea what she wanted.

"Miss Dorlane," he said as he stepped onto the main floor. They stood in a short, dimly lit hallway off the lobby area. "What can I do for you?"

"It's that door you said you'd fixed. You didn't. The knob or whatever it is doesn't work right, Mr. Ricci. The closet doesn't close properly."

"Miss Dorlane, I've explained that I can only do so much at this time. I'm not authorized to spend money on these types of repairs. It's the door, it's warped and has to be removed, planed, and rehung."

"Well, you know how to do that, don't you?"

She was older than him by a few years, thin and gaunt in clothes stylish forty years ago. Forty years ago, when she'd worked at the Bon Marche department store. Light years from today.

"Again, my hands are tied. If your toilet was overflowing, that would be different. But the door means sanding, painting, and new hinges." He shook his head. "Management won't okay the expenses."

"That is highly unsatisfactory. You're forcing me to go over your head."

"Be my guest, ma'am." Off he went. Crossing the lobby, he considered how many of the tenants in the Hope were like Miss Dorlane. Obsessing on this or that relatively minor nuisance in their apartment when, in fact, they would all be out of here by October. Their way of fooling themselves that if problems were being fixed like always, everything was okay, Ricci rationalized.

The new normal meant the old had to go to make way for millennials with their kitchen counter islands and their super-powered panini grills. What a world.

It was past one in the afternoon, and he sauntered into the Lamplighter, the restaurant-bar also off the lobby. Several regulars, including Carl Bullis wearing his ever-present Seahawks cap, were eating at the counter, a few occupying booths. The Bird Queen was there, too—a tall, willowy woman with long grey hair. Her real name was Sonya Martinero, and she was once a top model in Mexico City.

Ricci perched on a stool, setting his toolbox down at his feet. One of the others at the counter was Gibson Hodges. They nodded at one another. Hodges was the one paying him the hundred each month for nearly four years. He was going to miss that sweet little bump.

***

Hodges finished his lunch, drinking the last of his Arnold Palmer. He wiped his mouth with a paper napkin and picked up his check. This, though, was more out of reflex than anything, as he knew what the total was. At least twice a week, he had the tuna melt and coleslaw at the Lamplighter. He might splurge and have the fries too, but he hadn't today. He left bills on the counter and rose. He moved past the back of the seated Ricci.

"Gibbs," the older man said.

"Earl."

Hodges headed for the street-side door. Les Poole was coming in that way. He was the owner of the Lamplighter and its bartender. A valise in hand, he was returning from the bank.

"How's it going, Les?" Hodges held the door open for him.

"A guy came through here last night looking for you." Poole stepped inside and stood off to the side. Hodges joined him. "He was white, around your age." Both he and Poole were black. Hodges was younger, fifty-three or so, and about an inch or so taller than the other man.

"Negro, you just now telling me?"

"I look like Alfred to your Bruce Wayne?" he cracked. "'Sides, figured you'd be in sooner or later. Told him I'd seen you around because it seemed to me, he already knew that."

"What else he ask?"

"Nothing. He hung around some then split."

"Thanks, man, I appreciate the heads up."

"This guy just got out, didn't he?" Having been in this neighborhood for years, it wasn't tough spotting those recently released from prison.

"If it's who I think it is, yeah."

"Then he'll be back."

"Not if I get to him first."

"Handle your business, Gibbs."

"Ain't nothing going to happen to Anita." The other man was sweet on Anita Moss, the building's assistant manager.

"That means Dorothy too," Poole said. Dorothy Givens was the head manager.

"I hear you."

Poole headed toward his tiny back office reached through the Lamplighter's kitchen. Hodges walked up to Third Avenue where there was more than one hot sheet motel. If he'd just gotten out of the joint and had located a man he was hunting, he'd stay close, and he'd want female companionship, no matter how much young boy butt he'd had inside. Several working girls of his acquaintance were on the stroll in their short skirts and shorter jackets. He wasn't a customer, but they came into the Lamplighter some evenings for a drink and chat. While gentrification was transforming the 509, plenty of the same endured.

Hodges prowled about, hands in his coat pockets. At times he stood near the parking lot of a random motel to see who came and went. It was mostly the ladies with their johns but no sign of Russ Stallings. As he was certain it was Stallings who was looking for him. Hodges considered spreading some twenties around among the pros, asking had they seen or serviced him. But they'd string him along and play him for a chump to get more money out of him. He returned to the Hope.

Going along the fourth-floor hallway, he passed the Bird Queen's apartment. Through her door, he heard Martinero talking to her various caged parakeets and parrots and them tweeting at her vibrantly. Distracted, he only then noticed the fire door opening and out stepped Stallings. He came forward, a slight limp evident.

"How's it going, Hodges?"

"The fuck, man?"

"I came to collect."

"You ain't owed, man. Thought that was settled."

"That's not how I see it."

"You're the only one that does."

"I'm the only one that matters." He had on a bulky coat, maybe a gun in one of the pockets. But he had to be wondering if Hodges had a gun in his coat as well.

"This is what they call a standoff, Stallings." His hands were back in his pockets.

"You're not looking at this the right way, Hodges."

He hunched a shoulder. "Guess I'm myopic."

He frowned at that. "I'm'a give you a little time to consider what's right. You'll come correct." Like a gunslinger in the Old West, he backed up, eyes steady on Hodges. Still facing the other man, he pushed his hip on the fire door's crash bar and opened it. Using his foot to keep the door open, he sidestepped onto the landing. The door closing, Hodges heard his footfalls receding as he hurriedly descended.

Hodges removed his hands from his empty pockets and went into his room. Some four years ago, he ran a small crew that pulled a bank heist, though not an institution where you got a set of steak knives when you opened an account. It was an underground bank handling and laundering marijuana profits. This was all cash, and because of federal laws, these monies were not placed in usual banks as the feds would seize those profits. Naturally, such a set-up was fortified and guarded.

The heist was his last one after a string of them over the years. Stallings' brother was in on the job and was killed in the getaway. Hodges made sure the man's widow got his cut. But the brother had come around, saying since he was family, he should get a piece too. Get a piece, or maybe he'd go to the cops, he'd added. Hodges warned him off. The brother then leaned on his sister-in-law to come across. Hodges busted Stallings' kneecap with a crowbar and took the money back. Soon thereafter,

Stallings got picked up on an old beef so was out of sight and mind. Until now.

Hodges weighed his next moves. He could set a trap for Stallings and kill him. It wasn't as if he hadn't killed in the past, but he'd never developed a hardness about doing such, and now, years out of the game, he was reticent to take such a harsh approach. But he damn sure couldn't wait around because he knew Stallings would work himself up, and when he came around next time, he might shoot first and worry about finding the scratch afterward.

Later out on the streets, Hodges walked several blocks over to an area once replete with storefront businesses, mom and pop concerns ranging from hardware stores to nail salons. Now they were vacant, and a new mall and promenade was on the books to be built. Several buildings already had plywood boards in front of their facades. It was at one of these fences that Hodges paused. Ignoring passersby, he inserted a blade screwdriver between two of the boards. Some time ago, he'd loosened and removed the nails in one of these boards. He'd drilled in screws where the nail holes were. Then he'd replaced those screws with the next size smaller. In that way, the board stayed in place but could be removed if leveraged free as he was doing now.

He went through the gap. On this side of the board, he'd attached straps so he could set the board back in place. It wasn't secured, but he didn't intend to be in here long. This particular building had already been gutted. Hodges put on a flashlight and wended his way around several iron beams until he came to an area on a rear wall. He bent and, using his screwdriver again, wedged out a section of remaining drywall. In the cavity was a metal box where he kept a gun, an extra magazine, and a couple of other items, a burner cell phone, and an object encased in a square of foam.

Hodges had determined that living in a place like the Hope meant you never knew when the cops might sweep through on a humbug. Better to keep such things as a cold piece off the premises. Along with the foam casing, he slipped the semi-auto into the other pocket of his coat and the magazine in his pants pocket. He went back out, a couple passing by but not paying attention to him. Given he wasn't returning, Hodges didn't bother to put the screws back in place, only propping the board back in place. He walked away.

***

Toward dusk, Stallings watched Earl Ricci, wearing gloves, exit through a side door of the Hope from the lobby. He had Hodge's trunk from the storage room strapped to a dolly. Despite the cold, he was sweating from the effort and breathing hard. A 2001 Sable station wagon with several dents in the body was parked in a No Parking zone at the curb. One of the plastic taillight covers was gone. Instead, there was red tape covering the cavity. Stallings appeared, this time with a gun.

"I'll take that, old-timer."

"Mister, I don't want no trouble, but this trunk doesn't belong to you."

He gestured with the gun. "This says it does. Load that bad boy up."

Making a pained face, Ricci opened the back of the car and wheeled the trunk over. He undid the straps and leaned the battered piece of luggage against the car and tried to lift it up but couldn't.

"I'm going to need some help," he said.

"Fine," an irritated Stallings said. "But don't try nothing."

"I won't."

Together they got the trunk up and slid it into the rear cargo area.

Stallings stepped away and, gun back in his hand, said, "Keys. And don't even think about calling the cops."

Ricci handed them over.

Stallings got in the car, its springs squeaking. After a few cranks, the engine started, and he drove away.

Reaching the Astro Motel on Third Avenue, he parked the car on the lot and got the back open. He pulled the trunk out, letting the other end thunk onto the asphalt. He noted the contents of the trunk shifted about some as he dragged it to his room. He got the door open using his card key. In he went with his prize and closed the door. Stallings then put it on the bed. Having been so excited before, it was only now he noticed the two padlocks securing the lid.

"Shit," he said.

He didn't have any tools with him. He'd arrived in town by bus. In a joint like this, the old man behind the bulletproof glass in the manager's office wasn't going to lend him a pair of pliers. Where the hell could he get a hammer or some damn thing? Maybe one of those big, serrated knives for the kitchen at a Rite-Aid. For sure, he needed to be gone from around here as soon as possible 'cause Hodges was going to be looking for him and the cash. That goddamn car, what was he thinking? Hodges would spot that for sure.

Back outside, making sure the door clicked as he pulled it close, he got in the station wagon and turned the ignition. The battery was weak, and at first, his initial effort produced a lethargic rotation of the crankshaft. He cursed again, hitting the steering wheel.

"You piece of shit, start."

Stallings turned the key again, and this time the car responded. He backed it out and drove the vehicle several blocks over. This time when he parked, he left the keys and headed back toward his room. It was dark now, and Stallings was anxious, staring at passing cars, straining to see if Hodges were at the wheel. More than once, he had the feeling he was being followed but doubling back, he didn't see Hodges. But what if Hodges had a partner, not the old man, some young buck he hadn't accounted for?

Jittery but focused, Stallings stopped at a supermarket and bought a big kitchen knife. At a liquor store, he got a pint of vodka in a plastic bottle. He took a different route back to the motel, wary and on the lookout. In his room, he took a swig from the bottle and got to work on the cracked leather of the trunk. The knife wasn't serrated, but it was sharp. He began cutting through, but it soon got stuck. Stallings had the trunk on the floor and a foot on it as he took the handle in two hands. He began sawing again but couldn't make headway. He withdrew the knife and peered closer at the slit he'd made. Beneath the leather was wood. He had no choice but to keep going. Stallings began sawing again with the knife. He was able to lengthen the slit more, but the knife kept bunching up in the opening. He paused to catch his breath and take another pull on his booze. He got back at it, and this time when the knife stalled, the plastic handle snapped in two, and the blade bent in the process.

"Motherfucker," he said.

Stallings checked the time. The Rite-Aid was still open. He would have to chance it. He chastised himself for ditching the car earlier. He should have loaded the trunk up again and driven further away. But where to? It wasn't like he had a lot of money, having just gotten out of the joint. All his life Stallings had come up short but not this time. Every day when he was down, he'd imagined getting his, and surely not some old ass hunk of luggage was going to stop that from happening. Reaching for the doorknob, he heard a raucous laugh. Stallings froze.

He went to the window, keeping low and easing the curtain aside a fraction. Out there off to the side of the driveway, seen partly in the glare of the motel's neon sign, one of the working girls talking to a man who could be Hodges. But he was in gloom, and Stallings couldn't make out his features, couldn't see his hands to tell if he were black or white. Did he look toward the rooms? Stallings moved back, trying to keep his heartrate in check.

Picking up his gun, he decided if he heard footsteps, he'd blast whoever it was on the other side of the door and make a run for it. Minutes ticked by, but nothing happened. He went to the window again and peeked. Nobody stood near the driveway, at least no one he could see. He couldn't just sit here on his hands, he had to get to the store and get another knife. Gun in his jacket pocket, Stallings left the room, looking all around. At Rite-Aid, he bought two large knives and a screwdriver. It was colder now. Coupled with the gnawing sense that time was against him, he hurried back to the Astro.

Entering the room, he gaped, stones in his stomach. The locks on the trunk were open. Dropping his plastic bag of tools, he fumbled for his gun, visualizing Hodges coming out of the bathroom pumping rounds at him. But the bathroom was empty. The door to the room was ajar at his back. He glared at the interior of the trunk. There was a quilted pad in there like what movers used. It was partly wrapped around three cinderblocks. There was also a grenade and a stack of banded hundreds.

"That sonofabitch," he said, swallowing hard and putting his gun away. He knew a grenade had been used to blast out a section of wall in the heist his brother had been part of. He also knew it was illegal for a civilian to possess one. Particularly a guy out on parole. He grabbed the hundreds and the grenade. He'd used his real name to rent the room, and he had to get rid of it. He turned to see two cops crowding the doorway.

"Is that a fuckin' grenade?" one of the cops said as both drew their weapons. "Don't even think about tossing that thing, Sgt. Rock."

"I can explain this."

***

Sitting in his car across the street, Hodges watched as the two officers marched a handcuffed Stallings out of the hotel. Using the burner, he'd called in a disturbance at the Astro. He'd figured Stallings would keep watch on the Hope. For five hundred dollars, he'd paid Ricci to wait until almost dark and take the trunk up from the basement and load it in the beater of a car he'd borrowed from the Bird Queen. Hodges had promised her if anything happened to it, he'd buy her another one so she could continue to drive her birds around in the cargo area. Every week she'd take them to the Cascades and set their cages on the rocks for the view. He'd removed the money from the trunk except for the one stack and replaced the swag with the cinderblocks and the grenade.

Stallings wanted to be part of the robbery, now he was.

In his car, Hodges had followed Stallings in the station wagon. Night was a good cover, and with its discolored taillight, the Bird Queen's car wasn't hard to keep track of either. The Astro motel was used regularly by the ladies, and Hodges had recruited a working girl he knew from the Lamplighter who called herself Cherry Rose. He paid her to tell the old boy behind the glass she was there to see the man in Number 15, Stalling's room. She laid a twenty on him, and he used his passkey card to let her in. She'd unlocked the trunk with the keys Hodges had given her and left. Hodges wasn't worried about the manager going to the cops. Stuck in his dotage at the Astro, he'd no doubt learned long ago to keep his head down. And if the police got around to believing Stallings who for sure was diming Hodges out, they needed evidence to sweat him. There was none given the underground bank he stole from had covered its tracks. Otherwise, all the money they handled would have been taken by the feds—who, given the explosive being used, investigated.

***

"Guess this is it," Hodges said to Les Poole the following day. The two men shook hands, standing at the lobby entrance to the Lamplighter.

"Better not ask you where you're heading."

"I'm not looking over my shoulder anymore. Well, not too much at least."

He'd settled at the Hope to stay off the radar. Now he was going to enjoy his ill-gotten gains. He wasn't getting any younger, and Stallings had shown him best to do what he wanted, no sense living with regrets.

"Miss the sun, huh?"

“Something like that,” he chuckled. Hodges walked away from the Hope for the last time.

The Rumor in 411

Frank Zafiro

We had a good thing going, really.

What did I mean by that? Could be I meant the Hope Apartments. The place wasn't The Davenport, but most people in Spokane couldn't afford The Davenport, anyway. Gavin and me, we didn't have enough money on any given day to even risk walking into the lobby of the place, but we could afford to live at the Hope. Barely. At least, we could until the same suits who could put themselves up at The Davenport for weeks on end came in and turned this old girl into another refuge for hipsters with cash. For a little while longer, though, we had a place to lay our heads, and that was a good thing.

I could just as easily mean me and Gavin when I say a good thing. Gavin Dane was a good friend. There weren't many of those in the world, at least not of the true kind. Lots of so-called friends that were only there when the ride was smooth. Not Gavin. He was a thick and thin motherfucker.

So yeah, I could mean him.

But let's face it.

I didn't mean the Hope or Gavin.

I meant the drugs.

***

The pounding on the door woke me up from a vague, dark dream. All I could remember was that I was being strangled. Whoever had his hands around my throat was also slamming the back of my head into a brick wall repeatedly. As I came out of that half-reality, the drum beat of my head bashing into the wall was in perfect time with the banging on the door.

"Ronnie! Wake the fuck up!"

I groaned and blinked. Gavin's bare feet were two inches from my face, but that was nothing new. These units only had one bed, so it was either sleep in flip-flop fashion, or one of us had to take the floor.

I slid off the bed. Gavin pulled the blanket over his head and turned to the wall.

"Ronnie Rossovich! Answer the door!"

"All right!" I yelled. "I'm coming!"

I swung the door open. Oberg stood in the entryway, his fist raised to pound some more. He wore a pair of faded dingy white boxer shorts and a Winger concert T-shirt that didn't cover the last three inches of his ample belly.

"What?" I demanded. "You're going to wake up the whole place."

His eyes narrowed. "It's one-thirty, Ronnie. Everyone except the junkies has been up for hours. And you know what I say about junkies?"

I did, but he was going to say it anyway.

"Fuck the junkies," Oberg pronounced. Then, without waiting to be invited, he walked into our tiny apartment. He looked around at the sparse furnishings. He sniffed in disgust and muttered, "What a dump."

Oberg lived in one of the corner units. Those were a little bigger and, unlike ours, had its own bathroom.

Somehow, Oberg equated not having to walk down the hall to pee as being anointed as nobility.

I closed the door. “What do you want?”

Oberg held out his hand. “I need the ten dollars you owe me.”

I held up my empty hands. “I don’t have any money.”

“Bullshit. I saw you pay rent yesterday.”

“Which is why I don’t have any money.”

Anita, the assistant manager, had been all over the tenants to pay for the month of October in advance, and we were no exception. Everyone had to be out after Halloween, so she didn’t want anyone skipping on the rent.

I’d been expecting Dorothy, the manager, who usually collected. She was older than Anita, but the years had made her kinder, not meaner. I had an appeal all set to go, but when the knock came, and it was Anita at the door with her hand out, things fell apart. I tried my line about needing food money.

Her eyes narrowed with her customary suspicion. “Naw, what you buyin’ is going straight into your arm, Rossovich. Don’t try to con me.”

If Elvis had told Anita Moss he could sing a little, she’d have regarded him with suspicion. She trusted no one. In my book, that was a vice, not a virtue. The fact that she was right about where the money would go didn’t change that.

I bargained to pay half now and half at the end of the month.

“Okay,” she said.

Surprised, I repeated dumbly, “Okay?”

“Sure. You pay me half now. Then you and Gavin get your skinny white asses on up out of this apartment for the next two weeks. I'll slap a padlock on the door, and you can come back on the sixteenth. How's that?"

I paid her. Turned out I was still a dollar twenty-eight short, which she dutifully noted in her ledger before moving on to the next apartment.

Oberg had been staring at me as the image of Anita's visit flashed through my mind. He seemed to be considering my logic. Eventually, he shrugged. "It don't matter. I need you to pay me today."

I rubbed the sleep from my eyes and moved to the kitchen. I thought we might have some packets of coffee left over from the box we swiped off the housekeeping cart at the Lincoln Motor Court last week. As I rummaged through the drawers, I said, "What's the rush? I've owed you that money for months, and you've only asked for it, like, twice."

"I figured you'd get it to me eventually." Oberg jerked a thumb toward Gavin. "And if you welshed, I knew your boyfriend here would pay off."

"He's not my boyfriend."

"Whatever. I knew he was good for it."

He was right. Gavin would cover the debt.

I opened another drawer. No coffee.

"Is this because of the eviction?" I asked, figuring he was worried that once we got booted out, we'd all scatter to the winds, and he'd never see his money again. Which was probably true.

"If that was the case, I'd be here two weeks from now," Oberg said.

I checked the final drawer. Empty. I slid it shut and gave Oberg a weary look. "I'm tired of playing guessity-fuck-fuck with you, Obie. I don't have your money. I'll try to get it today or tomorrow, okay?"

Oberg shook his head. "You ain't gonna make it to tomorrow, Ronnie."

"What's that supposed to mean? Are you threatening me?" I knew I couldn't take Oberg by myself, but I was also pretty sure Gavin and I together were a match for him. He struck me as the kind of guy who only needed one poke in the nose to go crying to mommy anyway. Or, in this case, probably crying to Dorothy.

But Oberg's demeanor didn't change. "I don't threaten," he said. "But there's plenty of people around who are gonna want to punch your ticket."

"What the hell are you talking about?"

Oberg grinned, showing his yellow-stained teeth. "You shouldn't sleep so late. Word is all over the Hope, and it came in off the street."

"Word?"

His grin widened. "That you're a rat, Ronnie. A fucking rat."

***

After Oberg left, Gavin got up. We sat at the rickety kitchen table on hard metal chairs, me with my face in my hands and Gavin comforting me.

"It'll be okay, Ronnie," he said in his easy, gentle voice.

"It's not true."

"I know."

"But people will believe it, won't they?"

Gavin didn't say anything. He didn't have to. We both knew the answer. On the street, especially in the smaller ecosystem surrounding the Hope, a rumor like this was an insidious virus. The rumor didn't need to be true for people to catch it. Maybe that was because they feared snitches so much or because they hated them. Maybe they just wanted to believe it. Or already believed enough crazy shit that believing this was easy. But I think it might just be a combination of all of that and more. Having a common target gave them something to direct their anger toward and someone else to feel superior to, all the while being part of the tribe while doing so.

"You've got to face this head-on, Ronnie."

"I can't."

"You have to. If you don't, people will believe it for sure."

"They already do."

"Some maybe," he conceded. "But if we come out strong with a denial, that might convince most people that it isn't true."

We?

I glanced up from my hands to look Gavin in the eye. Gavin Dane, who I always thought should have been a private eye or a movie star with that name. Instead, he was a quiet, resolute junkie who might be the only true friend I'd ever had. Or would ever have.

Gavin stared calmly back, a trace of his quirky smile playing on his lips. There was always something mysterious in those eyes of his. I was pretty sure where his love for me came from, that it was like Oberg said. Either way, it was a deep connection. I decided years ago that why didn't matter. Gavin loved me and was loyal. I didn't need to label it. When the most important thing in your life is how you're going to find and pay for your next fix, labels kinda lose their usefulness, anyway.

Except for *rat*. That was a label that stuck. One that could break love and loyalty.

"I just need to lay low," I said.

"For a *month*?"

"A few days, is all. Let things blow over."

"This isn't going to blow over." Gavin squeezed my shoulder. "You gotta face it. Tell people it isn't true. It's the only way."

"Oberg's right. Someone'll kill me."

"Oberg's an idiot."

"You don't think someone would kill me over this?"

Gavin let go of my shoulder. "Nobody will believe it. We'll make sure of it. Now, let's go."

A shot of panic lanced through me, the first powerful thing I'd felt since waking. The sensation flashed me back to the dream of being strangled.

"We gotta cop first," I told Gavin.

"Duh."

***

We took the stairs. Ever the optimist, Gavin punched the button for the elevator, but I just kept walking. That thing rarely worked, and no way did I want to be inside the tiny box when it decided it was time to break down again. Didn't stop Gavin from trying, though.

Except for the ground floor, each level of the Hope was a carbon copy of the others. There wasn't any benefit to living on the fourth floor, not unless you were a fitness freak who liked climbing stairs. As we descended, the slap of our tennis shoes on the steps echoed slightly in the old building. Each floor had its own smells as we passed.

As I reached for the door to the lobby, it opened on its own. Earl Ricci, the stocky maintenance man for the Hope, stepped through with a toolbox in one hand. I noticed a plunger in his other.

Earl saw us but made no effort to step aside. Instead, he lumbered forward, letting the door swing shut behind him.

"Hi, Earl," Gavin said pleasantly, moving out of the way.

Earl grunted.

"Toilet problems?"

Earl slowed, then stopped. He looked over his shoulder at us. "Men's bathroom on two. Again."

"Yeah?"

"Yeah. Probably all the homos flushing their condoms. *Again.*" His eyes flicked back and forth between Gavin and me. Then he grunted and gave a half shrug. "Anyway."

Without another word, he turned and trudged up the stairs toward the second floor.

"See?" I whispered to Gavin. "Even Earl doesn't trust the elevator."

We made our way into the lobby. The manager's door was closed, so no Dorothy. That was probably good. She was tuned into the whisper stream of the street. If she'd heard the same rumor as Oberg, I knew she'd stop me to talk about it, to ask how she could help.

She couldn't. Someone gets called a rat, no one can help.

Outside, the crisp October air bit into me immediately. I was never fat to begin with, but years of riding the horse had stripped away most of my weight. Cold cut through me easily. The battered orange OSU hoodie I wore was better equipped for a brisk spring day, not the winter weather that was settling in over Spokane already. Gavin's jacket was no better. We'd have to hustle up some heavier coats soon.

If I survived.

I pushed the thought away, but it swung back like a punching bag after an ineffectual blow.

"Come on," Gavin said, rubbing his hands together and blowing on them as he turned to walk down the sidewalk. "Let's take care of this now. Then we fix."

"Where to?" I asked, but he didn't have to answer. Where else could we go to solve this?

The Lamplighter.

I wrapped my hands around my upper arms and fell into step beside him.

***

Stepping into the Lamplighter was the closest thing to time travel you could ever experience unless the laws of physics change. Due to the low lighting inside, the stale tang of decades-old cigarette smoke was the first sensation to wash over me. I'd been coming into the Lamp for several years but still wasn't entirely used to the intensity of that first blast of ancient, embedded smoke. The low bass drumbeat and plucked strings of the Fleetwood Mac hit "The Chain" played on the vintage jukebox in the corner. Only it wasn't vintage, just the original, and the song playing now was one of the newest it featured.

Gavin was already moving across the dirty golden shag carpet, following the pathway worn by countless patrons. The 1970s décor meshed perfectly with the carpet and the cigarette odor. My eyes adjusted as I followed Gavin. I kept my head down, not meeting anyone's gaze. Even over the sound of the music and low chatter, I heard a few mutters of "rat."

I was in trouble.

"Hey!" Lester Poole, the bartender, barked at us.

We both turned. Lester was a tall, thin black man. His clothes were stylish and more recent than the Fleetwood Mac tune on the juke but still hit their peak before Clinton was President.

Les pointed his bony finger, staring hard at me. “Don’t even think about shooting up in my bathroom.”

I opened my mouth to answer, but Gavin beat me to it.

“Of course not, Les.”

Lester’s gaze shifted to Gavin and softened softly. “Well, good. But no loitering, either. Paying customers only.”

Gavin nudged his head toward Laszlo Nagy in the corner booth. Lester followed the motion. He scowled slightly, then turned back to his busy work.

“Come on,” Gavin said in a low voice.

I followed him toward Nagy’s corner booth. Laszlo Nagy sat in the short-back black vinyl chair alone. Even though the man was almost as skinny as I was, no muscle stood guard. Nagy didn’t need it. He didn’t hold dope or money. Anyone stupid enough to mess with him would see it paid back times ten within an hour, and everyone knew it. None of us knew for sure who was backing him, but that didn’t matter. He’d shown his power on several very public occasions, so we knew it was real. Him sitting alone in the bar nursing a drink like this was an expression of that power, or at least flaunting that he had powerful friends.

“Hey, Laz,” Gavin said. We stood at the table, not daring to sit without permission.

Nagy ran his hand over his long, stringy hair and eyed us both with contempt. The faded remains of a pair of black eyes was still evident on his face, punctuated by the greasy sheen of his skin. Honestly, it irked me. I didn’t believe him to be any more than a half-step above a user himself, but he tried to pose like he was the white Frank Lucas or something. I guess in our small world, he kinda was. The idea that someone dotted his eyes for him gave me some measure of joy, though.

"Ain't you two just popular these days," Nagy said. He glared at me. "Especially you, Ronnie Rosso*snitch.*"

"It's not true," Gavin said.

Nagy didn't look away from me. "The fuck you know."

I started to repeat Gavin's denial, but Nagy held up a hand.

"Don't bother. You'd just be diggin' a deeper hole for yourself." He grinned, revealing his ugly teeth. "Which ain't a bad idea, now that I mention it."

"Look," Gavin said, "I don't know where you heard this, but it's bullshit. Ronnie's not a snitch."

"I'm not," I added.

Nagy's smile pressed into a tight-lipped scowl. "So you're gonna lie to my face, too? What, you think I'm stupid?"

"No," Gavin said easily. "I think you're smart. That's why we came straight to you."

Nagy absorbed the compliment, seemingly unsure how to react. I knew he liked his ego stroked, but I could tell he didn't want to let go of this rumor, either. Finally, he said, "You ever go to court, Gavin?"

"Once or twice."

"No, like *real* court, not first appearance or bail shit. With witnesses and evidence and shit."

"No."

Nagy's lizard-like gaze flicked to me.

I shook my head. "Me neither."

“I figured.” Nagy took a sip of his drink, obviously relishing the superiority of the moment. Then he continued, “See, it’s kinda like TV when they do that shit. I mean, it’s boring and all, but some of it’s the same. Especially when it comes to witnesses.” His lips peeled away from his teeth again in a grin full of malice. “Last time I was there, the prosecutor had what she called ‘an irrefutable witness.’ You know what that is?”

I did, but that wasn’t what Nagy wanted to hear. “No idea,” I said.

“Figured that, too.” He leaned forward. “That’s a witness who’s a stone-cold lock. You get me?”

Both of us nodded. I didn’t like where this was going.

Nagy raised his hand and waved over a rail-thin kid who looked fourteen. He wore round glasses and a faded denim jacket. His expression was all bravado, but it was easy to see the scared boy underneath.

“This is Scooter,” Nagy told us.

You need a new nickname, kid.

“Scooter here saw something a few days ago. He just told me about it last night.” Nagy motioned for him to speak. “Tell ’em.”

Scooter cleared his throat and shifted from one foot to another. “Uh, I was over a few blocks, walking back from Dick’s Burgers. I turned into an alley to take a shortcut and saw a couple of guys.”

“Who’d you see?” Nagy prompted.

Scooter pointed at me.

“Bullshit,” I said.

“Shut up,” Nagy ordered. He waved for Scooter to continue.

Scooter cleared his throat again. “It was you. I recognized the orange hoodie.”

"There's plenty of people who wear—"

"I said, shut up," Nagy growled.

I did as I was told.

Scooter watched the exchange, waiting until he knew it was safe to continue. "So, uh, I didn't know what was going on exactly, I decided to leave the way I came, but before I could, the other guy turned away and walked toward his car. He got in and left." He swallowed. "Then you looked around and left in the same direction."

We all sat in silence for a moment. The Fleetwood Mac tune had been rising to its climax during Scooter's description of events and now trailed off. Some R&B deep cut replaced it.

"That's it?" Gavin asked.

Scooter nodded.

Gavin turned to Nagy. "*That's* what made you think Ronnie's a rat?"

Nagy waved Scooter away. When the kid was gone, he said, "Scooter said the other guy looked like a cop."

"That's crazy."

"And so did his car."

"Still crazy."

"It ain't crazy," Nagy said. "Cops have a look. And so do their cars."

"So maybe some cop stopped Ronnie in an alley to fuck with him. That doesn't make him a snitch. We've *all* been hassled by the police."

"Scooter said it didn't look like he was being hassled. It looked… cozy."

Gavin rolled his eyes. "You're taking what a fifteen-year-old kid said over—"

"He's eighteen."

Sure he is, I thought, but kept my mouth shut.

Gavin didn't argue the point, either. "You're taking what he thought he saw as gospel? You didn't even want to ask Ronnie about it before letting him get tagged as a rat?"

Nagy shifted slightly in his seat as if he hadn't considered this before. "Scooter is solid," he said, though I could hear a sliver of doubt in his tone. Then his eyes bore into me. "But, fine. I'm asking you now, Ronnie. What the fuck with that guy in the alley? Convince me."

I swallowed, suddenly cold. I could feel the beginnings of sickness creeping in. All I wanted to do was get away from Nagy and the Lamplighter and just fix and then deal with this all later. It would be better later if only I could—

"Don't just stand there like you're making up lies on the spot," Nagy growled. "Today, motherfucker."

"I… I don't really remember for sure," I said haltingly. "I had some business-type hit me up in the alley a few days ago. That might have been it."

"Business type?"

I nodded.

"Not a cop?"

"No. But this guy had, like, a car sort of like cops drive. A Lincoln or something."

"What'd he want?"

I glanced away. "A blowjob," I muttered.

"What? Speak up."

I cleared my throat. "He wanted head. Offered me forty bucks for it."

Nagy studied me closely, suspicion wafting off of him. "You're just walking through the alley, and some random business dude asks you for a knobber?" He smirked. "Come on."

"He didn't just blurt it out. He waved me over, and then he danced around it for a minute or two before he finally asked."

"Did you do it?"

"No!"

"You sure?"

"I didn't!"

Nagy considered. "Then what?"

"Then he left, and so did I."

"Like the kid said."

"Pretty much."

Nagy stared at me, clearly thinking over what I'd told him. After a while, he leaned back. "I don't know," he muttered.

"It's true," I said.

Nagy sucked on his teeth. "You do put out that vibe."

"The truth vibe?"

"No, the kind that says you'd suck a dick for money." Nagy spoke absently, thinking. He stroked his greasy face. "And the kid's description of the cop and his car weren't very specific."

I felt a small surge of hope.

Nagy shrugged. "I guess it all comes down to who I believe. And I don't believe you, Ronnie. I think you're a fucking snitch."

"He's not," Gavin said.

Nagy turned to Gavin. "How do you know?"

"I'm closer to him than anyone."

"Yeah, so I've heard."

Gavin didn't react. "He's not. I guarantee it."

"You're vouching for him?"

"Yeah. And you know I don't lie."

"Oh, I know that, huh? Now you're telling me what I do or don't know?"

"I guess so," Gavin said. "Because it's the truth."

Nagy leaned back. He glanced around the room, surveying it. Even though the thub-tump of the bass bounced through the air, the main ingredient I sensed was a watchful tension. What Nagy decided here would be a pronouncement with the same weight as any judge had down at the courthouse. If he said the rat label stuck, I might as well run straight out of the Lamplighter and not look back.

He knew it, too. Not only that, but he was eating it up. The power, the attention. A medium fish in a tiny pond. I felt grateful for whoever gave him raccoon eyes.

"I need to think on this," he finally announced, loud enough for everyone in the place to hear.

"What's that mean?"

"It means I gotta think on it," Nagy repeated. "You and your boyfriend come back tonight. Around eleven. I'll let you know then."

We stood there. I don't know what was going through Gavin's mind, but relief was pouring through mine. Following fast on the heels of that was *Good, now we can score and get right.*

"Eleven, then," Gavin said. "We'll be back."

"You better," Nagy told him. "Don't make me find you."

He wouldn't, of course. But he had access to muscle who would, and it was just a phone call away.

"We'll show."

"Good for you. Now get the fuck out of here." He raised his voice for the crowd. "Like Lester says, paying customers only."

There was a smattering of chuckles at that. Gavin and I didn't hang around to hear them taper off. We got the fuck out while it was still an option.

***

"Ho-ly *shit*," I said as we walked down First Avenue. I rubbed my upper arms against the cold. "I can't believe that worked."

"Until tonight, at least."

"Thanks, man. You really saved my ass."

"It was nothing."

We rounded the corner onto Cedar. I stopped in front of the Rocket Bakery and grabbed Gavin, swinging him around to face me. "No, it wasn't, man. It was a lot."

Gavin gave me one of his quirky smiles. He lifted his shoulders in a slight shrug. But his eyes burned with something I'd seen more and more often lately.

Yearning.

"You stood up for me," I said. "No one else ever has."

"Well, you're worth it, Ronnie. You're worth it."

I felt a sting of tears in my eyes. "I wish I could give you what you want," I said quietly.

Tears sparkled in his eyes, too, but didn't fall. "I've got everything I want."

I didn't know how to answer that. I just stared back at him until someone from the bakery patio seating yelled, "Get a room!"

Gavin laughed at that. He started walking again and pulled me along with him.

"What so funny?" I asked though I was already laughing a little, too.

"The fuck does he know? We've already got a room."

"For another thirty days," I said, "and then we're out."
"There's many a slip twixt the cup and the lip."
"What's that supposed to mean?"
"It means that anything can happen between now and then. Anyway, it doesn't matter. You wanna score now?"
"Duh," I said in my best Gavin voice.

***

We got lucky on our way over to the Browne's Addition neighborhood. Some idiot left their car running, probably to warm it up, without locking the door. Gavin was in and out of it so fast I was surprised he didn't blur. But as we walked away, he opened his jacket to show me a small purse. A block later, he rummaged through it, eventually holding up a few bills in triumph. It was more than enough to score. The rest was all makeup, a driver's license, and two credit cards. He examined the name on the credit card. If it was Terry or Stacy or some other name that'd work for a man or a woman, we could use it ourselves for a few purchases before it got canceled.
"Tonya," he told me with a shrug.
Oh well. We could still sell them for a few bucks to someone else.
Gavin slipped the bag into a garbage can, pocketing the cash and the credit cards.
"Here's what I'm thinking," he said. "We score, get back home, and fix. We can ask Dorothy to wake us up by ten tonight. That'll give us plenty of time to make it back to the Lamp."
"Sounds good."
The first dealer we tried was dry, but then we spotted Liliya Scrimshaw. The bony addict walked with a purpose

along Pacific Avenue. Scrimmy was a prostitute who mostly worked out on East Sprague, so if she was in Browne's Addition, odds were it was to find dope. Maybe things were tight out east.

"She's going to Teague's," Gavin said. "Up on Cannon."

"I heard he went to prison." That was the rumor, anyway.

"Won his appeal."

We followed her, keeping almost a block behind.

"Maybe we should see if she wants to buy these cards," Gavin suggested.

"I don't want to deal with that skank," I said. "She scares me."

"Her money's good."

"Her money's about to be gone."

Sure enough, Scrimmy went straight to the squat brick two-story building and disappeared inside. We hung around up the block until she left before going inside ourselves. Dealers don't like it when you crowd the door.

We knocked and waited. Teague unlocked a couple of deadbolts before swinging the door open. He eyeballed us for a moment before recognition set in. I could tell the fat man was baked. They say not to get high on your own supply. Teague took that seriously, and to my knowledge, he never touched heroin. But he smoked enough pot to put any Rastafarian to shame.

"Money up front," he said, dispensing with any pleasantries.

Gavin handed him the cash for both of us. Teague contemplated it as if he'd never seen a dead president before, then closed the door. The deadbolt thunked. We waited. I started bouncing from foot to foot, partly from the cold but mostly from need. Gavin hopped in place a little like he always did.

"You think he forgot about us?"

Gavin shrugged. "Hope not."

I was about ready to knock on the door again when the deadbolts flipped. Teague eased the door open and handed it to us.

"You never saw me before," he told us.

"Saw who?" Gavin said.

Teague gave him a confused look. "Me. You never saw *me* before."

If I had any sense of humor instead of a full-on, raging heroin desire, it might have been fun to say "who?" and play stoner games with him for a while. But I could feel the nausea coming on. We split without another word.

On the way back to the apartments, we picked up the pace. I was already feeling the joyous rush of warmth that waited for me. Floating in a sea of forgetfulness. Not just escaping my problems but escaping to another world. None of this life even existed there.

It was heaven.

We cut through the alley between Adams and Jefferson. Halfway to the other side, I heard a car accelerate behind us. I turned around to see a boat of a car lurch to a stop. Two hard men piled out.

Every last bit of me screamed *run*, but I stood rooted to the spot. Maybe in the deepest reaches of my being, I knew this was inevitable. Someone slaps a rat label on you, it ends this way.

"Go!" a voice yelled. I thought for a second it was my own, hollering at Gavin to run away. It wasn't his fight. He didn't need to stay and suffer for my bullshit.

But it wasn't. It was Gavin who screamed it at me, and then pushed me toward Jefferson Street.

Instincts took over, and I bolted. I cast one quick glance over my shoulder to make sure Gavin was keeping up, but he wasn't running. Instead, he charged at the driver of the car. I slowed, but the other man was sprinting after me. His stoic expression was cold, and I knew in an instant what would happen if he caught me.

I ran.

I burst out of the alley and across Jefferson, ignoring traffic. A delivery truck slammed on its brakes, horn bellowing. A rush of air buffeted me as it sailed past, barely missing me. I didn't break stride, hauling ass down another alley, before hooking left and into the lobby of the Hope. The manager's door stood open. That meant Dorothy, and Dorothy meant safety. I made for the office.

Behind me, the lobby door kicked open. "Hey!" yelled my pursuer.

I got to the manager's entryway. Anita Moss glanced up sharply from the paperwork she was working on. "Rossovich! What's your problem?"

I glanced toward the lobby. The beefy man with the flat expression was in the middle of the big room. He'd slowed down once inside and now walked toward me deliberately.

"Help," I rasped to Anita.

"Help what?" she demanded. Then her eye caught the approaching man. "Excuse me?" she said, her tone clipped and full of edgy authority. Which was basically Anita all the time. She picked up her cell phone, her finger poised over it to dial. "Can I help you?"

The man hesitated. His cold eyes flicked from Anita to me and back to her again. Without a word, he turned around and walked away.

I watched him go. When the lobby doors had swung closed, Anita asked me, "What in the hell was that about, Rossovich?"

***

I waited more than an hour before venturing out. First, I peeked up and down Madison from the doorway of the Hope to make sure the coast was clear. Then I crept through the alleyway, watching and listening intently for that boat of a car. I heard nothing but the normal street sounds.

I found him lying against a dumpster, curled into a ball. His face was battered beyond recognition. Both eyes were swollen shut. He wasn't moving.

"Gav?" I asked softly.

He didn't answer.

I reached out, touching him softly on the shoulder.

He moaned but didn't answer.

I moaned, too, tears spilling down my face like rain.

***

I flagged down a car and got the driver to call for an ambulance. Then I returned to Gavin's side and tried to comfort him until the medics arrived. It was quiet in the alley, just him and me. I touch him lightly on the arm.

"You stood up for me," I whispered. "I'm sorry."

Gavin didn't answer.

Once the ambulance arrived, it got loud and busy. The medics asked their questions and did their thing. One of them suggested they should call the cops, but I convinced him not to. He didn't like it, but he listened.

When I realized they weren't going to let me ride in the ambulance with Gavin, I lied and said he was my brother. The medic hesitated but eventually shrugged and allowed it.

On the way to the hospital, the medic kept working on Gavin. He spoke non-stop into a microphone, muttering a constant stream of medical jargon. I didn't understand any of it, but the whole thing was unnerving.

At the emergency room, the nurse peeled me away from Gavin and started asking me a bunch of questions. I didn't know the answers to most of them, and my claim to be his brother started to fall apart. When the nurse finished with me, he was clearly exasperated. He pointed toward a room full of small, hard-backed chairs. "You can wait there."

"Is he going to be all right?"

"I'll let you know when I know," he said. "Or the doctor will."

I found a chair in the corner and pulled my knees in tight to my chest. I rocked there, trying to soothe my fraying nerves. The hunger for a fix scratched and clawed at me while I sat. I found myself wondering if Gavin still had those two little balloons Teague had given him. Would the hospital staff search his pockets and find them? I hoped not.

Across from me, a woman and her small child sat waiting. The kid might have been three. She had to keep finding things to entertain him. When he got interested in me, she made sure to immediately distract him with a treat from her purse.

That made me think of the purse Gavin took to get us money for this afternoon. He was always so resourceful, and luck seemed to follow him. Things had never come so easily for me, and I had to fight and struggle and compromise to keep my head above water. Gavin seemed to just float.

After two hours, I was ready to climb the walls. I glanced up at the clock for the thousandth time. Fifteen more minutes, I decided.

Fifteen minutes and I'm out of here.

I'd find a way to score. There was still time before the meeting. Would I still go? I had to, right? It was either that or leave town. And even then, a long arm might still reach out and find me wherever I ended up.

Besides, I couldn't run without Gavin. He was loyal to me, and I was loyal to him. It might not be everything he wanted, but it was everything I had to give.

The clock crawled on.

Five minutes.

Ten.

I was about to stand up to leave when a doctor came through the door. A mask hung from her throat, the top straps undone. "Did you bring in Gavin Dane?" she asked me.

I nodded. "Is he going to be okay?"

She didn't hesitate. "He's gone. I'm sorry. I did all I could, but there was bleeding on the brain, and…"

Her voice faded out even though her lips kept moving. I stood there in shock, trying to make sense of what she'd said.

Not Gavin. In this world of shit that I lived in now, he was the only thing that was good in it. He made me forget sometimes how bad my life was. Forget the impending eviction from the Hope, the endless cycle of scrounging for cash just to—

"His things," I said, interrupting the doctor.

"Excuse me."

I swallowed. "He had some things of mine. I'd like to get them if I could."

The doctor pressed her lips together in disappointment. "If you mean the narcotics in his pocket, then the answer is no. We'll be calling the police to deal with that."

I left the emergency room without another word.

***

I walked for a long time, turning blindly at intersections, weaving my way back downtown. The ache in my veins had shifted from desire to need to an absolutely excruciating requirement. Even as I walked along, I shifted and jittered, doing the addict dance. I badly needed to fix.

But I had business first. When I glanced at the digital clock on a nearby bank sign, I was surprised at how much time had passed. I was going to be late, which wasn't good. But it couldn't be helped.

Gavin.

I may have moaned the name. A pair of young women eyed me strangely as I passed, then burst into giggles after I continued on. I didn't care.

Meet.

Then fix.

Deal with the rest later.

My wandering had landed me in Riverfront Park. The Spokane River branched into two parts briefly to flow around the center of the park on both sides. I made my way over a wooden bridge and past the pavilion. A short walk from there, a long narrow concrete bridge spanned the river again, leading toward the Spokane Arena.

I trudged slowly across.

A solid man stood in the center of the bridge, leaning his forearms against the railing and gazing down into the water below. For a moment, he seemed to resemble the stoic thug who'd chased me earlier, but I knew it wasn't him.

He ignored me as I approached. He wore jeans and a leather jacket. His features were hard and confident.

I stopped, leaning onto the rail next to him and following his gaze downward. I thought of Gavin, his body now just as cold as the dark, icy waters below.

"You're late," Detective James Morgan said. "I don't like to wait."

Billy's Plan

James L'Etoile

Billy Love didn't want to die in prison, but life on the streets was killing him. Living was easier when there was nobody to tell you when to wake up or when to lockdown. But, without someone looking over his shoulder, Billy didn't make the best decisions.

Inside the deteriorating single-room occupancy hotel for society's castoffs, ironically named the Hope, Billy paused on the second-floor landing to catch his breath. He felt the rattle deep in his lungs. He knew the signs—he'd let this round of pneumonia set up camp, making it hard to get a good breath. He'd traded the last of his HIV meds to a scrawny white kid for two gray lumps of meth and a bottle of fortified wine, the next best thing to prison pruno he could find, and it didn't attract a swarm of fruit flies like the homebrew did fermenting in his prison toilet. He could make do without the meds for a few days. All he wanted was to crash on the thin mattress in his room and disappear for a while. The cold sweats predicted he might not make it to the top of the stairs.

After a deep cough loosened up his chest, he made the trek to the third floor, where the familiar faded yellow Notice to Vacate sticker in the hallway greeted him. The eviction orders were plastered on the doors when he rented the room four months ago. The property owner was out to make a quick buck and expected the Hope vacated by the end of the month. Lost Hope was more like it. Seemed like a rush to toss a bunch of people without means out on the street. Folks who have were always in a hurry to get more, and it didn't matter if the have-not's suffered along the way.

Billy patted the baggie of meth in his pocket. The way Billy had it wired, he planned on being out of here before anyone knew he was gone—back inside a familiar prison cell for a violation. Billy's plan for a little in-prison tune-up and getting on the prison's HIV meds was literally in the bag. The antiretrovirals, and the therapeutics, were easier to come by in prison, and he didn't have to worry about a roof over his head. Dodging the shady multi-agency Street Crime Abatement Team was getting harder too. Cruising around in their shiny black taskforce SUV's every time he went to make a buy made dealers nervous. If you were holding and got picked up by the task force—you were looking at hard time. A short parole violation meant he could wipe his debt clean with Little Eddie, the local dealer, by going back to prison—a convict bankruptcy. The way his life unfolded, Billy figured he was doing time on the streets as much as he did in a prison cell. There was nothing out here for him except a different view. No one was going to hire a sick ex-con on parole. It was harder to get a slice of government handouts because everyone needed help nowadays. At his current pace of drug use, alcohol abuse, mounting drug debt, and outright neglect of his medical issues, he'd be in a stainless-steel drawer in the coroner's office within a month. Going back inside on a violation would give him a chance to hit the pause button, get healthy again, figure out a new life; maybe find one of them jobs down at the Amazon warehouse. Decent pay and whatever he could lift from the shelves—just like a regular guy.

He fished a key from his pocket and found the lock to #304 wouldn't turn, leaving Billy locked out of his apartment. It was really more of a room than an apartment. His old prison cell had its own toilet, not one he shared with everyone else on the floor like this dump.

Billy rapped hard on the doorframe of #306. "Anita! Get Earl up here!"

Anita, the Hope's Assistant Manager, unlocked the door but left the chain secured. She peered through the crack, brushing a wisp of graying hair out of a face glistening with a thin sheen of sweat.

"Billy, what are you doing? Keep it down."

"Get that lazy-ass maintenance dude, Earl, up here. He needs to fix my door."

"Billy, you gotta—"

"This rundown rat's nest of a building. I know you think it don't matter 'cause it's being sold, but you guys ain't put a dime into the place since Nixon was president."

"There's nothing wrong with your lock."

"You callin' me stupid, woman? I'm telling you my lock's busted."

"Billy, you owe me last month's rent. You had 'til today to pay up. I warned you. I changed the locks."

"You can't do that! All my shit's in there."

Anita reached behind her door, "Wait a minute." She closed the door, and Billy heard the chain slide before she reappeared. She heaved a black plastic garbage bag at his feet. "There. Take your worldly possessions and leave."

From the clank of empty wine bottles in the bag, Anita didn't bother sorting trash from his belongings, not that there was a great difference between the two. She tossed everything in and tied it shut. A whiff of stale booze meant one of the bottles wasn't quite empty or sealed.

"Man, why'd you have to be like that? What am I supposed to do now?"

"Start by paying your rent. Two hundred bucks for the week, in advance, and I'll give you a new key."

"Two? It was one-fifty."

"Inflation. Now go away, Billy. It's late."

"Where am I supposed to stay tonight?"

"It ain't that cold outside yet."

"You're so full of yourself. Gimme the key, or I'll go get Miss Dorothy to open my place up. You know she'll come do it."

"Don't you be bothering Dorothy with your drunk-ass self. She gave me the go-ahead to change the locks. One less room we gotta empty out before the developers take over."

"That ain't right."

"Talk to me in the morning about paying your rent or be gone." Anita slammed the door in his face.

Billy heard a crash on the other side of the door, and a wisp of plaster dust wafted from under the threshold. "Place is fallin' apart anyhow," Billy said through the door.

He hefted the black garbage bag that symbolized what his life had become. He was a cast-off, one of society's unwanted. He wasn't even good enough for the Hope.

The bag was heavier than he thought it would be—the sum of his life's burdens. He dragged it behind him and trudged down the stairs to the lobby. The wine bottles clanked with each step, and he heard one break against a stair tread. The odor of stale booze confirmed it.

He camped in one of the lobby chairs and stared out the nicotine-coated windows figuring out the right time to pull the trigger on his prison vacation plan when his parole agent, Theresa Costa, stepped through the front door. She was five-five, at best, but carried the attitude of a six-foot street-brawler when she was pissed. Billy tried to read her expression to find out which personality he was about to face.

"Did Anita call you? She's blowing it up. It's no big deal."

"No, she didn't have to call me. You forget something?"

"I'm behind on my rent, is all. I've got it covered, though. I'll be square with her tomorrow."

"You need to get square with me."

"What you mean?"

"You forgot to charge your ankle monitor again, Billy."

Billy's neck burned. He'd let his ankle bracelet battery run dry—again. It wasn't part of his plan; a parole violation for the dead monitor wouldn't buy him enough time inside to get healthy. It might end up getting him tossed on a community service detail, picking up trash along the freeway. The very thought made him want to run out into oncoming traffic.

"I'm sorry, Miss Costa. I was on my way back to the room to plug in, but they done locked me out."

"You been drinking?"

"That ain't no violation of my conditions."

"No, it's just you tend to make bad decisions when you drink."

"I'm staying cool," then he remembered the baggie of meth, and it suddenly felt hot. If she searched him, as she had the right to do, he'd get popped for possession, a Class C felony, and a one-way trip for up to five years back inside; way longer than Billy planned.

Billy pulled open his garbage bag and fished around for the charging cable.

"Don't bother."

"You're taking me in? For not charging my monitor?" Billy grinned but looked away, hiding his relief from Agent Costa. The great state of Washington did offer free medical care in prison to make up for a lifetime of bad choices. Little Eddie couldn't threaten to cut his throat for his unpaid debt if Agent Costa took him away. "I guess I had it coming. Probably for the best, you're sending me back in. I can get back on my HIV meds and clean up a bit before I make a fresh start."

"No, I'm not taking you in. In fact, I'm cutting you loose." The parole agent knelt and removed the ankle monitor.

"How come?" Billy stiffened with the unexpected news.

"The state doctor said you went to your appointment the other day. Told me you weren't doing so well."

"What happened to patient privacy?"

"He's a state doctor, and you're state property—or you were."

"I'm not following."

"You're off parole. We've discharged you. Seems the state thinks you're more trouble than you're worth. We're done paying for your medical care. You're the county's problem now."

"Wait. I need a refill on my meds. My t-cell count—"

"Ain't my problem no more. Do what everyone else does—go find a job and pay your own freight. Find a free clinic somewhere. They're popping up like weeds around the city." His former parole agent gathered the monitor and set for the door.

An unexpected hollowness fell over him. He'd been on some form of probation or parole supervision since he was twelve. It was a safety net when Billy's drug debts regularly got out of control or when he needed a little detox. The last year he used a quick parole violation jolt behind bars to control his HIV-related medical issues. Amazing what a little time could do for plummeting t-cell counts and opportunistic infections. This time, he planned on a ninety-day tune-up and then he'd be good to make another run at the straight life.

Billy watched his plan go up in smoke. He traded the pills for the baggie of meth so he'd test positive and violate his parole conditions—earning him a trip to the slammer where street dealers like Little Eddie couldn't touch him, the doctors would put him back on meds, he'd eat right and get healthy. A positive test wasn't considered possession, so he'd only catch a little bit of time, and Agent Costa ruined it.

Going to the local county hospital emergency room for his meds wasn't going to give him the three hots and a cot he needed. Billy sat back in the chair and noodled on another scheme to get locked up long enough somewhere warm for the winter and straighten up his medical situation, but not a new beef serious enough to buy him hard time. The answer flitted across the lobby in her church clothes. Dorothy Givens, Hope's resident manager, made a path for the door and froze when Billy spotted her.

"Evening, Miss Dorothy."

Her cheeks flushed the same pale red as her hair used to be. In her mid-sixties, Dorothy ran the Hope like a rescue for stray cats; always open and willing to overlook a transgression or two.

"Why Billy Love, you startled me so. What are you doing here at this hour?" Dorothy said with a hand over her heart.

"Anita's being an ass again--"

"Billy, language."

"Sorry, Miss Dorothy. Anita done locked me out of my room on account of I'm behind on the rent."

"Got to be more to it than that. More than half our tenants are a little late."

"All's I know is I got nowhere to go."

"It isn't seemly to have you camping in our front window. We'll figure out what to do with you in the morning. Find a place to spend the night, maybe the Front Street Shelter?"

"The shelter is always full by this time of night. Gotta be there before dark to claim a bunk. I planned on getting prison medical care. I'm not sure what I'll do now that I'm off parole. I'll find a way. Where you off to, all prettied up?"

Dorothy blushed again. "Just never you mind."

A red Cadillac pulled to the curb in front of the building. The flare from a match to a cigarette illuminated the driver briefly. Billy recognized Chester Caldwell, whose family owned the Hope, and pushed the redevelopment project forward. Billy shot a glance to Miss Dorothy, who straightened the hem on her jacket.

"Why, Miss Dorothy, are you and Chester—"

"Hush. You're not to whisper a word of this to anyone. You keep my secret, and you can sleep down in the laundry tonight."

"I guess that'd be all right," Billy said.

"Just you keep this to yourself."

"Yes, ma'am."

Billy wasn't interested in the family tree of Dorothy's gentleman caller. Chester Caldwell was a twenty-year Spokane Police Department beat cop, and he'd busted Billy five times since he was a kid stealing hubcaps off cars parked at the funeral home, to the last time when Billy tried to rob a mom-and-pop market. The mom in the market swung a mean baseball bat, and Billy was unconscious on the floor when Caldwell responded to the robbery in progress call.

Dorothy's new boyfriend hadn't let Billy live down the fact he got his head cracked by a sixty-five-year-old woman. Not exactly the hard gangster image Billy wanted.

Caldwell's glare cut through the grimy window, and he tensed when he spotted Billy and Dorothy together. The fact he wasn't in uniform didn't make the cop less threatening.

"Chester don't like me much," he said.

"Oh, come now. His bark is much worse than his bite."

"I dunno. Last time he barked, I went inside for three years."

Caldwell knocked on the window, showing his impatience.

"He have anything to do with me getting locked out of my room?"

Dorothy blushed again. "He may have mentioned you being a bad seed..."

Caldwell rapped on the windowpane, harder this time.

"I should go. Set yourself up in the laundry room for the night, Billy, and we'll talk this out in the morning."

She pulled an elastic stretchy ring from her wrist and held the key to the basement to Billy. No one ever trusted him with anything like this before. He puffed up his bony chest, stifled a cough, and took the key. He felt Caldwell's eyes burn through his back.

Dorothy didn't wait for a response and trotted to the waiting Cadillac. Caldwell held the door open for her and scowled at Billy.

It was Billy who broke first, looking away from the off-duty cop.

"Asshole," Billy muttered.

Grabbing his wine-soaked garbage bag, Billy trod to the basement to abide by Dorothy's wish that he not be in public view. The basement was originally a speakeasy during Prohibition, and over the decades, the fine mahogany bar tops, brass rails, and trimmings were scavenged and sold for scrap. All that remained was a damp cavernous space where the Hope installed a bank of coin-operated laundry machines.

The dryer on the end of the row had an exposed wiring panel, allowing the residents to hot-wire the machine and use it without dropping a quarter in the slot. Billy got the machine running and leaned against the metal side, soaking up the heat that chased off a bit of the basement dampness.

The hum of the machine couldn't lull him to sleep. He hugged his knees and drew a ragged breath. He needed to get back inside and on his prison meds soon, or it would be too late. He'd seen what happened to men who let themselves go without treatment. Billy didn't want to end up like them—a long and painful death. Or he could wait until Little Eddie came after him. Same result either way.

He rubbed his hands over his legs to warm them and ran across the baggie of meth. Here he was, tossed in a moldy basement with the leftover debris no one wanted. Struggling to stay warm, hustling a place to sleep tonight, and his deteriorating health didn't leave him any other option. A possession of controlled substance charge was risky. With luck, a good public defender could talk a judge into a year, maybe eighteen months tops. He could do a year-and-a-half standing on his head. When he got out, he could start over.

He stood and pulled the meth baggie from his jeans. Two crystalline pea-sized rocks reflected in the fluorescent light. He tightened his grip on them and strode upstairs to the lobby. The clock over the front desk marked it as almost five in the morning. Billy knew where to go.

The corner market, not the one where the bat-wielding woman put him down, was a pit-stop for cops during their patrol of the area. They'd manage to chase most of the overt drug and sex traffic back into the shadows, and Billy supposed it was to help gentrify the neighborhood for the pending redevelopment of the community around the Hope.

Billy pushed open the market door, and a bell tinkled as he entered. Two uniformed patrolmen stopped refilling their insulated coffee mugs and watched him approach the counter.

The sandy-haired cashier nodded at Billy, making sure he knew the two officers were eight feet away.

"What can I get ya?" the cashier said.

"Can I trade these for a bottle of Mad Dog?" Billy slid the meth on the counter.

"What? Dude, no. Get that shit outta here." The cashier tried to speak in a hushed tone urging Billy to stop.

"Hey, I know they don't look like high quality, but it'll still get you off."

A hand clamped on Billy's shoulder, and one of the officers spun him around.

Billy smiled and began to relax. He'd be in a nice warm cell, with food and meds before lunchtime.

"What's wrong with you," the cop asked.

Billy shrugged. "I guess you gotta do what you gotta do. I need to go back inside, anyhows." Billy put his thin wrists out for handcuffs.

The second cop picked up the baggie and looked at it under the light. To Billy's surprise, the cop started laughing. He showed it to his partner. "Johnson, take a look."

The officer palmed the baggie, turned it in his hand, and tapped his finger on a label Billy never noticed. "Contains real cane sugar."

"I guess I can't take you in for possession of rock candy." The officer tossed the baggie on the counter. "Lucky for you. Let me guess you bought it off someone who said they were selling you the real deal?"

Billy twitched. "What? No, you got it wrong." His plan was turning to shit—again.

The cop pulled a card from his pocket and handed it to Billy. "Give this outpatient treatment center a call. They might be able to help you."

"Bullshit. I don't need no drop-in center. It's real. I got this shit from a blonde kid yesterday."

The two cops exchanged a look. The taller cop asked, "When was this?"

"Yesterday, like I said. Sometime after six."

The tall officer nodded to his partner, who stepped closer to Billy and spun him around facing the counter. The officer gave Billy a thorough pat-down.

"That's more like it," Billy said as the officer snapped handcuffs on his wrists.

The taller cop led Billy outside by his elbow and parked him on the curb while his partner made a phone call.

Billy looked across the street at the Hope. The structure stood tall in its heyday as a hotel for the rich and powerful, thrived during Prohibition, survived the economic collapse, and now sat ready to reinvent itself as a boutique hotel for hipsters. The brown brick face was starting to crumble, but there was a feeling about the place and its history that gave him hope. He was ready to reinvent himself too—a new beginning.

Billy's personal urban renewal plan took a left turn when a sleek black SUV and a second patrol car pulled into the market's small parking strip. Now in uniform, Officer Chester Caldwell stepped from the car and strode to the gutter where Billy waited.

"Thanks for the call. What'd you have on this dirtbag here?" Caldwell asked the officer standing over Billy.

"He tried to pass off a bag of rock candy. Said he got it from a blonde kid yesterday. We field-tested the stuff, and it ain't methamphetamine."

Caldwell stiffened.

"Billy, you stepped in it this time."

"Yeah, I know. Take me in. You and I both know that ain't a bag of sugar."

Caldwell glanced at one of the officers. "You read him his rights yet?"

The tall one nodded.

"I don't care about some plastic bag of shit. When did you get it from the kid? What'd he look like?"

Billy scrunched his forehead. He knew Caldwell was trying to trick him out of his quick tune-up in a prison hospital bed.

"I bought it from a shaggy-haired blonde kid. Skinny, not too tall, I guess he's in his twenties." Billy closed his eyes and tried to picture the kid. "Bit of a smartass, wore baggy shorts and a Vancouver Canucks jersey."

Caldwell nodded. "How much you pay?"

Billy had him right where he wanted him. The cop was trolling for a confession to lock it all down. Billy could almost feel the familiar warmth of a rough woolen jailhouse blanket. "Not cash money. We traded for it. Don't matter, I know I'm still in possession, a Class C beef. I'll cop to what I done." Billy tried to look contrite, lowering his gaze to the pavement.

"What'd you trade for the baggie?"

"I had some prescription pills I gave him."

"Pills? Like fentanyl or hillbilly heroin?" Caldwell asked.

"Oh no, you ain't gonna trick me into copping on some sales of controlled substance charge. They was HIV meds, retrovirals. Kid mighta been made to believe they was oxy. That's on him. Listen, you think you could move things along, Caldwell? My ass is getting cold on this concrete."

"I think we can accommodate you, Billy. How you feel about a Class A felony?"

Billy whipped his head up at Caldwell. "What the hell you talking about?"

"Thing is, the kid took those pills like they were oxy like you told him."

Billy laughed. "What a tool! Bet he was surprised he didn't get high. Serves that smug-ass college-boy right. Him being a dumbshit don't make a Class A felony unless you're calling him felony stupid."

It was Caldwell's turn to laugh. "Someone's felony stupid, all right. Tell me Billy, what do you pill heads do when you don't get high from your oxy?"

"Take more, I guess."

"Um-hum, and that's what Scott did. Scott Bartlett, the kid you gave your pills to, he ended up taking eight of them. Found your prescription bottle right next to his body."

"His body?" Billy stiffened.

"Medical examiner's preliminary take is that the kid had a bad allergic reaction to the prescription pills you gave him. His throat swelled shut."

"That ain't on me."

"The law says otherwise. Recklessly causing the death of another is first-degree manslaughter. Comes with a life sentence."

"I just thought, if I got back inside, I could make things right, get back on my meds, and make a go of it again." Billy's voice cracked.

"Yeah, Dorothy told me about your dumb-ass self-improvement plan." Caldwell lifted Billy from the curb and started walking him to the patrol car. Billy's knees buckled.

Two officers dressed in black tactical gear stepped from the SUV. Their raid jackets were emblazoned with the S.C.A.T. taskforce logo.

"This our boy? We'll take him," one of the task force officers asked.

Caldwell held him upright while the second taskforce officer opened the SUV's rear door. "Timing has never been your strong suit, Billy. The kid, Scott Bartlett, was one of their C.I.'s."

Billy's knees quivered when he sat in the SUV's caged back seat, and his stomach turned to quicksilver as he caught a construction crew draping a banner on a storefront next to the market. "Opening soon—Spokane Free Clinic and Pharmacy." Bold lettering proclaimed funding for the HIV clinic from the Elijah Hope and Veronica Caldwell Foundation.

"Opens this week, if you'd waited a couple of days, Scotty Bartlett would still be alive, and you wouldn't be looking down the barrel of life in prison. I guess you won't have to worry about getting your meds for the next forty to fifty years."

The other rear door opened, and the task force cop shoved a second handcuffed man in the seat next to Billy.

"We've been street sweeping. Brought you some company," he said.

It took a moment for Billy to register the man was Little Eddie.

"You can't skip out without givin' me what's mine."

Little Eddie slipped his handcuffs and gripped a razor blade in his free hand.

Billy didn't want to die in prison, and the streets made sure he wouldn't.

The Hope of Lost Mares

Paul J. Garth

The woman known as Talia Johnson thinks of horses when the man is on top of her.

She remembers their skin under her small hands, bristly and soft, the smell of the mare's mane catching in the flatland air, and the sounds of their hooves treading through swaying grass. But mostly, she remembers their eyes; black and wet and deep, like underground rivers, each containing currents, a pull to drag you under or wash you clean.

Then she thinks of home and shudders beneath him.

Rain beat against the building when the man finally left. She went to the window, the light from the other apartments turned a sickly shade in the night's gloom, then lit a cigarette. Music came from another cracked window somewhere up on the fourth floor. Jazz, the music her mother played around The Ranch, squealing saxophones and shrieking trumpets, the sound of insanity. She exhaled, the smoke thicker in the heavy air, and watched as it moved in front of her, amorphous, like ghosts. The beginnings of a headache swelled in the back of her head. She took another drag then flicked the butt into the courtyard below.

Brett came in without knocking, liquor on her breath, eyes glossy. She carried two tumblers in her fingers, stolen from the Lamplighter. "He gone?"

Talia gestured at the empty bed. Outside, the rain picked up, percussion for the floating brass.

"I was thinking we could party, but if you're not in the mood..."

Talia nodded. "I'm fine. Just."

"Ready for something else?"

"Yeah."

Brett sat at the small dinette set on the other side of the room. The lone chair wobbled underneath her like it was contemplating bucking her off. Brett was in her early thirties, ten years older than Talia, but in the dim light of the apartment, she looked a hard forty, with the kind of craggy face and thin lips that suggested a woman who would put up with exactly zero shit, and the knife handle that stuck from the lip of her ankle boot confirmed the impression. But when she smiled, Talia saw the Brett she'd come to know showing underneath the cracking outside, the real Brett. The one that made her feel safe and seen.

She sat on the bed, the window still cracked above her head, the discordant music still creeping in. "I'm just tired," she said, head meeting her knees. "I just don't know how to keep doing this. Every day I think about how it shouldn't have to be like this. I know I can't, but I think part of me, a big part of me, wants to go home."

Brett leaned back in the chair, one leg crossing in front of her. Her hand came down and began stroking the knife handle absentmindedly, and her eyes turned up toward the ceiling. "I wanted something once." She sounded sad while she spoke but weary too. "And you know what I learned? You gotta cut that shit out. Nothing's going to change. What you want is never going to happen. So to survive, to keep going, you find something every day, doesn't even have to be something you liked, just something you didn't hate. That's it." She shrugged and was silent for a while. "Listen to it or don't, honey. But if you choose *don't*, there are a whole lot of dead girls who can tell you how it ends. Dreams, in this kind of life, aren't for us. Dreams are just a slower way of dying."

Talia lit another cigarette and lay down on the bed.

The first year, before she met Brett, had been awful. More filled with hunger and terror than she'd ever imagined a person could take. Sixteen years old and on the road, no money, no ID, only a sturdy pair of riding boots on her feet and a fraying backpack with a couple pairs of extra clothes slung over her shoulder. The black highways and moonless nights, the lecherous drivers, their eyes as hungry as her belly, her shivers given way to fear sweat. She still remembered the face of the first man she took in her mouth, how he grinned at her and patted her on the head and called her Priscilla, a name she'd never heard a girl her age possess.

And then, months later, searching for enough change to buy a soda and a sandwich, Brett had found her.

What started with a jug of Dr. Pepper and a gas station burrito soon turned into something else, a recognition of oneself in the other, a helping hand offered to another girl drowning in the world. Brett had helped her. Taught her. Gotten her settled in the Hope. Had been there, her rough hands showing Talia how to start putting together something that resembled a life. Not that this new life could replace what had been left behind, but some days, Talia convinced herself, it was a life worth living. Brett had taught her how to conduct a business from a single location, inside, to keep the cops away. How to talk to men. How to be prepared for what happened when they became violent. How to talk to the Spokane cops, if they ever showed up. To stay away from the other girls in the building, especially after the pimp the girls were always recruiting for ended up dead. Had even taken Talia to city hall and bribed a clerk with a stolen check to marry them, just in case they were ever both arrested, so one could not be made to testify against the other—a handy ace in the pocket for two professionals who lived across the hall from one another.

"I know," Talia said. "But now that this place is going away, it feels like a chance to get out. One I should take. But I don't have enough money. I'm not going anywhere. So I can't help feeling like it'll just seem like another mistake. Like something I should have been ready for but wasn't."

Brett stood and walked to the wall. They'd tacked the eviction notice up one night after drinking in the Lamplighter, giggling, certain it'd just been a scare tactic, that the Hope could never really go away. It hung there, the edges of the yellow paper curled inwards, like some kind of wicked Oleander, blooming in reverse. "Guess I kinda forgot we did that," she said, shrugging. "It's still a month away."

"That enough time to get an ID, a job, and an apartment?"

"Might be," Brett said. "If you used your real name."

She thought of the horses again. The horses and The Ranch. The way it looked at night, sixteen hundred acres of open land and almost twice as many grazing cattle, the skeletal shapes of pumpjacks extracting mineral wealth from the earth, and the main compound itself, a small scattering of soft shapes underneath that stretched out starry dark. She knew them by heart, the angles of those buildings forming a constellation she carried with her in her soul's own sky.

Talia said her real name in her head, felt it move silently on her tongue, the vowels working softly against her teeth, a prayer and a curse at once. "No," she said, finally. "There's no going back to that."

***

The banging on her door started sometime after 2 A.M.

Talia was still awake, sitting in bed, the last of her cigarettes smoked an hour before, a copy of Cheryl Strayed's *Wild* Brett had stolen from the library then insisted Talia read open in front of her. She reached into the flimsy nightstand and pulled the drawer open as slowly as she could, then reached in and gripped the can of pepper spray she kept in case any of the men grew overly insistent. She had not had to use it in a year, had not even had to threaten to use it in months, but the shape of it in her hand was familiar and calming like the small tube was made to be carried by her.

The banging started up again.

She held the pepper spray behind her and moved to the door. There was no peephole, and the chain was thrown, but she'd learned not to open the door unless you knew who it was, that even a peek could be dangerous. She'd learned that men could be feral creatures, that some of them carried not love or lust in their hearts, but chaos and a taste for blood, and that sometimes, years later even, they came back.

Still, she put on a cloying voice, a voice designed to appease and ingratiate. "Who is it?"

The pounding on the other side of the door stopped, but she could still hear him out there, the shifting of feet in the dim hall, the deep breaths of someone second-guessing themselves, running their hands over their beard and comparing the number on the door to the number in their head.

"This is 313," Talia said. "And I'm sorry, but I'm not expecting anyone tonight."

"Yes."

Sweat broke over her brow and her skin bunched over her stomach. The voice on the other side of the door had provoked a familiarity in her that could not be placed. It was like something she knew, something she knew *well*, but different too. She squeezed the pepper spray tightly in her hand, her finger heavy on the nozzle.

"You have the wrong apartment, whoever you are."

"Charlotte," the voice said from out in the hall. "I know you're in there."

It was recognizable this time, the voice the same as she'd grown up with, mocking in her ear. A voice she'd heard her entire life until she ran. Until she left The Ranch. Matthew. Her brother.

"Charlotte, open the door so we can talk. Or," she could hear it, the frustration rising in him, that quick rise to anger he'd gotten from their mother. "Open the door, Charlotte, or I'll kick the god damn thing down."

Hands shaking, she tucked the pepper spray in between the elastic waist of her pants and the small of her back, then slid the chain and threw the lock before stepping back into the darkest part of the apartment.

"Come in," she said. "Slowly."

It'd been five years since she'd seen him, but, as he entered, she saw he'd changed. He was heavier, to start;

the weight some men get on the downside of their mid-twenties hanging from his gut like frosting drooping from the edge of an over-rich cake. He wore an expensive black blazer with stains of some kind on the lapels and cuffed designer jeans over thick hide work boots. His hair was longer, hanging down in his eyes, and he'd grown a patchy beard that bloomed from his overround cheeks. But his eyes, though bloodshot now, dimmed by the exhaustion and grind of hard living, still reflected that same cruel intelligence as he stepped into the dim light of apartment 313. She wondered if she were to step closer if she would be able to smell home, to catch a scent of The Ranch's thick, black Nebraska dirt, or if he'd just reek of sweat and rage and the madness their mother had given him in the womb.

He pushed the door closed behind him, the chain clattering in its track.

"You found me," she said, her voice strong, refusing to be cowed by him.

Matthew studied the floor, the window, her bed, the dinette set. He moved to it, taking a careful seat in the chair Brett had been tipping in hours before, his eyes never meeting hers.

The sweat on her brow had chilled, and her hands drifted uselessly by her side. "What do you want?" Talia tried again.

The gun came out of the blazer like a train approaching a car stuck on the tracks, inevitably and filled with routine menace. He set it on the table, brushing the dirty tumblers aside, the black carbon grip and cold metal barrel sucking light from the room, a collapsed star placed where she ate ramen and rib sandwiches from the Lamplighter. "Mom's dead," he said. "Esophageal cancer. Wasn't quick, either.

First showed symptoms," he shrugged and paused. "Six, seven months after you left."

She thought of leaving. The silent ride Joe, one of her father's ranch hands, had given her to the interstate. His worried advice, as they sat in the parking lot of a truck stop: to get to Omaha and get on a bus for somewhere far away. Her certainty, that in a few years, there would be a new Sheriff and that whoever it was would believe her, would protect her, the only thing that gave her enough strength to place one foot in front of the other. The fear she'd felt inside the long hauler's cab as they moved west, a certainty building in her with each passing mile that it did not matter which direction she went, that eventually, the remains of her family would find her, would bring her back and ensure she, too, had an accident.

She answered Matthew in a flat voice, as though she were talking to a ghost. "Can't say I'm sorry to hear it."

He shook his head, the hair unwashed and sticking to his head. "Didn't think you would be."

"And you came here to tell me this so I could come back home. Get my half of the inheritance, right? So we'd take over The Ranch together. Ride horses on fucking Sunday?"

Matthew nodded at the gun. "She never liked you. Not even before. But after you told, after you told, then ran, she hated you. We spent years looking. Omaha. Denver. Kansas City. Figured you'd have stayed close. And then nothing, so we went bigger. L.A. New York. Chicago. The places runaways go. She didn't expect you to go far, and if you did, she didn't expect you to go far and be smart about it."

Talia smiled through the acid that had pooled in her mouth, her teeth a threat. "So she underestimated me, and now the bitch is dead."

"Got a hit on you a month ago, finally," Matthew continued. "Some old cop saying he'd seen you outside this building." His hand moved, crawling across the tabletop toward the gun, then stopped, fingertips almost touching the black grip. "You know what she wanted? What her last request was, right before they took her throat?"

She dry swallowed. Felt hot tears at the corners of her eyes. In the back of her head, she heard her father's voice, talking her through how to settle a skittish mare. How to talk to her mother in a way that didn't invite wrath. How it was all going to be okay, even as he lay dying on the floor of the barn. "I figure I can guess. And this way, you keep it all. All the land. All the money."

"Well," Matthew said. "You know, we were close. So I have to. Nothing personal." His hands moved, fingers draping themselves over the grip of the gun. "Doesn't mean I'm gonna like it. But I don't imagine I'll hate—"

The can was up and, in her hand, and she was halfway to the dinette and her brother before her brain realized what her body was doing, molecules in motions, cells surging at a chance for survival. A scream was leaking from her, and the room took on a crystalline clarity, the scuffed wood floors, the paint-chipped window locks, the two stolen tumblers on the table and the slow turning fan and the bone yellow brick of the wall and her thumb finding the release of the spray and the shock of it hitting the room as it ejected out, bursting across Matthew's face, into his eyes, his nose, his screaming mouth.

The gun waved in front of him, and he squeezed the trigger, but the safety was on, and it just silently pulled, the barrel flapping at the ends of his arms.

Talia crashed into her brother, hands finding a tumbler, raising it, then smashing it down on the side of his face. Matthew fell from the chair, the gun catching her jaw. She stumbled back, vision out of sync with her brain, and hit the ground, knocking the air from her.

Pepper spray misted the room. It crawled into her lungs. Pried the bronchioles up and into her throat. Matthew lay on the floor, grabbing at his eyes, a weak coughing scream coming out of him, everything unintelligible except for *kill* and *bitch* and *Mom*. She rolled onto her stomach. Saw the gun. It'd clattered to the floor and slid halfway under her bed. The sting began in her eyes then. Tears bled. She tried to blink the pain away, but each attempt only drove the burning further inside her skull. Head on the floor, she crawled toward the gun.

A hand grabbed her foot and jerked her back. She kicked at it, but it held, and then her brother was on top of her, grabbing at her shoulders and hair, wrenching her from the floor. He flipped her on her back and smashed her head down into the floor.

Her vision shook. Faded. Reset. Just in time to see his face, eyes swollen and barely cracked, blood dripping into his beard from a tear on his cheek, and his fist swinging for her head. She kneed up. Found his nuts. He writhed on top of her, screaming.

His hands were around her neck then. Squeezing. She tried to draw air in, but all she could get was more burning mist in her lungs.

"You fucking whore," Matthew said, coughing, and even through his slit eyes, she could see the hate that had come to the front, a dark gray bitterness he'd held for her since she'd found out. "You could have died quick, instead."

Her legs kicked underneath him, feet beating out a death rhythm on the dirty floor. She gripped his wrists. Dug nails in. Felt blood slide under her hands, but they would not slip from around her neck. Her thighs bucked. Up. Into him. But he would not move.

Blackness dimmed the edges, then everything but the tiny center of her vision, filled with only her brother's twisted face, and in her last moments of consciousness, she remembered the day she'd come home early to find him with their mother in her parent's bed, naked and twitching together under white sheets; she remembered the gasp she'd made, mixed with the sounds of their moans, and the quiet tiptoe away, hoping she'd been unobserved. She remembered the look on her father's face when she told him, three days later, shock and loathing so clear on his face that, for a moment, she'd been convinced it was her he hated. And she remembered the barn. Her father, waving to her, a smile over his mouth but his eyes, sad and broken, as she walked the stalls to feed the horses, and her brother looking down from the hayloft, a smirk on his face as he inched an oat barrel closer and closer to the edge. She remembered the sound it made, the wet crack, as it split her father's head and the feeling of his hand in hers as it went cold. "It'll be okay," he'd said, his mouth a broken thing, the words only half-formed. She'd been unable to look at him in his ruin and had instead turned, meeting the eyes of a lonely mare in her stall, losing herself in its eyes. "It'll be okay."

Her vision was almost all the way gone, and stars danced in the blackness, and for just a moment, she thought she was back there, standing once again under that Nebraska night, tracing the outlines of The Ranch as it stood underneath an open and sprawling starfield when a jet of blood hit her face, hot and rancid and thick, and her brother's hands released from around her neck, and he slumped over on top of her, torrents of gore spilling out across her chin, down into her mouth, and she coughed and coughed and looked up and saw Brett, standing there, the knife from her boot dripping blood, the door open behind her.

***

Five A.M. by the time her hands stopped shaking. Hours until Talia could open her eyes more than a crack. Brett had wrapped her brother's body in a pair of red sheets and mopped up most of the blood on the floor while Talia showered in the small bathroom at the end of the hall, but even hours later, Talia could still smell it sitting in the small room, could still taste it in her mouth, no matter how many of Brett's Camels she dragged down her bruising throat.

When she spoke, her teeth interrupted her, clattering together like she'd been standing outside for hours on The Ranch. "We-we-we're going to jail," she said.

She'd imagined the reunion with her family a thousand times since the night she left, but in all her imaginings, in all the scenarios she'd envisioned in which her mother or her brother found her, she had never seen it going this way. That she'd still be alive and that her brother would be dead on the floor, his throat sliced out by her sex worker mentor.

"Stop that talk," Brett said. "We're not going to jail. No one knows he's here, I don't think. And even if they do, no one knows he walked in here and didn't walk out."

"There are ways, though," Talia said. Her throat felt lined with setting concrete, and every inhale burned. "Cell phones. They can track them. Why I left the one I used back home. Why I didn't have one when we met."

"You're thinking too big, honey." Brett pointed toward the yellow eviction notice they'd tacked to the wall. "This place isn't gonna *be* here in three weeks."

"So?"

"So," Brett said, her bloodstained fingers brushing against Talia's as she pulled the cigarette away. "So there's not going to be anything here. If his body doesn't get found for a couple weeks, and trust me, honey, I've got an idea, a place in the woods, somewhere far away we can stick him where no one will ever find him, but even if they do, as long as it's a few weeks from now, this place? It'll be gone. Demolished. So there won't be any forensics. Nothing cops need to give either of us a murder charge."

"It was self-defense, though. We should call. I said we should call."

"Honey," Brett said. "Some rich guy from out of state ends up with a hole in his throat from the girl he wasn't strangling? And it turns out the girl he was strangling is his sister *and* a whore? No. I told you, that's not the way it works for us."

Talia felt her head nod. "Fuck," she said, the word hanging in the air between them.

Brett smiled. She reached up and smoothed away one of Talia's flyaways with rough, callused fingers. "No one is going to jail. God damn promise you that. And plus, even if we get talked to, remember, we got the paper from the county. Doesn't matter if they come around asking. They can't make us tell anyone about what the other did, remember?"

"You think that applies to," her teeth started chattering again, finding the edges of the word for the first time after becoming a participant in its meaning. "To murder?"

Brett stood. Kicked the bundle of red sheets at her feet. "No point in it if it doesn't," she said.

Exhaustion fell on her, and Talia slipped into the corner of the bed. Her eyes closed tight, she thought of her mother, dead, a tube down her throat, her father, gasping out last words with a broken neck and a stoved-in skull on the barn floor, her brother, wheezing as blood had jetted from the screaming mouth underneath his jaw. The horses, skittish in their stalls, waiting for her return for years. She was alone now. Alone and forgotten by everyone except Brett.

She felt her friend climb in bed with her, and fingers slowly, peacefully traced the exposed skin of her shoulders.

"He had a lot of money in that wallet of his," Brett said. "I'll split it with you."

Finally, she slept.

***

They woke at noon, then waited until nightfall, both of them in that small apartment, stepping around the body at the foot of the bed. They'd discussed going to Brett's apartment, but neither wanted to leave what was left of Matthew alone. It wasn't superstition, but a kind of self-preservation that played in the backs of both their heads on a constant loop; their problems could not get worse if both of them were there.

Talia sat with her back against the brick wall. The shades were drawn, and late September Spokane heat climbed up through the floorboards of the Hope, turning the apartment into a charnel house. She lit candles to keep the smell down, but they weren't enough. She noticed Brett had cleaned while she slept. The floors were scrubbed, and everything, her phone, any pictures of herself, the clothes she'd been wearing, anything that could have even hinted at anyone who might be related to or have any knowledge of the body on the floor, had been thrown away.

Finally, the sun dove down, and night sounds began to drift against the windows. More jazz music. The laughter of girls and the shouting of men. "This is going to work?" she asked. The words came out a wheeze through her swollen throat. "You're sure."

"Trust me, baby," Brett said. She was wearing different clothes now. Jeans and a dark flannel, and, Talia saw, the knife that'd killed her brother in her boot. "I took care of it all while you slept."

They stood and contemplated each other over the body between them.

"When he's gone, and you feel safe, what are you going to do?"

Talia stared down at the bundle of red sheets at her feet. Imagined she could see through them and that Matthew's frozen, shocked face was staring back at her. "Wait," she said. "Live somewhere far away. And then, when enough time has passed, and I can say he's dead without people thinking I killed him, go back home. It's beautiful there. And I guess, now, with Matthew dead, it's all mine. I can live a life. You could come if you want. Live comfortably. The Ranch makes really good money."

Brett smiled, and just for a moment, Talia thought she saw something awful in that movement, a kind of brutal joy at what she'd done for her friend, maybe, at the act itself. "Let's get him out of here," she said.

They slid what remained of Talia's brother into a sleeping bag, zipped it, then worked him into a rolling recycling container Brett had taken off the street.

Full dark now, and the halls of the Hope were empty. Brett nodded, and Talia opened the door, pushing the container over the rough floors, the weight inside shifting with every bump. They passed no one while they worked the container down the hall, to the elevator, then out through the lobby, and on to the street.

Outside, Talia saw the truck Brett had borrowed, an early 2000's Ford, and together, they muscled the container into the bed, where it came to rest against a pile of picks and shovels.

They drove east through Spokane, taking I-90, before cutting south several miles outside of town. The radio in the truck was broken, and they'd left their phones at the Hope, just to be sure, so there was nothing to do but look at the looming shapes of trees stretching across the flat blackness, the stars too timid to come out, the music of tires and the road the only sound.

A half-hour later, Brett drove the truck into a stand of firs, cutting off the sky above.

"This is it," Brett said.

"And then he's gone."

"And you can start over. The life your family tried to take from you. That you should have had all along."

Talia rubbed her hands over her jeans. She'd been gone so long and knew she couldn't go straight back to The Ranch, but that going home was even a possibility felt overwhelming, made her skin tingle all over, as though, over the years, her entire body had become a scab, and finally, it was starting to heal. She got out of the truck, smiling, and went to the back, pulling down the gate. Brett appeared beside her, reaching in, grabbing the sleeping bag.

Talia reached out and grabbed Brett's hand. "Thank you," she said. "I cannot thank you enough. For this, and for everything. You were family to me. Are family to me. In a way, they never could be. It's all…" The tears that had been building since bundling up her brother and removing him from the Hope finally burst free, and she stood in the middle of the woods, the cold dark pressing down, sobbing. Somewhere in the back of her mind, it reminded her of how she'd left, of some night standing outside the reach of some truck stop's halogens, crying in rage and despair, beating her chest at everything her brother and her mother had taken from her. At what they would do if they found her. But it was over now, and this woman in front of her had seen her through. Brett had saved her life, both on the street and in the Hope. She'd killed the man hunting her. And now, she was helping Talia get rid of the body so, someday, hopefully, sooner than later, she would be able to return home to claim what was hers. "It's all too much. And I meant it, what I said back there. You should come with me. We'll live easy. We'll never have to look at another man if we don't want to."

Brett leaned in and placed a small kiss at the corner of Talia's teary eye. "Of course I will, honey. I'd do anything for you. And I'd be happy to do it."

Together, they pulled the body from the back of the truck, then gathered the shovels.

Joy rising in her, Talia picked up one of the shovels and swung it toward the night above. "I'll start," she said, breathing hard. "I'll dig—"

The bullet tore through her chest before she could finish, shredding muscle and bone and tissue and bursting it out behind her against the trees and the dirt and the shadow of the sucking night.

She hit the dirt next to her brother's body, all the air suddenly gone from her lungs. Blood filled her throat, slicked her teeth, and her eyes scoured the shape beside her, searching for the upraised hand, wondering how he'd gotten the gun back, how he'd played dead for so long. She tried moving her arms. Her legs. But everything felt tied to the earth, too heavy to move.

Brett stepped forward then, Matthew's gun hanging in her hand. She did not smile, but the look she wore on her face reminded Talia of the grin Brett had shown outside the Hope, the one that just barely hid a deep satisfaction. She looked lupine, filled with hunger and rage and a hunter's elation.

Talia tried to speak. To ask. But her throat was filled with blood, and all she could do was wheeze. Her hands reached out, grabbing at the dirt like vines caught in a cold wind, but were too weak to hold anything.

"You didn't talk about it a lot, but I know enough to find it, and I'll take good care of The Ranch, I promise," Brett said. "Couple of months, you two will get found out here, his gun, your knife." She reached into her boot and tossed the knife at Talia's feet. "Cops'll figure it out. They ain't dumb when they don't want to be. And then I'll go east. I've never been to Nebraska, but it seems quiet, and, after all these years, I think I'd like quiet."

It took everything, but Talia finally managed to wheeze out words. "What are you talking about?" she said.

"You forgot, honey. We're married. Won't be too hard to prove Talia Johnson is really Charlotte Jensen. And, you know. What's mine is yours."

"I wanted you to come with me," the woman known as Talia Johnson tried to say, but her throat was filled with blood, and her eyes were heavy, and the words came out like only the kiss of a soft breeze.

Above her, the stars had finally started to poke through the night, each of them crowning the top of a tree she lay beneath. Her eyes slid shut, but the points of light remained, all a candle in a window as she rode her old mare back to The Ranch, her father, just a shape somewhere up ahead in the darkness, waving her in.

Under her body, the ground tremored, the dirt bouncing beneath her bloody, grasping fingers, and as the light faded and the wind began to blow, she realized she was feeling their movements on the earth, the horses she'd left behind, and in her dark, some part of her ran to them, hoping one would be there, waiting for her, ready to take her home.

Across the Board

John Shepphird

Manny's bookie was late. The longshot didn't win but came in second. He had bet the maiden claimer across the board—win, place, and show which meant he'd collect for second and third.

Today's winnings would cover his next bet plus a Quarter Pounder from the McDonald's on Third Street. What he really liked was the warmed apple pie that came in the cardboard sleeve. He'd get one of those for sure and hoped the McDonald's would still be open by the time Gary arrived.

Where is that guy?

Back in the seventies, Manny Gomez started playing the horses at Spokane's Playfair Race Course. But, as the century came to an end, Playfair closed.

Now, Manny mostly played Emerald Downs. He'd gotten to know the trainers and horses over the years, and that gave him an edge. He knew that in horse racing it's about beating the public, and luck has very little to do with it. It is a four-hour drive from Spokane to Emerald Downs in Auburn, Washington, just south of Seattle. That's why Manny had a bookie.

To take his mind off it, he passed the time reading one of the many Western paperbacks he kept around. His apartment was full of them, books from Louis L'Amour, Larry McMurtry, and modern-day Westerns from Cormac McCarthy.

Finally, there was the knock.

The old man climbed from his recliner, one of the few pieces of furniture he owned, and confirmed it was Gary through the peephole. He opened the door with, "Where the hell were you? You're late."

"You sound like my ex-wife," Gary said.

"I've been waiting all night."

"I had shit to do, I'm a busy man."

"Busy doing nothing," Manny grumbled before he shuffled aside to allow the middle-aged Gary to enter the apartment. The bookie said, "Nice score old-timer. Too bad your horse couldn't get up to win."

"That damn jockey went too wide at the turn, should have saved ground." To watch the race replays, Manny had to go to the library to use the computers. It was part of his routine.

Gary pointed to a faded photo on the wall—a much younger Manny beside a blonde in a snug black dress and heels. "But that horse won, right? Where was that?" The photo was the crowning moment, the jockey mounted on a majestic thoroughbred beside Manny holding a trophy.

"The Spa," Manny said.

"The what?"

"Saratoga. New York."

"And you were the owner?"

"Long time ago."

"Who's the girl?"

"Some broad. I forget her name," Manny grumbled.

Gary pulled his pants up over his beer gut and handed over the envelope of cash. Holding up his mini spiral notebook, he asked, "What do you want for tomorrow?"

Manny thumbed through his winnings before handing Gary twenty-four dollars and the slip of paper he'd carefully prepared that afternoon. "I'm betting the pick-six."

"I can't take that action."

"Why not?"

Gary said. "That's picking six winners over six consecutive races. I'd have to lay it off."

"So lay it off," Manny said.

"I'll take your straight bets all day, pops, but no crazy exotics."

"My money's good."

"Sure, it is, but I can't take it without laying it off somewhere, and then I'll have to charge you twenty percent for the hassle."

Manny did the math in his head. He dug into the envelope for a five-dollar bill and handed it over. There goes the Quarter Pounder. He still had enough for the apple pie.

"Hold on," Gary said. "Think about it. The payout from a pick-six… if you hit it, they'll send me a ten ninety-nine, and I'll need to pay taxes. All of that will cost you sixty cents on the dollar by the time I combine my vig with what I'll have to hand over to the government." Manny said nothing so Gary continued with, "At the risk of losing the only client I've ever had that plays the ponies, take my advice. Open an online wagering account for yourself. You can bet whatever you want, whenever you want, and not have to wait for me to come around."

Manny said, "I can't."

"Why not?"

"Because they'll need a Social Security number."

"So"

"I don't have one."

"Why not?

"I was born in Mexico. Never got one."

"What about the jobs you had? And paying taxes?"

"Most of my jobs were under the table. The times I did have a real job, I'd invent a number."

"So you're not collecting Social Security?"

Manny shook his head.

"How do you get by?"

Manny bit his lip before he confessed, "I had some retirement tucked away, but I'm all tapped out."

"And I thought you were betting your Social Security check." There was an awkward moment between them before Gary said, "You've never bet the pick-six with me before."

"It's because they're evicting me."

"Who?"

"The landlord, who else?"

"When?"

"At the end of the month. Everyone out by Halloween."

"That's next week."

Manny nodded.

"What'd you gamble your rent away?"

"Just bad luck. They're clearing us all out. Everyone's got to go." Overwhelmed by the thought, Manny plopped down on the recliner. He wasn't feeling good, suffering from heartburn. He chalked it up to not eating all day.

Gary said, "Can they do that? I mean, just kick you out?"

"They can do whatever they want."

"How long have you known about this?"

"They've been threatening for a couple years."

"So you're betting the pick-six," Gary said, "throwing a Hail Mary into the end zone. You realize that is like playing the lottery or keno. At least with keno, there's a leggy chick that comes around to take your money. Remember Keno girls?"

Manny snapped his fingers. "Mary. That was her name. Mary from Cincinnati."

"Who?"

"The blonde in the picture. Saratoga."

"Oh… right. You stay in touch with her?"

"No. I forgot her name, didn't I? I got no place to go," a defeated Manny lamented. "I'll end up at the Salvation Army sleeping on a cot."

"No family you can ask for help?"

He waved that off with, "Everybody long gone."

"Seems to me like they should be giving you some sort of stipend to move out. It's only fair."

"They've been coming around with paperwork to sign. I avoided that. My neighbor Larry… he talked with the lady. They made him pack up and move into some state-run old folks' home, the poor bastard."

"You need to ask for help," Gary said, concerned.

"I'll figure it out."

"You have my phone number if you need anything. I can lend you a few bucks."

"Just take my bet. That's what I need."

"Alright, old-timer. Call me if you need anything."

Manny nodded silently.

"And good luck."

After Gary left, Manny set out for McDonald's in the dark. By the time he crossed under the freeway, he'd lost his appetite but pressed on anyway. The McDonald's was combined with a Chevron gas station. By the time he arrived, the heartburn was so bad he had to sit down.

***

The next morning, Gary the bookie dropped into the Lamplighter before the games back east got underway. Since it was October, the NFL season was still fresh so there'd be early Sunday action. Later in the season, after Thanksgiving, the bets would taper off and not pick up again until the playoffs.

Seated at his regular barstool, he ordered his usual Bloody Mary from Les, the bartender, before pulling out his phone to open a horse racing wagering account. As suspected, he had to provide a social security number. He funded the account with his credit card for the amount of Manny's bet. There was a fifty-dollar sign-up bonus, so he pocketed that for himself, already in profit for taking Manny's bet. He feared Manny was throwing away good money but what the hell. It's what the old man wanted. Gary felt bad for the guy. He was his only client that bet the ponies.

Some of his regular customers trickled in, the familiar neighborhood drunks and degenerates. Some would stay for the games nursing their beers, and others would drift off after handing over their cash or adding to their marker. Gary made his rounds dropping into a few other downtown bars before the start of the Seahawks game. His clients made small bets, so his business was about volume.

Later that afternoon, he was waiting on the scores when he checked the track results. He was surprised to see sixty-three thousand dollars in the account. At first, he thought it a mistake. Gary called the customer service number. They confirmed the amount. Manny had hit the impossible bet.

Gary rushed over to the apartment and knocked on Manny's door. There was no answer. He called on his cell phone and could hear Manny's landline ringing inside the apartment. A thin, older woman carrying a clipboard came down the hall and upon seeing Gary approached. She introduced herself as Dorothy Givens. "Are you family of Mister Gomez?"

"What's that?"

"Are you related?"

"No, just a friend. I've got some good news for the guy."

"Oh," she said gravely. Dorothy fingered the crucifix that hung from her turtleneck. "I'm sorry to be the one to inform you, but we lost Mister Gomez last night."

"Lost?"

"Cardiac arrest."

"A heart attack?"

"Outside the McDonald's not far from here. Can you direct me to any family members of his? I've been unable to find any."

Gary was at a loss. "I don't think he had family."

"Why do you say that?"

"What he said. That everyone was gone." Gary wondered if Manny had told anyone about the bet. Would the money be his to keep?

Dorothy said, "We've been trying to contact Mister Gomez to arrange assistance for quite some time. I've knocked on this door many times, but he never answered, even though I could hear him inside."

Gary nodded. "He mentioned the eviction."

"I've been assisting with the transition of the residents. How long have you known Mister Gomez?"

"A couple of years."

"The police are going to need someone to identify the body. Can you do that for him?"

"But I hardly knew the guy."

"I've been asking the neighbors. Everyone is either not willing or preoccupied with having to move out. When did you see him last?"

"Yesterday."

"What was the good news?" she asked, hopeful.

He didn't admit that he was a bookie and that Manny had won a bet. Instead, Gary said, "Nothing important, considering all of this."

She explained, "The police have been notified and will be here this afternoon. Since you were his friend, I'm sure they'd like to speak with you."

"Like I said, I hardly knew the guy."

"I've seen this procedure before. They'll do an inventory to determine any next of kin if there's a will or trust or any insurance policies. To complete the death certificate, his remains will have to be identified. Can you help with that?"

The last thing Gary wanted to do was look at a dead body. "I can't. I've got to get to work."

"It doesn't have to be today. Tomorrow or the next day would be fine."

Gary cringed at the thought. Dorothy continued, "You saw him yesterday, right? I've already tried the emergency contact Mister Gomez provided when he signed the lease years ago, but that number has been disconnected."

"There's got to be someone here that can do it," Gary said, "A friend or neighbor."

"None willing. If his body is not identified, they'll cremate him. And if nobody claims the remains after a while it will be disposed, thrown out with the trash. An unmarked grave. Out of respect, I'd prefer to avoid that."

Because she put it that way, Gary agreed to make the identification.

Less than an hour later, the bookie was standing in the Spokane County Medical Examiner's Office. They pulled back the plastic tarp. It was Manny alright—his jaw open in a frozen, sardonic grin, his gray hair matted. Even though Gary was in his mid-fifties, this was the first time he'd seen a dead body. It put him back on his heels.

They gave him a document to sign. He asked what would happen to Manny's remains but couldn't get a straight answer. Before he left, Gary offered to cover the expense of cremation and a proper burial. He figured it was the least he could do. The woman at the counter let him know somebody would contact him.

After that, Gary needed a stiff drink. He made his way back to the Lamplighter and ordered a double in an attempt to get the image of Manny's ashen corpse out of his mind. He bought everyone in the bar a round and toasted with, "In memory of Manny." None of the day drinkers knew who he was talking about, but they lifted glasses in the man's honor.

***

Later that week, Dorothy phoned and said, "The police were not able to find evidence of next of kin, and we need to clear out his possessions today. I wouldn't normally do this, but… I don't think there's really anything of much value. If there's something you'd like to keep, a memento for sentimental reasons, you're welcome to take it before everything goes into storage."

Gary was reluctant at first but figured if he was going to collect Manny's winnings, he should go through his belongings out of respect because maybe there was a family member the police had missed. He'd figured he'd feel less guilty if he gave a percentage of the winnings to a relative. There had to be someone.

As Gary came upon the apartment building, there was a construction dumpster full of ratty couches and bags of trash piled at the curb.

Upon entering the apartment, Gary was mortified. The cops had tossed the place, drawers pulled out, contents dumped everywhere as if he'd been robbed. A moment later, he wondered if some cretins had done this after the police searched the belongings.

Among the debris, he found nothing to imply that Manny ever had a wife or children and no correspondence to family or friends. There was clearly nothing to retrieve, but before he was about to leave, something caught his eye. The recliner had been toppled, and under the cushions, there was a hidden scrapbook. Gary pulled it out. There were more winner's circle photos like the one on the wall and a few snapshots of a much younger Manny wearing a wide tie at Expo '74. Since Gary grew up in Spokane, he recognized the World's Fair from 1974. It was a big deal. He remembered it had an environmentalist theme, way ahead of its time.

Beyond the photos, he found pages of yellowed newspaper articles. What he thought strange was that the clippings concerned burglaries of jewelry stores, museums, and pawn shops. The newspapers were all from random cities, including Phoenix, Denver, New York, and San Francisco.

Gary wondered why Manny would keep these in a scrapbook.

Dorothy appeared in the doorway beside a clean-cut man in his late thirties wearing a button-down shirt. She said to him, “This is the man I told you about, a friend of Mister Gomez.”

He thanked her and said, “I’ll take it from here.”

Dorothy offered a polite smile, thumbed the crucifix at her neck, and moved on.

The man introduced himself as Agent Monroe and displayed FBI credentials. Unconvincingly he said, “I’m sorry for your loss.”

FBI? Gary thought. Then it occurred to him. Maybe Manny was responsible for these heists. Was he hiding out? That would explain his hesitation to provide a social security number. If a number pinged somewhere in the system… that could lead back to him. “I didn’t know him that well,” he said and closed the scrapbook.

“What was your relationship with Mister Gomez?”

Gary was well aware that bookmaking was a class B felony in the state of Washington punishable to up to ten years in prison and/or a twenty thousand dollar fine. Even though the legality of sports betting, other than horse racing, was rolling out in more and more states across the country, Washington was not one of them. He was certain the local police wouldn’t enforce the law, but who knew how the Feds saw it? For that reason, Gary said, “Just a friend.”

“What did you share in common?”

“I don’t know. He was a good guy.” Gary pointed to the photo on the wall of Manny in the winner’s circle. “He knew a lot about horses, used to own thoroughbreds back in the day. We’d handicap and compare picks.”

Agent Monroe glanced at the photo. “How often did you see each other?”

Gary shrugged. "Mostly weekends."

"Did he ever speak about jewelry?"

"What do you mean?"

"Did he ever mention anything about luxury items such as diamonds or precious stones?"

Gary motioned the surroundings. "Does it look like Manny was living in the lap of luxury?"

"If you don't mind me asking, what do you do for a living?"

"I'm on disability."

Monroe nodded, said, "The Medical Examiner's office pulled fingerprints from the deceased. They matched to a man by the name of Milos Ivanov arrested fifteen years ago. Does that name ring a bell?"

"No," Gary said.

"Milos Ivanov came to Spokane to staff the Russian Pavilion during the World's Fair."

"Expo Seventy-four," Gary said. "I remember."

"When the fair ended, and it came time to return to Russia, Milos defected. About the same time, ballet dancer Mikhail Baryshnikov defected after a performance in Toronto. That may have inspired Milos to do the same."

Gary said, "But Manny was Mexican."

"It appears Manuel Gomez was one of his many aliases."

"Could have fooled me," Gary said. "I think you've got the wrong guy." It occurred to Gary that Manny did not necessarily have Hispanic features, but he didn't mention it. Instead, he asked, "So the Russians are still looking for this guy?"

"I assume they were at one time. With the collapse of the Soviet Union, I doubt anyone cares much anymore. Records show he was a submariner."

"Like... submarines?"

"Yes, before he was staffed to serve as a host at the World's Fair. So he never spoke of the Soviet Union, jewelry, or of his travels?"

"No."

Monroe produced a photo of a diamond necklace. "Approximately twenty years ago, Milos sold this necklace to a diamond wholesaler in Miami for pennies on the dollar. Records indicate that the necklace was once owned by famed fashion designer Coco Chanel, so it had historic, collectable value. Milos didn't know that at the time. The necklace had been burglarized from a home in Beverly Hills. Authorities in Miami tracked Milos down and arrested him, but he jumped from a third-story window and escaped."

Gary caught himself glancing at the scrapbook before he said, "You're telling me this guy was an international jewel thief?"

"According to the file. What seems odd is that he came back to Spokane after all these years. The landlord says Milos has been living here for over fifteen years."

"So you're thinking he sold off his loot over the years to get by?"

"Fencing his goods, yes. People are creatures of habit," Agent Monroe glanced around at the piles of junk. "He returned to Spokane, what was familiar. What we're trying to figure out is where he kept his stash of jewelry. We found a shovel in the closet, and so we're assuming he may have buried it somewhere."

Gary said, "He told me he was tapped out."

"What's that?"

"He said he was broke. That his retirement was gone."

"Other than horse racing," Monroe asked again, "what else did you have in common?"

Gary said truthfully, "We talked about horses. That's it." He picked up the scrapbook, "I was looking around and came across a photo of him in here." He showed Monroe the page. "I remember what Expo Seventy-four looked like because I was there too, as a kid." There was an image of Milos standing next to a massive bust of Lenin inside the Russian Pavilion, "but I also noticed something else." Gary turned the pages to the newspaper clippings. "I was wondering why he kept all of these articles about burglaries."

Agent Monroe found great interest in the scrapbook. After thumbing through it for a moment, he said, "You may have just discovered the playbook."

After almost an hour more of questions and rehashing what he'd already told Agent Monroe, Gary asked if he could go home. Monroe took the scrapbook. Gary grabbed a few of the newer-looking Western paperbacks before they went into storage and, eventually, the dumpster.

He craved a drink so stepped into the Lamplighter. Seated, he got the call. The woman from the Medical Examiner's Office said, "You mentioned you'd handle the cost of cremation and burial. Is that still your intention?"

"Yes." Gary arranged to pay for the cremation and urn. He figured it was the least he could do.

"What are you doing?" Les, the bartender asked, having eavesdropped on the conversation.

"Taking care of Manny Gomez's burial. Remember that guy?"

"Sure."

"What did you know about him?" Gary asked.

"Nothing, other than he drank vodka. Never ice."

"Of course he did," Gary said. "Did you know he was Russian?"

"Could have fooled me."

"Fooled everyone."

It was dark by the time Gary left the bar. Even though it was Halloween, this wasn't a part of town where kids trick or treated. Old downtown was devoid of youth. There was nothing there for them.

Gary turned up his collar against a cold wind.

Outside the apartment building, he passed the dumpster. He saw that the recliner had been tossed out, sitting atop a pile of rubbish. Didn't Dorothy say Manny's possessions were going into storage? But then it made sense. They would discard large items like old, broken-down furniture and mattresses. Of course. Then the thought came to him, and he stopped in his tracks. Since the scrapbook was hidden in the recliner, what else could there be?

Gary climbed up into the dumpster. He found a discarded bread knife and cut into the upholstery to discover a deep pocket below the seat cushion. From inside, he pulled out a handful of velvet bags, cases, and jewelry boxes, all empty. There were jewelry store price tags and diamond appraisal forms. There were lock pick sets and plastic gloves. He was certain this was the stash. Lastly, he pulled out a military medal of some kind. When he was sure there wasn't anything more, he tossed the contents into a plastic bag and made his way home.

It wasn't until he was seated at his computer under the illumination of a desk lamp that he examined the gold star medal. He searched Google to learn it was the Hero of the Soviet Union medal. The medal honored heroic feats in service to the Soviet state and society.

This guy was a hero?

The next morning Gary called a funeral parlor to arrange the burial plot. He took the medal to the headstone mason to embed it into the memorial. People needed to see the medal. He wasn't about to bury it with the urn. The headstone was expensive but paying for it relieved the guilt of collecting the pick-six payout. Gary had no idea what year Milos was born so in honor of a guy he hardly knew, the inscription read:

Milos Ivanov
Horseplayer, Jewel Thief,
Hero of the Soviet Union
Across the Board

*"You forget what you want to remember,
and you remember what you want to forget."*
- Cormac McCarthy, *The Road*

The Air Shaft

Dana King

Celia blew smoke out the window. "Thank God for this air shaft."

Dave smiled from across the way, as much as he ever did. "I had no idea it got this hot in Washington. You see the pictures, and it's all trees and mountains. This is—well, it's not desert, but it's sure not trees and mountains."

"You ever been to Hanford? Where that reactor is?" Dave had not. "Rattlesnakes. Swear to God."

"Nope. Never been there. Only been here a couple weeks."

About how long she'd known him. "What brought you?"

"You mean here to Spokane? Or to the Hope Apartments?"

"I call them the 'Hopeless Apartments.'" Celia glanced down to the base of the shaft three stories below. Cracked concrete and debris from people who treated it as a trash chute. Last week Celia noticed what she insisted to herself was the biggest mouse she'd ever seen. "You know they're throwing us out by Halloween, right?"

Dave nodded. Sipped from a can of Olympia. "I don't figure to stay more than a month or six weeks. Long enough to find something more stable. This place is in transition. So am I. It suits me." Another sip. "What about you?"

"I'm between places." Left her last apartment, three in the morning with the clothes on her back and what she could carry in one trip. Life savings in her pocket. Seventy-eight dollars and fifty-seven cents. Had to blow three guys and turn two tricks to get up the deposit for her one-bedroom at the Hope. An efficiency wouldn't do for a girl in Celia's line of work, not with having to share a bathroom down the hall. "I'll be out by the end of August. September at the latest. Find someplace with air conditioning."

"Yeah. Air conditioning." Dave wiped his brow with the back of his hand. "What do you do to keep ends together?"

"I guess you could say I'm part of the gig economy. You?"

"For now, I'm working midnights at the convenience store a few blocks from here."

"The Seven-Eleven?"

Dave shook his head. Pointed southwest. "Other direction. On Third. Next to Starbucks."

"Across from the grocery store?"

"That's the one."

Dave didn't seem eager to volunteer much more about himself than Celia did. Fine with her. He seemed nice. Quiet, but not creepy quiet. It was nice to have someone to talk with like this, the air shaft separating them. He'd never tried to invite himself over or hint like he wanted her to, Celia often as not sitting in a half-slip with one foot on the window ledge. Woman who lived across the way before was a dried-up old bitch. Never spoke, not even to return a hello. If she paid Celia any mind at all, it was to look down that ski jump of a nose at her.

Celia crushed out the cigarette. "I better get going. Talk to you later."

Dave looked at his watch. "Yeah, I should try to get some sleep. Wish I fit in the refrigerator." Grunted at his joke and turned back inside his room.

Celia went in to finish her makeup. It was a bitch to apply in this heat, her face sweaty in the time it took to walk from the window to the bathroom. Dark enough in the Lamplighter not to be a big deal if she displayed the rest of the merchandise well. Reminded herself—again—that working the Lamplighter was better than walking the streets—swore she'd never do that, drink bleach first—even if she did have to blow Lester Poole once a week for the privilege of picking up guys in his shitty bar. Refused to call him "Les." Made it too obvious how he symbolized everything connected to her life right now.

Standard of living? *Less.*

Housing arrangements? *Less.*

Prospects? *Less.*

Celia smiled as her mind flashed to her mother. "Not less, Ceel. *Fewer.*"

Gave the apartment a quick once-over before locking the door. Not enough there to merit more than a brief look. The bathroom was cleaner than it appeared. Nothing she could do about that. She'd made the bed. Left the window to the air shaft open. No rain predicted, any that fell would have to come straight down to get this deep in the shaft. Locked the door and started getting her mind right. Looked once at the elevator as she heard the car pass her floor. She'd been stuck in it twice, once just a week ago. Shook her head to reinforce her decision and took the stairs.

Too early for the Lamplighter to be busy except for the usual day drinkers. Men who had their priorities straight:

liquor before pussy. Maybe if one of them hit a number. Jack Gilstrap treated himself for a week after his mother's life insurance cleared, drank up the rest.

Lester saw her as she came in. Nodded. Dipped his head a couple of inches. "Evening, Candace. Have a little free time later?"

Bad enough she had to blow the old letch. No way was he getting her real name. "We already had some free time this week, Lester. The new week starts on Sunday."

Lester showed disappointment. Didn't argue. "The usual?"

"Yes, please."

Celia took her regular seat near the end of the bar farthest from the door. Lester brought over her Seven and Seven. Set it on a cocktail napkin just so. "Ever wonder why they call them cocktails?"

"Not since the first time you told me." Lester looked puzzled. "Surest way to get your cock in her tail, right?"

"I told you before?"

"About twenty times."

Lester's face stiffened. "Ain't true, anyway. The quickest way might just be to drop a fifty on the floor in front of you."

"Go fuck yourself, Lester. This isn't the only shitty bar I can work out of."

Celia sipped her drink. Let the tang of the Seagram's slide alongside the fizz of the Seven-Up. Thursday was Pete Singer's usual night, though not for a few hours yet. Pete was a nice enough guy, tipped her an extra twenty if he had it. No one with a lot of money to spend ever came to the Lamplighter. A couple of law firms nearby, though their clients were more likely to patronize the dump. Police arrested an armored car robber as he walked her toward the door a few months ago. Big fun. She had to go to the station and explain what she was doing with him without saying she was about to fuck him for money. Sometimes her marketing degree still paid off.

The guy walked in as she was about to pay for her own refill, a promising sign. Wore a suit, which was unusual for the Lamplighter, but it had seen better days and hadn't been a great suit to begin with. The tie was frayed at the tip. The briefcase had been expensive once, long ago. The guy himself was average height, maybe a small paunch. Early forties. Pleasant looking, not handsome. His smile showed a misaligned tooth. "Is this seat taken?"

"It is now."

Celia didn't milk the play. No fooling around like he was trying to pick up an amateur, then the awkward moment when the topic of money arose. That's what she missed most about the outcall service. The price was set, she showed up, he got laid, and she got paid. Now she set aside any confusion about her professional status and got down to business once the first drink arrived. Get him upstairs, get him off, take a shower, and the night might still be young enough for at least one more.

He rolled over on the price so quick it irritated her, knowing she missed out on another fifty. Now it was time for the ground rules. "Before we go upstairs, let's get a few things straight. No bondage, no pain, no water sports. Everything else is fair game. You okay with that?"

He was. She'd seen it before. Her directness made him hot. He wouldn't last half an hour. She'd be back trolling by eight-thirty.

Celia used her pass key to the service entrance and stairway the Hope's maintenance man, Earl Ricci, had given her. Allowed her and her dates to bypass the lobby, where Anita gave the stink eye to anyone less righteous than a nun. Tried to have Celia thrown out a few weeks ago just on suspicion. That key cost her another hummer a week, but Earl was a nice guy, and he'd lose his job if either Anita or her boss Dorothy found out. Plus, Lester detested Earl, so she liked thinking how pissed off Lester would be if he knew he wasn't the only one getting freebies.

The apartment wasn't stifling, thank god for that. Might even get some unexpected rain, the way the sheer curtains she'd hung flowed out the window. She led him into the bedroom—he said his name was Ray—and asked if he wanted to undress her.

"I want to watch you do it. Put on a show for me."

She could do that. Preferred it, actually. Gave her a chance to show off the parts of the merchandise she wanted to show. Thought of it as how the butcher displays the best-looking side of the meat on top. She turned her back and took her time removing her stockings. Let him see her ass was still tight. Stayed that way while she shimmied out of the thong.

Turned around to pull the dress over her head and saw the handcuffs. Two sets. She said, "Look, I told you the deal. I don't get restrained," and he hit her before she got the last syllable out, a slap across the face. Not an attention-getter. The real deal. Followed it up with a punch, a left cross, before she got over the shock. She tried to scream, thinking the thin walls would let the sound out. He put one hand over her mouth, the other on her throat.

She kicked him as hard as she could between the legs. Felt her shin drive through his erection. His turn to scream.

She broke away and ran to the living room. Got the entry door unlocked but not open before he grabbed her by the arm and threw her across the room to crash in the corner. He lunged at her, and she scuttled away under him, the threadbare rug scratching her bare ass. Made another lunge for the door. He grabbed a handful of hair and jerked her back, hard. She lost her balance and fell to the floor. He straddled her, pinning her arms. Punched her face a few times.

She tried to turn away from the blows but guessed wrong and turned into one. Saw stars, tasted blood.

He leaned over to attach a handcuff to her right wrist. "You would've liked what I had planned. You're not going to like what happens next nearly as much." Snapped the cuff closed. Reached for her other wrist.

Celia tried to get her legs up far enough to wrap around him, pull him off. That level of flexibility was years in the past. She felt the second cuff around her wrist. The hasp scratched her wrist as she jerked it away. The idea she would die tonight exploded in the back of her head. She started to cry. Hated herself for it but couldn't stop.

She felt him reposition himself. Heard a sound she couldn't place, and Ray was off her altogether. She held her eyes closed, waiting for what came next. Another noise she didn't recognize. Risked a look to see what else had gone wrong in time to see Dave from across the way hit Ray and send him onto the couch hard enough to tip it over.

This new shock required recovery, good news or not. Celia watched Dave hurdle the couch. Saw his right arm rise and fall, each downward stroke punctuated by the sound of impact. Celia recovered the presence of mind to try to pull Dave away. "Dave! *Dave!* Stop! You'll kill him!"

Dave came away easier than she expected. Put one hand on the overturned couch and stood. Turned to look at Celia.

His breathing showed both exertion and adrenaline. His voice was steady. "Are you all right?"

Celia nodded.

"Did he…?"

She shook her head.

He gave her face a quick inspection. "Let me get you a towel and some ice for that nose. Sit in the chair and tilt your head back."

It occurred to her as he went to the back of the apartment, he hadn't seemed to notice she was naked. She was wrong. He came back with a dish towel full of ice and the bedspread. Eased her into the wing chair and wrapped the spread around her. "Anything else you need? You have any aspirin? Tylenol? That face is going to hurt pretty soon if it doesn't already."

Celia still a little disoriented when Dave went over to check on Ray. Watched him try to turn the couch upright. Then he tried to lift Ray. Stared at the situation, puzzled. Celia had about regained her faculties when Dave climbed over the couch and knelt on the other side. She couldn't see his hands. His face showed more confusion than before. She said, "What is it?"

Dave didn't move. His voice was as bewildered as his face. "I didn't hit him that hard."

A different kind of fear crawled up Celia's back. "What's wrong?"

Dave's head wagged a bit. "I *know* I didn't hit him that hard."

"*Dave!* What's wrong?"

Dave still looking at Ray. "He's dead." His head tilted up, searching the wall. Moved his hands somewhere behind the couch. Sighed. A word escaped that Celia couldn't make out. "He must've hit his head when the couch went over. There's blood on the molding."

Celia's voice had no substance. "He's dead?"

Dave still stared at a spot she couldn't see. "Far as I can tell."

Hot as it was in the room, Celia felt cold even wrapped in the bedspread. The first signs of nausea took hold. As confused by Dave's reaction as by what had happened. No concern on his face. No remorse. "Disconcerted" came to mind. Something didn't make sense, and he was trying to figure it out. Celia said, "Dave." Quiet, not to disturb his concentration.

Ray on the floor still held Dave's attention. "Were you seen with this guy?" When Celia didn't answer, Dave turned his face toward her. "Did anyone see the two of you together?"

"Some drunks in the Lamplighter. Lester Poole."

"Who's he?"

"The owner."

Dave looked back toward Ray, not quick enough to hide his dissatisfaction with Celia's answer. Didn't say anything for a minute or more while Celia was afraid to speak. "How drunk was this guy?" Nodded to indicate Ray.

"Not very. At least he didn't seem to be. We had one drink in the Lamplighter. He looked sober when he came in."

Dave nodded once. Repositioned himself and dropped down to one knee. Lifted the back of the couch to an upright position. Ray's body went to the floor like icicles slipping off a roof on a sunny day. Dave came around the couch, went through Ray's pockets. Came up with a wallet on his left hip. "Raymond Donnelly. He's from Dishman. What the hell's he doing in the Lamplighter?"

Celia didn't recognize her own voice. "Maybe he came in looking for a whore to kill. We don't draw a lot of attention when we go missing, you know."

Dave pored over the contents of the wallet. "How much was he supposed to pay you?" She told him. "There's not half that much here. Did he bring anything else with him?"

The foreign voice said, "There's a briefcase. In the bedroom."

Dave stood without a word. Started for the bedroom. Celia called him back. "Aren't you going to… I don't know. Put him on the couch or something?"

Dave looked at her, then Ray. Back to Celia. "It don't matter to him, either way. Besides, he might have killed you. Fuck him."

Celia didn't want to say what she really meant. *He's right there. The dead man not six feet away.* Dave must have figured it out. He came back from the bedroom carrying Ray's briefcase and a sheet. Set the case on the eating table, draped the sheet over the body. Unlocked the cuff from her wrist.

She couldn't decide what to make of Dave as he opened and went through the case. He didn't seem mad. Nor scared. He seemed like… a guy doing his job. Had the demeanor of a plumber or electrician. Someone who worked with his hands and fixed things. She felt another, stronger wave of nausea. Worked up the gumption to ask what she wanted to know—and didn't want to know—most in the world. Unhappy with the way her voice sounded when she started to ask. Tried again, and it came out better. "You've d—you've done this before. Haven't you?"

Dave paused his inspection of the briefcase's contents. Didn't look at her. Might have pursed his lips before he spoke. "Once." Went back to work.

Celia was scared before. Dave's answer took things to a new level. Afraid to say any more, terrified not to. "What are you—what are we gonna do?" Making them a team. Teams stick together.

Dave still sifted papers from the briefcase. Spoke as if his mind was elsewhere. "You're going to take a long shower. Clean yourself up. You have any bleach? Strong disinfectant?"

"I have some of that spray Clorox stuff in the kitchen. Under the sink."

Dave jammed the papers back into the briefcase. "That'll have to do." Gathered the papers back into a bundle. Looked at her for the first time in what seemed like weeks. "Get yourself cleaned up. You'll need to get the blood off the wall and every other place there might be any. Vacuum all the rugs. Wash all the bedclothes. Anything he might've touched or where fibers of his clothes might've come loose. You have a carpet shampooer?" She shook her head. "Then vacuuming will be good enough. Do not," raised an index finger, "do *not* rent a carpet shampooer. Leave it go at vacuuming but vacuum the shit out of the place. In the morning. Not now. Not unless you make a habit of housecleaning at night."

Celia nodded for each new instruction. Her head kept going up and down like a bobble head doll set down too hard even after he finished. Made herself stop. She whispered without meaning to. "What're we gonna do?" Pointed to Ray. "With him?"

"We're not doing anything with him. Where'd you pick him up?"

"The Lamplighter."

"Get cleaned up. Make up your face the best you can and stay out of the light, which shouldn't be too hard in there. Be seen. Act like you're done with him, and you're looking for a relaxing drink. Do not pick anyone up, but don't be too obvious about shooting them down. Maybe go to a couple other places. Make sure people see you, but don't be obvious about it. Whatever you do, don't come back here before one or two in the morning." Paused. "Two's better."

"What will you be doing?"

"Never mind what I'll be doing. How long will it take you to get ready?"

"Half an hour. Forty-five minutes."

Dave did math in his head. "That works. Don't leave until I get back."

Celia couldn't help but glance at the sheet-shrouded corpse. "What about him?"

"He won't bother you in the bathroom. Stay in the bedroom if you want, I'm not back yet."

Dave left without another word. Celia took a hot shower. Felt the water sting the bruises on her face. Took special care with her make-up. It didn't hide the marks altogether, but she'd get by given the kind of light she'd find where she planned to go. Dressed and finishing with her hair when she heard Dave come back.

He didn't waste words. Didn't ask how she was. Celia not sure if his brusqueness meant anything more than acknowledgement of the high-stress situation. "You ready?" She nodded. "Where are you going?" She told him. He relaxed half a notch. Nodded toward Ray. "He'll be gone when you get back. So will I."

"Where are you going?"

"I wouldn't tell you if I knew. Remember, clean the wall, vacuum the floors, and do the laundry first thing in the morning. Not too early. Nine, ten o'clock should be all right. Throw the vacuum bag away when you're finished. Not here. Somewhere between here and the laundromat, maybe."

Celia grasped his forearm. "Why are you doing this for me?"

"If the police come looking for him, tell them you two came up here, did whatever it is you want to tell them you did, and he left. Might be just as well to let them know he was a john. Maybe they'll think he was out places a nice suburban man shouldn't be and trouble found him. Also makes it sound more like you aren't hiding anything. If they come back with a warrant, give me up. Tell them I was jealous of you sleeping with another guy. Whatever. You're not going to know where I am so nothing you tell them can hurt me."

"You just told me to say you killed him. Didn't you?"

Dave nodded.

"That won't hurt you?"

Dave looked at Celia as if deciding how much to say. "Once you're on the hook for natural life, everything else is free." He must have seen the look on her face. "There's already a warrant out for me. One more won't matter. Deflect everything you can to me if it comes to it. I don't think it will, but you never know." Opened the door. "Go now."

Celia pushed the door shut with a foot. "You're not a killer."

"A killer is someone who kills people." The edge left his voice. "One might be an accident. Two?"

"You might've saved my life."

"And that might've mattered if this one had come first. Maybe."

"What happened?"

"It's getting late. You need to go."

Celia planted herself in front of Dave. Gripped his arms tight as she could. "Tell me. Please. I got you into this. I need to know."

He looked her straight in the eye. "My sister was in an abusive relationship. The whole family, all her friends, we tried to get her to see this guy for what he was and get out. She wouldn't leave. She'd come to my parents' house in tears, beat up. Once, she was missing a tooth. She always went back.

"One day, I went over to drop off some nice corn I'd found at a farm stand. Walked in on him, beating her with a belt. The buckle end." Jerked a thumb toward what used to be Ray. "It wasn't like with him. I beat Donny until I saw brains. Then I called the police."

"Wasn't that defending your sister?"

One corner of Dave's mouth turned up. "Not the way she told it."

Celia raised up on tiptoe to kiss Dave on the cheek. He didn't lean in or away. Squeezed her wrist for a second, then moved her through the door.

She turned back to him in the hallway. "Drop me a line when you know you're safe. So I know."

"Where should I send it?"

Celia said, "I'm not going anywh—" before she realized she was, no later than Halloween. "Write down my cell number."

For the first time, she saw an emotion from Dave, sadness in his eyes. "It's better if I don't. This way you can think what you want about me. If I tell you I'll call or text and I don't, you'll think the worst. You really need to go. I have a lot of work to do."

She did exactly as he told her. Went back to the Lamplighter. Let the word out she was tired and was taking the night off, just didn't want to be alone. Went to a couple of other places she hadn't been for a while. Made a point to speak to anyone she knew, even just by sight.

Celia walked into her apartment at a quarter to two. The living room furniture was where it belonged. The bed clothes Dave used were in the hamper. The bloody smudge on the wall behind the couch was gone. The vacuum cleaner sat in the middle of the living room floor.

***

Cops were in the Lamplighter when she walked in the next night. A detective named Higgins showed her a photograph. "Do you know this man?"

Celia gave it more attention than she needed to. "Yeah. He was in here last night."

"Did you talk to him?"

Celia forced herself not to reach for a cigarette or her drink. Before going out, she'd worked on her story, practiced it. Not so much detail she could be tripped up. Not so vague she'd seem evasive. "We left together."

Higgins's face didn't change. His pen hesitated before jotting the note. "What time was that?"

Had to tell the truth. People had seen her. "Seven. Quarter after, maybe. I didn't really check."

"Where did you go?"

"My place."

"Which is where?"

Celia's mind flashed to the cleaning she'd done. She watched enough crime shows to know they'd find evidence if they looked hard enough. Her job here was not to give them anything that might make them want to look. "Upstairs. Hope Apartments."

"When did he leave?"

Had to lie now. "Eight, eight-thirty."

"He wasn't up there long."

"We didn't hit it off."

"Why not?"

Celia shrugged. "You know how it is. You meet someone, and once you talk a while, you don't like each other as much as you thought you would."

Higgins let his skepticism show. *Please, lady. I know why a man goes to the room of a woman he just met and only stays an hour.* "What did you do then?"

"You mean after he left?" Higgins nodded. "I watched a little TV. That was boring, and it was still pretty early, so I came back down here."

"What time was that?"

Celia pretended to think. "Nine-thirty or so. Les would know. He served me a drink when I came back."

"What did you watch on television?"

"One of those hoarders shows." Shook her head. "I can't believe people watch that shit all night."

Higgins's notepad rested in a position where he could check out Celia's legs and still appear to be working. She'd seen enough of that to recognize it, though most men worked their props so they could keep tabs on her tits. "How late did you stay?"

"Not long. Just one drink. I was restless, and that guy—his name was Ray, right?—I wasn't in the mood to see him again in case he came back. I went to a couple other places where I might be around someone I knew and could relax."

"What did he do?"

"What do you mean?"

"You said you weren't in the mood to see him again. Did he do something? Scare you? Try to hurt you?"

Celia couldn't stop a sigh. *Enough already*. "It was just—he was an asshole, okay? He seemed nice in here, but once we started talking, he turned out to be a real jerk. Struck me as the kind of guy who'd make a scene if I ran into him again."

The cop tapped his pen against the notepad, and Celia worried he wasn't ready to let it go. He said, "What time did you leave here?" and she felt as relieved as the last time a pregnancy test came back negative.

Celia moved her hands like she was trying to remember she'd left at 10:24. "Quarter after ten? Ten-thirty?"

"Anyone see you leave?"

"I said good-night to Les. I have no idea if he logged the time. What's all this about anyway?"

"Just a few more questions. Why did you come back here if you were worried about running into Ray again?"

Celia made a small pout. "Habit, I guess. I'm so used to stopping here first when I go out, it's just where I went. I was halfway through my drink when it occurred to me Ray might come back."

"Did he?"

"Come back here? No. Not while I was here, anyway."

"Where else did you go?" She told him. "Anyone there you knew?" She told him. "They can vouch for you?"

"If they remember. It's not like I walk into a place and everyone yells, 'Ceel,' like they used to do for that fat guy on *Cheers*. You ever see that show? It had that actor who was on *The Good Place*. That's a funny show, too."

Higgins put his notebook in an inside jacket pocket. Used the opportunity to check out the rest of Celia's goods. Called over to his partner. "Hey, Dallas. You want her for anything?"

Dallas didn't look up from whatever he was doing. "Cut her loose. Get her in for a formal statement if you think it's worth the time."

Higgins turned his attention back to Celia. "You mind coming by the station tomorrow for a statement? It's routine. You saw him, spent some time with him, we'd like it for the record."

"Like I asked you already, what's this about?"

"Someone killed him last night."

"Oh my God! Where?"

"Body was found down by the tracks."

"What was he doing over there?"

"That's what we'd like to know. Here's my card. Stop by tomorrow between ten and noon if you can. Shouldn't take us an hour, and we'll get you back to work. What is it you do?"

"I guess you could say I'm part of the gig economy."

Higgins smiled for real. "If that's how you want to put it. I'll look forward to seeing you tomorrow morning, Ms. Snow." Tapped a finger against the card in her hand. "That cell number goes directly to me. You think of anything that didn't come up today, call me. Or call the station. Either way."

Celia promised she would. Higgins's partner was already at the door, looking at his watch. Higgins got a move on, and they walked out together.

Celia relaxed—not all the way; she doubted she'd ever relax all the way again—and ordered a Seven and Seven. Let it slide down her throat. That went better then she'd hoped. A girl in her line of work had to be able to read people. She doubted Higgins suspected her of being anything more serious than a second-rate hooker. She couldn't blame him for that.

Disco Drops a Beat

Matt Phillips

Disco slapped his hands on the bar, punctuated a timed beat with hisses and clicks of his tongue. A quick beat to impress the drunks hanging their heads over warm beer and empty shot glasses.

Les, digging in a file cabinet behind the bar, looked at Disco and said, "Will you shut that down, young buck?"

Still carrying the beat with his hands, Disco said, "Gotta get my beat on, Les. Practice for when I'm making them for K. Lamar—you know how it is, pops."

Les shook his head, found what he wanted in the cabinet—a crinkled manila envelope. He straightened and tossed it onto the bar. "There you go. That's the last bit I got to pay that mother—"

"Better all be here, Les," Disco said as he snatched the envelope and graced the bar with silence. He dug a hand into the envelope and felt the small stack of money between thumb and forefinger. "Feels like two hundy, but do I need to count it?" He centered his cockeyed gaze on Les and waited.

"Fuck yourself, Disco."

"Yeah. I better count this mess." Disco slid the cash out and counted it slowly on the bar, exaggerated the amount when he landed on a small bill. Knew he was getting on Les' old man nerves. But Disco also knew what it would be if he didn't get Monster the full two hundred. He'd get himself a beat-down. Like to make it so he couldn't get with Sharon tonight. Somehow, she let him kiss her a couple weeks back, and that was that. Tonight, maybe, Disco thought he could get it in. Fingers fucking crossed. He finished counting and dropped the money into the envelope, folded and tucked it down the front of his pants beneath his black hoodie. "It's all there. You pay just like the bitch you are."

Les narrowed his eyes. "The fuck I had to pay Monster all these years for? So I could deal with smart ass little kids coming in here?"

"I'm fifteen years full-grown, Les. Got a hundred-dollar bill in my pocket. More where it came from, too."

"Shit. You're just a bug with a boss. Someday gonna get smashed."

Disco gulped, bit the front of his tongue, and reminded himself what Monster said to him the other day: Get my money and don't cause trouble. Okay, leave this shit alone. Disco spun and started for the door but heard Les call after him with that shaky old-man voice.

"How you get the name Disco, anyway?"

Before crossing through the lobby and exiting onto Madison Street, Disco shouted over his shoulder. "Sly and the Family Stone was my momma's favorite group!"

Les shouted after him, "That ain't disco—it's some old school funk! You dumber than you look!"

Disco stepped outside onto Madison, licked the cold October air from his lips. It wasn't until he started walking down the street that it occurred to him: Nobody at the bar said shit, except for old ass Lester.

Quiet as a church up in that motherfucker.

Like, everybody praying or something.

***

Monster didn't bother counting the money. He tossed the envelope onto his coffee table—next to a crumpled McDonald's bag and a few portioned dime bags—and sat back with his legs spread ball player style. Wore his standard Adidas sweatsuit tonight and a pair of old-school track shoes from the same brand. Monster's place was a third-floor walkup—pimp-status with the 75-inch flat-screen and surround sound. All this fancy modern furniture that made Disco afraid to sit on it. Monster raised his eyebrows and said, "Sit your ass down for a second, brah. Stay awhile."

Disco looked around, uncomfortable with all the fancy-ass chairs staring him right in the face.

"Right here, brah," Monster said as he pointed at one of the confusing gray chairs. "Take my favorite spot."

Disco sat and hunched forward, elbows on his knees.

"Ain't nothing left from the Hope, am I right?"

"Yeah—they're saying everybody's out next week."

"Halloween."

"That's it," Disco said. "Make it a haunted joint, I guess."

Monster said, "You take your twenty already?"

"You said I should. So, that's what I been doing. What I did tonight." Disco was afraid to look at Monster, not sure how to talk to the older guy—almost thirty—and concerned he'd fucked up somehow. On accident, maybe. But still.

"That's good, brah. How you like to make a little more?"

Disco shrugged, elbows still on his knees. Still looking at the plush beige carpet, he said, "I like me some money."

"Look at me, youngster."

Disco looked up and met Monster's eyes—brown and flat. He licked his bottom lip and tried to hold his own browns nice and steady.

Monster leaned forward and said, "There's something I want you to do. Kind of an extra chore before the Hope gets turned into some fancy joint for all them hipster kids and lawyers."

Disco grinned, thought it funny—in a perverse way—that him and his mom had to give up their shitty studio so the city could turn the Hope into some fancy hotel. Not that his mom was home much. Because who wanted to live in room 216 and share a bathroom with a bunch of dirty street motherfuckers?

Not that the next place would be any better.

Disco knew it wouldn't be.

And his mom, she was never going to get better. All that junk she put into her arm. Disco might as well give it up, pretend she was dead.

"What you want me to do, Monster?" he said.

One eyebrow tilted toward the ceiling, and Monster smiled, his iced out silver grill plate flashing. "I know there's somebody up there, has something I want."

"Money?"

Monster didn't answer, but instead stared holes into him.

Disco got a twist in his stomach. "I ain't a stick-up boy, Monster."

"No, you ain't." He leaned forward and slid a key off the glass coffee table. He reached across the table and held it out for Disco to take. "You take this with you. I need you to get something from the old man. He's got a drawer behind the bar, takes this key."

Disco took the key, looked at it in awe.

"I don't want Les to know you took it. It's why I'm giving you the key." He sniffed hard and leaned back into the sofa, laced his hands behind his head.

"I got to sneak into the Lamplighter?"

Monster grunted. "There's a C-note in it, you do what I need."

Disco nodded, looked up at Monster, and cocked his head. "What is it you need me to—"

"Envelope. Like this one here." He lifted his chin at the money.

Disco nodded again. He thought for a moment and said, "But ain't it true that Les don't take no shit?"

Monster laughed before saying, "He don't take no shit? What you call it when the man pays me for four years, just because I tell him he has to? What you call that?"

Disco shook his head. "Fuck if I know."

"I call that taking shit, D. That there is taking shit, brah."

***

Sharon ran a fingernail along Disco's shoulder. She chuckled and said, "You a good kisser."

He put his head up, shifted on the bed. Met her eyes and those big eyelashes looping over them. "Yeah? Shit—you think I didn't know?"

She shook her head, used a hand to flatten his head onto her tits. Brown and flat with purple nipples. "You all talk, Disco."

He smiled, tried not to laugh. "When we gonna take this all the way, make it official?"

"Make it official? You need to get a girl all the way to call it official?"

"I'm saying is all… You know you—"

"Me and you are gonna take this shit slow."

Disco lifted his head again, rolled his eyes at her.

She stared at him, unblinking. "We gonna take it as slow as I want. Tell me you hear me."

"I hear you," he said as he rested his head again.

"You be lucky to lose it here at the Hope."

"Lose what?"

"Disco—I know you're a virgin."

He didn't respond.

"I think it's sexy."

"Really?"

"Yes."

Disco felt her reach for the key on the nightstand, heard it slide across the fake wood. Imagined her looking at it, studying.

She said, "What's this for?"

"A thing for Monster."

She dropped the key onto the nightstand. "Another thing for that loser, huh? Pretty soon you gonna—"

"It's not like the other shit, girl."

"Oh, yeah? What's it like then?"

Disco rolled off her, sat up in the bed. He scooted backward and rested against the wall. Rubbed at dry skin on his forearms. "It's the old man at the restaurant."

"Lester," she said.

"Yeah—old man Les. He's got something belongs to Monster."

"What is it?"

Disco shook his head. "Fuck if I know."

"You ever wonder why Monster keeps on charging Lester for protection, or whatever it is?"

This was a conversation Disco wanted to end. He was supposed to crush it with Sharon tonight. Not walk away with blue balls and an argument. Man, he just didn't understand girls. "Look, I don't ask about shit that don't concern me."

"It's gonna concern you when Monster gets your ass locked up."

"I'm not gonna get locked—"

"Gonna have to bail your ass out." She nudged him with an elbow. "You better save some of that scratch if you want out of the clink. God knows I ain't gonna pay for that shit."

Disco put a hand on her bare shoulder, felt her fingers close around his. "I promise you: This thing is no big deal."

"You know what they say about a gangster's promise."

Disco said, "I ain't no—"

"You know what they say about it?"

He sighed and shook his head.

"It's like a prayer: Worth half a shit, and a waste of breath."

"You got a dirty mouth."

She said, "Come down here and let me whisper in your ear."

***

Disco knew most people counted on their apartment building lobby being empty after one in the morning. Silent. But the Hope was anything but that.

Disco watched from just outside the stairwell and bobbed his head to bass coming through the floor. Every few minutes, somebody walked into the lobby, passed him, and entered the stairwell. Mostly people in their twenties and thirties. People up to no good. Like the hooker who walked in, gave Disco a brief look and shrugged—a white girl wearing big ass stilettos and black tights under her white mini skirt. She had long black hair and a purse swinging from her shoulder.

"The elevator working, or what?"

Disco shook his head. "Does it ever work?"

She popped a bubble of pink gum between her lips and said, "You know if it takes you and me up, they're gonna make it so it don't work."

"I heard that."

She clicked toward him and entered the stairwell, cussed under her breath as she started to climb.

Seemed like all the Hope was these days was a joint for hookers and drug dealers. And people like his mom—fiends. Crackheads.

Fucking losers.

Disco looked at the key in his hand, swung his eyes toward the entrance to the Lamplighter. The doors were never locked. He knew that, but the restaurant was off-limits past one or so, depending on when old man Les told people to fuck off and drink in their apartments. All the liquor locked in a steel cage, and the beer fridges locked up too. Through the glass doors, Disco could see the shapes of tables in the dark, the bar beyond them. He did wonder what was in the envelope Monster wanted. Best bet was money or drugs.

But, shit, it could be something else.

What though?

Disco shrugged, though nobody was there to see it. He said to himself, "Man, fuck if I know. I just want that hundred bones."

He started across the lobby, made it to the restaurant entrance, and stopped. He squinted to see better through the glass doors. No movement or lights on inside—old man Les probably upstairs in his room. Watching a taped football game or something. Disco entered the Lamplighter, almost sneezed as the scent of wet dust hit his nose. He shuffled through the tables and came around the bar, started searching for the locked drawer. He found it—a gray cabinet heavily-scratched—and inserted the key. He turned the key, and the drawer slid toward him. Funny, only thing inside was the manila envelope. Kind of thin and flimsy. Disco picked it up and thought it didn't feel like money.

Or drugs.

No—something else.

Paperwork, maybe.

He closed the drawer and turned the key, stood up, and heard Lester's voice from across the restaurant.

"You don't even know what's in that envelope, do you?" He was sitting at a table, less visible than a shadow in the night.

Disco squinted and could almost make out the shape of a man. "You scared me, pops. You like sitting in the dark all night?"

"He paid you for this?"

"He's gonna pay."

"And you don't know what it is you're doing."

"All I need to know," Disco said, "is there's a C-note in it for me."

Lester chuckled, lit a cigarette. The cigarette's orange glow moved from his mouth to the table. He exhaled. "Kind of funny, he's gonna pay you. When all he had to do was come over here and ask."

Disco stood there and breathed.

"Like any man would have done. Come over here and ask."

Disco looked down at the envelope for an instant, searched again for Lester's shape in the darkness. "I'm not trying to get into any—"

"Go on, boy. Take it over to him." The orange glow moved up to Lester's mouth again, back to the table. He coughed. "You take it and tell him I said you could. That you didn't even really need the key. Tell him I just gave it to you. Because you asked."

"He said—"

"Or tell him whatever you want."

Disco sniffed the air and said, "You think he'll still pay me if I tell him what you said?"

Lester didn't answer. He sat there and smoked, the orange glow of his cigarette lifting and falling in the darkness.

***

Monster took the envelope and stared at it as he leaned back into the sofa. He sniffed hard through his nose and turned the envelope over, so he could unsnap the flap.

Disco stood there and watched him, didn't know what to say or how to act. He wanted to sneeze, but somehow held it in.

Monster slid his hand into the envelope and pulled out a white sheet, flipped it over—a picture. A girl in a purple dress and a kid next to her wearing a football jersey that stretched to his knees above bare feet. Disco could read the upside-down number from where he stood—a double zero. And he thought he recognized the background in the picture. Madison Street, right outside the Hope. Well, shit. A C-note for a picture? Damn.

Monster said, "You're still here. What the fuck for?"

"You said I was gonna get a hundy for it."

Monster reached into a pocket on his sweatsuit, came out with a few bills, and handed them to Disco across the coffee table.

Disco counted the money—tens and twenties—and shoved it into his pocket. He stared at Monster, who was gazing at the picture, breathing hard and loud. Disco said, "Who is it?"

"Why you care?"

"I didn't need the key," Disco said. "He would have gave it to you. He told me to tell you that—that the envelope was yours."

Monster didn't look at him, but said, "Get the fuck out of here, D. And whatever you do, don't bring your ass back."

Disco backed away, let himself out of the apartment.

***

"You do what you had to do?" Sharon burrowed into Disco under the blankets, groaned as she pressed against him.

He grunted, ran a finger along the small of her back. He had a key to her apartment and liked to sneak in late, wake up to her staring at him. Tonight, he didn't feel like sleeping—he didn't know what he felt like doing. "Yeah—I got Monster what he wanted."

"What was it?"

He paused and thought about what to tell her. Maybe, the truth?

“Well, what was it, Disco?”

“A picture.”

“A picture?” She was awake now and twisted her head to stare at him in the darkness. “Like, what kind of picture?”

“Some lady. And a kid.”

“Who do you think it was?”

“I don’t know. Maybe his family or something. That’s what it looked like. I feel like, maybe, it was his family.”

“You mean, Monster has a family?”

“I don’t know, Sharon. All it was… was a fucking picture.”

Sharon turned away from him. It didn’t take long for her to sleep. Disco, though, couldn’t sleep. He got out of bed, pulled his shirt and hoodie on—walked down to the Lamplighter.

***

He sat down across from Lester, watched the orange glow of the cigarette brighten at Lester’s lips. It lit his face slightly, those tired old man eyes and saggy cheeks.

Disco said, “You never sleep, or what?”

“I sleep in the morning—how it is when you run a bar for so damn long.” He yawned and cleared his throat. “You give him the envelope?”

“I did.”

“You get your hundred bucks?”

Disco looked at his hands. “I got it.”

“And you tell him what I told you? That the—”

“I told him, Les. He didn’t like to hear it none, either.”

The cigarette glowed, and Lester said, “I heard that.”

“Who was it in the picture?”

"My niece, Layla. Daughter to my sister. And her little boy—Maurice. Her sweet little boy."

Disco licked his lips and said, "What happened to those two?"

Lester exhaled and watched Disco for a minute. He shifted in his chair and cleared his throat again. "Your gangbanger pal killed them two. Slammed his car into a light post down the end of Madison."

"Drunk?"

"Not from what they tell me. An accident, they said. If you believe it. Happens that I do—what I think it was, an accident."

Disco crossed his arms.

"I think Monster killed two people I love, and then he didn't do a damn thing with the life he got to keep. Got into the drugs, stick-ups. Next thing I know, he's walking around here like a pistol's the only thing he's ever known."

"And the picture?"

"Only one we got left of them two. I told him come and get it like a man. I kept it for him. But he didn't never come—it sat in there for nine years, young buck. That's a damn long time. Mailed him the key and said, 'come on and get it.' Wanted him to talk to me, you know? But he never did—all he did was send his thugs in here to collect off me."

"And then he sent me."

"And then he sent you."

Disco said, "Maybe now he's—"

"I doubt it. It ain't about that. The Hope changing over—that just made him do something." Lester dragged from the cigarette and exhaled in Disco's face. "You got anybody, you do them right. Like that momma you got. She ain't right, but that don't mean she bad."

"Yeah… I don't think she's bad," Disco said.

"Most of us ain't," Lester said. "Most of us ain't."

***

He found her at the small table where they ate breakfast together. His mom. His momma. Facedown in a bowl of Fruit Loops. Her skin cold and tough. In her bra and sweatpants.

The apartment smelled like winter.

When the cops got there, he answered all their questions. After, he sat on the ratty couch, started tapping a beat with his fingers, picked up a rhythm part with his tongue. Let it run through him like a current—the beat. Just put his thoughts away in the back of his head. Like closing a drawer. And locking it. The beat became everything to him… A heartbeat.

From behind him, in the hallway, he heard the cops. Voices faint but audible.

"What's wrong with the kid?" A question followed by two hard sniffs and a grunt, the cop bringing the cold and drizzle in with him.

"He's in shock."

"Sounds like he's got a drum set in his throat." The cop cleared his throat again. Tried to take a deep breath, but it caught short with a bark-like cough.

"Yeah—it's a thing they do. Beatboxing, they call it."

"No shit?"

"Like I told you: He's in shock."

"Shock, I know." Two more short coughs before he said, "Right. Man, I hate to say it, but I can't wait for this place to turn into some fancy-ass hotel."

"The Hope?"

“Yeah. The fucking Hope. I want this shit to end.”

“The Hope ended a long time ago, pal. Even the kid knows that.”

Sulfur Rising

Carmen Jaramillo

The hallway had no smell at all.

The Hope building, where I lived, had fumes of musk and old vegetables and what seemed like sixty years' worth of fluids spilled in the carpets. Before that, the Glade was wet trees, soil, and maybe ash if a wildfire wasn't far off. And with my mom, years ago, it was wafts of dried rosemary and acrylic paint.

But Perenelle's brand-new building didn't even smell like Pine-Sol.

She let me into her white and pale gray condo. Her wide living room had almost no furniture aside from a smooth couch and a coffee table. She probably hadn't lived there more than a month.

Perenelle didn't hug me, but she did smile. Her voice sounded natural.

"I'm so glad you're doing okay, Addie Sage."

It rankled me that she used my real name after we'd lived together in the Glade for three years.

"Yeah, thanks… you too, you've got a nice new place, Perenelle."

I knew her real name, but I'd keep using the one Hermes gave her. I wouldn't pretend Splendor Solis never happened.

"Oh, I'm getting used to it." She paced away from me to the window, running a pinky finger along the rim of an empty white ceramic dish on the sill. Her parents probably paid for that, too.

Perenelle wasn't the only rich girl ever in Splendor Solis, but none of the others made it so obvious. She'd let sweat soak her long, fawn-colored hair while scraping turnips out of the dirt with the rest of us—after we'd all moved to the Glade, our compound out in Colville Forest—but we all knew Hermes still bought her twenty-dollar bottles of conditioner.

When I'd first found Splendor Solis, almost four years earlier, I didn't have a bed to sleep in that night.

"How about you?" Perenelle asked. "You're doing okay?"

I held up the binder clip I used for a wallet. "I've got thirty-six dollars here, it's all the money I've got in the world. Doesn't matter that I can't pay rent next month, though. They're evicting my whole building."

My mom had just died when I'd found Splendor Solis. Her family—the ones with all the Bible verses in their Instagram bios—hadn't bothered helping us out when she was alive, so I didn't want their help once she'd gone. I ignored the phone calls from Spokane Public Schools when I stopped showing up. I didn't want to stay in the house we rented, so I'd walked out the front door with just my phone and some packets of string cheese in my jacket pocket. I went to see an older friend, just for something to do. He'd let me tag along to what he'd said was a meeting for his environmentalist group. But at the building on Division, where they rented out space on the third floor, he'd introduced me to Hermes instead.

They ran dozens of pictures of him in the news after it fell apart, but none of them got Hermes' eyes right. They showed a man in his forties with a lopsided smile and gray chemistry teacher hair, but not the way he looked at you as if nothing else in the world interested him. That first night I met him, he didn't make me explain myself or ask me what my plans for the future were. He'd just had me share dinner with everyone and told me to spend the night on one of the office couches, no strings attached.

In front of me, Perenelle did look upset.

"O-oh... the entire building? That's so shitty of them..."

I waited; maybe she really would offer to let me crash in her spotless living room for a couple days.

"Do you know what you'll do?" she asked.

"Nope."

The morning after that first night in the Splendor Solis office, after Hermes had insisted I have breakfast, he'd made me the same offer as everyone else. I could join a cleaning crew, spiffing up houses for new owners or busy parents, and stay on as long as I wanted. No charge. I knew I'd take the deal, but I'd felt embarrassed about accepting in under twenty seconds. Instead, I'd pretended I had other options to weigh it against. I'd waved over at a shelf.

"What's with all the vases?"

Hermes had stepped to the shelf where three glass or ceramic containers sat in a row, all different shapes, all in different conditions. He lifted one that looked like it had been dug out of a shipwreck.

"You mean these flasks?"

"Yeah. I've seen a couple in like every room. Are they antiques or something?"

His eyes had lit up, thrilled to share it all with someone new.

"Do you know what alchemy is?"

"Uh... I guess I've heard the word before."

“People have used the science of alchemy to change the substances of the world for thousands of years.”

He hadn’t overwhelmed me with all his ideas at once. I’d learned about them over time—sometimes from the medieval books he’d translated or the papers he’d written himself—or heard it from other people on cleaning jobs. As the climate apocalypse washed over the world, alchemical transformations could bring the environment back into balance.

Perenelle’s voice lowered and softened. “Have you been able to do much since everything fell apart?”

She moved only a few inches over the floor. Now she was almost close enough to reach out and squeeze my shoulder.

“N-no, not since Hermes killed himself.”

She bit her lower lip and started rubbing her fingers, maybe thinking of hugging me, trying to decide if that would help me or not. I couldn’t tell if it would either since no one had hugged me in over a month.

Perenelle drew some hair away from her face, keeping her arms close to her smooth, gently-curving body. She didn’t need much to look glamorous, not even jewelry. Just a loose white tank top and jean shorts.

I’d never resented Perenelle for being Hermes’ preferred other half, or any of the other girls he paired with now and then since he’d singled me out for being careful and patient even from my first days with him. When Splendor Solis finally moved out to The Glade, where we would prepare the antidotes to environmental ruin, he put me in charge of handling and supervising all the most caustic chemicals. No one touched the lye or acetone without following my rules.

“Has Logan’s family been in touch with you?”

I blinked. "What?"

"I was wondering if any of Logan's family members tried to talk to you or get in contact with you or anything."

In Splendor Solis, Hermes had named him Citrine. Until I'd heard it again on TV, I'd forgotten his real name was Logan.

"Me? Why would they?"

I couldn't remember when it started, but at first, Citrine would gripe just to Mag, Quicksilver, or me about how many people had cleaned houses for no paycheck over the years. Weeks later, he would snap in group meetings that none of us even knew how Hermes spent the few pennies Splendor Solis had. He made his final threat to Hermes—that he'd been talking to his parents and sisters again and that they would help him bring a wage theft case to the state—two days before he died.

"Yeah, I guess there wouldn't really be any reason. Since Hermes killed himself, there's no one left to go after for what happened to Logan."

I knew Citrine's family had moved quick when they couldn't get a hold of him. And once the police started prowling around The Glade, Hermes couldn't take any more.

"Don't you miss Splendor Solis at all?"

She chuckled. "Yeah, I miss sleeping in a ten-year-old sleeping bag on a cement floor an hour from an internet signal."

Her laugh sputtered out when she saw that my face didn't change.

"I'm serious." My throat got tight and hot. "We lived in a forest. We supported each other. We all worked *together*. You don't miss any of that?"

"I don't miss trying to grow shit none of us knew about, I don't miss eating nothing but rice because we didn't have enough food stamps, and I don't miss every time Hermes forced us to sit down and listen to him scream for three hours because somebody forgot a rule he'd made up that morning. Fuck no."

I looked away for a second. Hermes really had worn us out in the last few months. Our potatoes and beets didn't come in the way we'd hoped, and Splendor Solis couldn't pay the taxes on The Glade's land. He'd always had time to listen to Mag or Quicksilver or me before, but by the end days, he'd throw things at us and call us traitors if we even suggested buying tent heaters.

"Addie, he killed Logan. You *know* that. And then he killed himself because the state police were gonna find out, and he couldn't stand going to prison."

"I... I don't get how you can say that. You used to believe in Hermes so much you'd talk the rest of us through doubts."

"He manipulated me! He lied to all of us to keep us in his *cult*!"

I bit my lips hard and stared, fixed, on the floor. If I kept my eyelids wide open, my eyes would re-absorb tears before they pooled.

I didn't want to argue with her. I'd had the argument with myself enough times.

"Look, Addie... what is it you wanted to see to me about?"

Perenelle sounded almost gentle again. Or at least, not annoyed with me.

"I need help. I need to find some way to make a living or start over or whatever... I want to leave Spokane, maybe go to California or Portland. I don't know."

I looked up. Perenelle's face was very still.

"Okay."

"But I need money. I want those gold bars Hermes transformed."

Perenelle's mouth parted. It hung there, open, at me.

"You... *you* cannot honestly believe any of that alchemy shit he made up ever worked."

"Of course, I fucking don't!"

Her neighbors might've heard that cracking childish shriek. I could keep my voice level or keep holding back the tears, but not both.

Perenelle sounded just like an old high school classmate I'd run into on a trip back into Spokane after the move. When he asked me what I was up to, I told him about the work of Splendor Solis. I couldn't tell if the look on his face was more disbelief or horror. I'd felt rattled when he used the word "brainwashed." It kept buzzing in my ears for hours until I'd realized how I felt, and my head had cleared.

"I know he *pretended* to transmute rocks into gold. I know he pulled all those tricks. I know he made every fucking thing up, and anything he didn't invent himself was made up by some medieval asshole! I don't *care*!"

Hermes had believed in me enough to give me responsibilities, and when they saw that, everyone else respected me too. He gave me a name that fit my place in Splendor Solis: Sulfur, the element of putrefaction.

"We all knew, Jesus Christ. That didn't matter." I took a breath. "Look, we all grabbed shit when we left. I did too. I'm not blaming you for taking the gold, even though you don't need the money, of all people."

Perenelle stood very still, her eyes fixed on me. She didn't raise her voice.

"What if I say no?"

"Then I'll go to the cops and Citrine's… *Logan's* family."

Now, finally, I heard a tremor in her voice.

"And… what're you gonna tell them?"

"That it was you who made me fill up a barrel of lye the night he died."

In all those shouting matches at our meetings, Citrine hadn't let any of us forget that, as the only other person allowed to handle Splendor Solis' money, Perenelle had stolen just as much as Hermes.

I hissed louder. "What? You think I *forgot* about that? The police treated Hermes' suicide as a signed fucking confession and never bothered to interview *me* about what happened to Logan's body. That's the only reason you're not already in jail. If I want, I'll go to the police station, I'll find Logan's parents and his sisters and tell them it wasn't Hermes who woke me up at one in the morning and ordered me to putrefy."

On our hikes together in the woods, my mom used to tell me how my name made me a beautiful force of nature. Perenelle knew it that night, dragging me out to the shed, maybe thinking I couldn't see the animal fear on her face in the moonlight. She'd clung to my shirt sleeve, and every vibration from her fingers screamed louder that she couldn't afford to have me refuse.

"So give me those goddamn hunks of gold so I can get the fuck out of here."

Her hands locked around my neck. The force of her elbows on my chest slammed me onto the floor, and my backbone crunched against the wood. One of her knees pinned down my right arm. Her fingers crushed my throat, and the cry I let out turned into a gargle.

"You're not telling anybody *anything*!"

Her lips had shrunk and stretched taut over her gums. I tried to peel her fingers away with my free hand. They clamped harder, her knuckles and wrists like iron until my tongue arched out of my mouth for air. She hissed, and spit from her teeth hit me in the face.

"That family won't want you anywhere near them! Why would they listen to poor trash? And you think you can go to the cops? Cops never listen to homeless pieces of shit like you! I could kill you right now and dump you on the sidewalk, and they won't do a goddamn thing!"

I swatted at her arms. My lungs were bursting trying to scream and breathe, and tears gushed out of my eyes.

"So get out of here, don't ever talk to me or come near me again. Don't ever say a thing about me or Logan again!"

Her fingers unlocked. She jerked her knee off my arm so I could suck down air and cover the sore skin on my neck, roll over and start crawling over the floor. I didn't try to speak. All I wanted to do was drag my legs over her rug and out of her door.

***

I'd stopped crying by the time I'd shuffled through the Hope's lobby to the staircase. I didn't have the energy to sob anymore. My throat still ached, and I just let my arms hang.

My mom had worked to keep me safe until melanoma drained her, but eventually, I still ended up hunting for the warmest part of an underpass to sleep in.

A surge of heat welled up from my raw throat and rushed over my face. My mom could've been an artist if she'd had more time to practice her painting and send work to shows. Instead, she waited tables while she raised me alone. But I had to crawl away from the smoking trash heap of the home I'd made for myself, grateful to still have my life.

I shoved my key into my door handle, rattling it to jiggle the lock. I had to be grateful I lived long enough to come back to a zombie of a building that smelled like greasy hair and dust that hadn't moved in forty years.

"Hi, Addie Sage!"

I spun around. Two doors down, my neighbor stepped into the hallway. I swallowed and kept my face still.

"Oh, hi, Iris…"

I didn't know her well, but we'd chatted three or four times over the past month. She was maybe five years older than me. She'd left a longtime boyfriend who liked to read all her text messages and throw her down their apartment complex's wooden stairs.

"Hey, I'm super sorry to ask this, but uh, my sink has been broken for like two whole days now, and I can't get maintenance to come up here and fix it until maybe tomorrow, they say…" She bit her lip, and I saw a cereal bowl in her hand. "Would it be a problem if I used your sink just really quick? I only wanna wash this one bowl, I'll only be in there like two minutes!"

I couldn't think of a reason to say no.

"Y-yeah, sure. No problem."

"Oh god, thank you *so* much. Not even two minutes, I promise!"

She kept on thanking me as I opened the door, her voice full of relief like I'd just canceled her credit card debt. She hustled past me once we'd stepped in, right for my empty sink. She turned on the faucet and called back toward me.

"How are you holding up? With the eviction and everything?"

I sat down on my folded-up futon.

"O-oh, uh, okay, I guess. I don't know…"

Putting words together felt like a full-body effort. I just sat there clenching my fists. My only stroke of luck was that Iris never seemed to mind doing most of the talking. Whenever she felt a little relaxed, she'd chatter freely, her voice hopping up and down, like a parakeet.

"Oh god, same here. *Same* here. Jesus… like we have to go to work every day just thinking *somehow* we're gonna find a place with a security deposit we can afford, right?"

She didn't notice—or maybe didn't care—that my attention faded in and out. Perenelle hissing "cult" at me still burned in my throat. I'd felt that bitter heat when I'd heard it from my old classmate, and every time I'd heard it on a TV station in a story about Splendor Solis, but not because I disagreed. Perenelle had been right. Along with everyone else, I'd spent most days exhausted, too hot or too cold, with a nagging anxiety burrowed so deep in my brain I could never relax.

And that was the best home the universe bothered to offer me.

"I'm worried I'm barely hanging on at work, too… like my manager and the other baristas are super patient but, I don't know, maybe one day I'll just screw up one too many orders…"

People listened to me in Splendor Solis, but that had been it.

The running water stopped, and I heard Iris clearly.

“Some weeks, I feel like I’ve gotten better at working through the panic attacks without mistakes, then the next day I backslide.”

I blinked. I remembered something she’d told me the last time we’d chatted in the hallway.

“You, um… you said you were looking into a free clinic for PTSD, right? Are you still on a waiting list?”

“Yeah, I am, which is something. I called them again this morning, and I guess I’ve moved up a few spots or whatever, but they say it’ll probably be at least another month before I can see someone. So I’m trying to be patient…”

Her voice trembled, a lot like mine had when I’d seen Perenelle. She shook water drops off her bowl into the sink and stepped away, crossing my room.

“Anyway, sorry, I’ll get out of your hair now! Thanks so much. If you ever need to use my sink—”

She stopped. She stared at the pile of about a dozen posters I’d dumped in the far corner, next to the doorway.

“Oh, *wow*… did you make these?”

She knelt in front of them. Her eyes widened at the drawing on top, a colored-pencil sketch of two red bodies, a man and a woman, and a blackened sun, all looking down on a curving flask full of sulfur over a flame.

“Well, me and some other people, yeah.”

She lifted the corner and peered at the other diagrams, drawings, and prints in the stack of posters I’d taken from Splendor Solis, all copied from medieval books we’d looked up online or from Hermes’ lectures. I couldn’t stand to leave the compound with nothing, but I hadn’t touched any of them since I’d tossed them there on the floor the day I’d moved in.

“It’s incredible! What is all this?”

A minute ago, Iris had thanked me as if it was the first act of mercy anyone had done for her in weeks. Had Hermes seen each of us like this when he first told us his ideas? Did he know how we'd cling to him?

I got up from the futon and knelt next to Iris. I looked her in the eye, curious and a little excited, and she stared back, ready to take in whatever I'd say. I imitated Hermes' face as best I could remember from that first day. The face that made people like Iris give themselves up.

"Hey, Iris... have you ever heard about the power of alchemy?"

Hope Evicted

Colin Conway

"What're those?" Dorothy Givens asked.

Fred Tresko leaned forward and dropped a hand onto a stack of yellow documents sitting at the corner of his desk. "You *know* what these are."

She scooted to the edge of her chair so she could read the header on the top paper. "Thirty-day notices?"

"Don't act surprised. We gotta do this to make sure no Gonzaga snotnose can buy one of these tenants another month. If that happens and the snow falls, we're screwed. We'll have to wait until spring."

Dorothy slid the top document out from under Fred's hand. As she read, she muttered, "I never thought."

Fred fell back into his swivel chair. It groaned and squeaked under his weight. "Are you kidding?"

She glanced up.

He asked, "What did you think we've been doing these past two years?" The question was filled with derisive nonbelief.

Embarrassed, Dorothy turned away and pretended to examine Fred's industry awards on the wall.

"Well?"

She continued to stare at the framed certificates. "You know how things are. I just thought maybe it might not happen. That maybe there might be a reprieve or something."

The swivel chair moaned as Fred leaned forward again. "You mean you *want* the Hope to stay the way it is?"

She might have answered honestly if that question didn't contain more of his derision. Dorothy looked down at the final eviction notice. The legal words blurred together.

Fred Tresko folded his arms and leaned on the edge of his desk. "Because of the housing shortage, the market is hot."

Not looking directly at him, she said, "I know."

"For nearly a decade."

"I know that, too, Fred."

Dorothy hated when he spoke to her in this manner. He ran Sterling Management and was her employer. She'd learned plenty of things from the man in their years together, but there were times when Fred Tresko lectured people as if they were obstinate children and he was a teacher in a one-room schoolhouse.

"Demand for housing is at an all-time high," Fred continued. "Marry that with the city council's delusions to implement socialistic rent controls, and what've you got?"

She knew, but no matter what word she selected, Fred would pick another just to show he was smarter. Therefore, she remained quiet and simply shrugged.

"Urgency." He slapped his hands together, and Dorothy looked up. It was an involuntary reaction, and she regretted it immediately. Fred's eyes narrowed now that they'd contacted hers. "Goddamned *urgency* is what we've got. How did you not know that?"

Another shrug.

"That's why we've had to work so closely with those commie bastards. Give them all sorts of concessions and do an ass-kissing dance any time one of them called. I'll tell you what." He pointed at her. "Whenever one of them found a camera, they'd wring their hands about what we were doing," Fred wrung his hands and made a sorrowful face.

Dorothy looked down again. Maintaining eye contact with Fred only encouraged him to rant. She needed to let it peter out, or she'd be there for an hour.

"But, oh boy, get them behind doors, and it was a different story. They loved how this project would clean up that cesspool. They loved what it would mean to the neighborhood and the city's coffers. Duplicitous bastards."

His voice had softened, and the engine for the anti-council express seemed to be losing steam. Had she continued to feign interest in his tirade, he would have moved onto some other soapbox—perhaps the tax implications of the whole thing. She hated when he talked about taxes.

Fred harrumphed. "Why this town wants to be like Seattle is beyond me. Give these people the power to vote, and what do they do? They vote morons into positions of authority." He grunted as if to signal the end of his diatribe.

She noticed the ticking of the clock on the wall. Fred began tapping in rhythm with the second hand. Dorothy looked up to find him studying her.

"Now," Fred said, "it's time for us to do our job and get that building cleaned out."

"Where are those people going to live?"

Fred shifted his weight, and his chair creaked its displeasure. "Not our problem."

"But that's a hundred and three apartments."

"Only seventy-two. The rest were smart enough to leave when we warned them."

"Well—"

"Our job isn't to play social worker, Dorothy—"

"I know—"

"Our job is to help the property owner make money."

"But—"

"But what?" Fred snapped.

Dorothy stiffened. She didn't know how to respond. She turned away from Fred's reddening face.

"Well?"

She offered, "This seems sudden," and regretted the words as soon as they passed her lips.

"Are you serious? This is in no way sudden. It's thirty-one days until Halloween, and we announced this event more than two years ago. Everybody's been on month-to-month leases for that whole time."

Dorothy's shoulders slumped. She did not look forward to delivering any of these notices.

"Twenty-four months," Fred said and tapped his desk harder. "Twenty-four months we've talked about this, yet seventy-two residents hung around until we have to push them out."

"A number of them were foreign families desperate for a place to live."

"They could have gone elsewhere."

"But the housing shortage. You said."

Fred waved her off. "We posted notices in the lobby. From day one. Over seven hundred days ago. And any time one of them got ripped down, you replaced them. Am I right?"

Dorothy reluctantly nodded. She or one of her staff had replaced the ripped-down notices repeatedly over the last two years.

“And still seventy-two stubborn and, might I add, foolish people decided to make us evict them. They caused this situation. Not us. This is their fault. Well, I’ll tell you what. If they want us to be the bad guy, that’s fine by me. We can do that.”

Dorothy didn’t want to be the bad guy. “I never really believed it would come to this.”

Fred clucked his tongue. “Don’t be naïve. Certified letters went out Friday, so the tenants should be getting them today. *If* they check their mail. That’s why you,” he pointed at her, “need to post these,” he stabbed the stack of yellow notices with the same finger, “on every door.”

“Yeah.”

“There are enough in here for the vacant units, too. I don’t want some mealy-mouthed lawyer saying we didn’t give proper notice to every damn tenant.”

“Even Lester?”

Lester was the owner of the Lamplighter, the bar on the lower level of the Hope.

“Oh, no,” Fred said. “I’ll deliver Lester’s personally. That sumbitch is going to be a pleasure to evict.” He tapped the stack of notices again. “There’re extras to put on the restroom doors, too. Don’t chintz out with where you hang them. Above and beyond. Got it?”

Dorothy nodded.

“Any questions?”

She felt silly asking it, but she did anyway. “Are they tearing it down?”

“Tearing it down?”

Lowering her head, she almost whispered. “For the new hotel.”

“The fuck?”

“Never mind.”

"Tear it down? No one is tearing anything down."

She kept her head lowered but lifted her eyes to him—the way a beat dog begs the forgiveness of its owner. "But some in the building have said—"

"You're listening to junkies and life's other losers? How would they have any idea what's going on? No wonder you thought this day would never come." Fred rolled his eyes. "Jesus, Dorothy, think, will you? Why would anyone tear it down? Construction costs are out the ass. No, they're going to gut the Hope to its bones and then start from the inside out."

"That's what I thought." She *had* thought that, but so many in the building seemed certain that it was getting torn down that she had begun to question what she knew.

Fred continued. "Two years ago, Mrs. Caldwell signed a master lease for the building with a developer out of Portland. I already told you this."

She nodded. He had explained it before, but she dealt daily with short-term apartment leases, not commercial contracts.

"It's a forty-year deal," Fred continued, "with a slew of options on the backend. Good for her, good for her estate, and good for the developer. But she can't turn it over until the building gets an enema. Understand?"

Dorothy winced, but she got his meaning. Her eyes hovered on the notice she still held. She had yet to put it back on the stack.

"You got another question," he said. "I can see it. Go ahead and ask. I don't want you wandering around in that building listening to those ding-dongs."

This question didn't feel silly, but still she whispered. "What about me?"

"Huh?"

Dorothy straightened, pulled her shoulders back, and repeated, "What about me?"

Fred crossed his arms over his belly. "What about *you*?"

"I have an apartment there. And my job."

"You'll be fine."

"What about Anita and Earl?"

"Don't worry about Anita and Earl. They're not your concern."

She looked away. Dorothy cared deeply for Anita and didn't know what the woman planned to do after this. Earl was a cantankerous man who made caring for him hard. She worried about him, but in a Christian way, not the friendship manner she had with Anita.

"You," Fred said, "you're the onsite manager, so you'll be taken care of. Trust me. The developer's gonna need your help, too."

Dorothy cocked her head. "How do you know?"

"What do you mean, how do I know? I know. I've been around these things before. They'll need your help finding where things are. Helping the subs learn their way around. Direct them to turn-offs and electrical panels. That sort of thing."

"That sounds like a better job for Earl, him being the maintenance man and all."

Fred's face pinched. "Earl Ricci is not a people person. Quite frankly, I'm glad we don't have to work with him anymore. After the contractor gets set up and firing on all cylinders, I'll find something permanent for you."

"Do you promise?"

"Oh, yeah." Fred Tresko closed his eyes and nodded. "Definitely. For sure. You're my girl."

***

Dorothy left the Paulsen Center's sixth floor where the Sterling Management offices were located and walked the ten blocks to the Hope Apartments.

It was cool out, but she barely noticed. Her mind was occupied with the conversation she'd just had with Fred. The notices in her hands felt like a bag of bricks—a bag of heavy, smoldering bricks.

At the apartment's entrance, Vernon Brown crouched near the door. When she neared, Vernon blew out a long stream of blue smoke and flicked his cigarette into the street.

"Sorry, Miss Dorothy."

She stopped and considered him. Vernon was in his late-sixties, and his once ebony skin was now an ashy gray. He wore a tattered sweatshirt, khaki pants, and blue running shoes. His yellowed teeth were visible behind a forced smile.

"For what?" Dorothy asked.

"Smokin' in the doorway. I know the rules."

Vernon had lived in the building for more than a decade. Currently unemployed, he filled his recent days by hanging outside the east entrance of the building. Throughout the years, Dorothy had helped the man find temporary work or necessary social services.

Her eyes drifted to the yellow notices in her hands.

"I won't do it again," he said and pulled open the door for Dorothy.

"It no longer matters," she muttered.

Vernon's smile faded as she passed by.

***

Dorothy sat in her office and stared at the stack of notices. She had set them on a chair along the far wall. A knock on the door refocused her attention.

"Yes?"

The door opened, and Earl Ricci stepped in. He was a short, pale man with a protruding beer belly. Underneath a canvas Carhart jacket, he wore a dark brown t-shirt and dirty blue jeans. "Why's the door closed?"

"I wanted some time to myself."

Earl watched her for a second before saying, "I can go."

She shook her head. "What do you need?"

"Nothing. That Vietnamese family on three keeps jamming crap down the sink then complainin' for me to fix it."

Dorothy sighed.

"It's not a race thing," Earl said defensively. "I'm just tired of them doing it, is all. They're fine people even if their food does smell kinda gross."

She lowered her gaze.

"What's wrong, Dottie?"

"They're evicting us."

"Yeah. Okay. That ain't exactly news, now is it?"

"It's finally official." She pointed to the stack of papers in the corner.

He grabbed the top sheet and read it. "What's this happy horseshit?"

"*Earl.*"

"Uh-huh," he said absently as his eyes scanned the page.

"Don't uh-huh me. We still have an example to set."

Earl waved the yellow paper now. "We're officially on the clock is what this is saying. Thirty days. But has anyone talked to us about jobs afterward? No. Not a peep.

You think maybe they already got something lined up for us elsewhere?"

"Don't be naïve," she muttered. Fred's voice echoed in her ears.

"What's that mean?"

She explained to Earl her meeting at the offices of Sterling Management and the lie told there.

"Fred lied?" Earl asked. "Are you sure?"

"As sure as this building is getting evicted."

Earl stared at the yellow notice he held. "But how could you tell?"

She bent over and put her head in her hands. "I just could."

***

Earl took the notices to post so Dorothy could remain in her office. She accomplished little more than moving papers from one pile to another as she waited for the inevitable first person to arrive and complain.

About forty minutes after Earl left, Alma Moore shuffled into the manager's office. Her hands gripped an aluminum walker that rattled and clanged with every step. Alma's gray wig was canted slightly on her head, and her thick glasses were dirty. A crinkled notice stuck out of the pocket of her muumuu.

"Doomsday is upon us." Her voice shook as she spoke. Alma pulled the notice from her pocket. "I got another one in the mail, too. Said the exact same thing."

"I'm sorry."

"Why? You didn't do this."

"Still."

Alma dropped the paper into the wastebasket. "I don't know why they gotta tell me twice. I got the message months ago."

"It's the law, Ms. Moore. It requires both delivery methods. Just to make sure."

The older woman made a dismissive snort before pulling a wrinkled envelope from her pocket.

"What's this?" Dorothy asked.

"Rent," Alma said. "It's the first, ain't it?"

Dorothy opened the envelope. Inside was a money order with no entry made on the payee line. Every month, she received many checks like this and often filled them in for the tenants.

"I thought about not paying," Alma said, "but it didn't seem right. God wouldn't approve."

Dorothy stared at the empty payee line on the money order and fingered the silver cross around her neck. "I doubt everyone will be as understanding as you."

"They won't be," Alma said. "I'm sure of that."

***

Anita Moss, the assistant manager, bounded into the office around ten, an hour before her shift started. She had an eviction notice in hand. "You forget to tell me something?"

Dorothy looked up. "Just got them this morning."

"I stayed up late last night reading a book. Thought I would sleep in this morning. Didn't figure anything this exciting would happen today."

"I didn't know it was going to happen, either."

"Earl woke me up as he was taping notices to all the doors. That is not a quiet man."

“I am sorry, Anita. I should have come told you right away.”

Anita dropped into the chair in front of the desk and reread the yellow notice. “We knew it was gonna happen. Hell, it makes sense it would be today being the first and all. Am I gonna find one in my mailbox, too?”

“Yeah.”

“Figures.”

Dorothy watched her assistant and a woman she thought of as a friend. “I’m embarrassed to say, I thought they might not go through with it.”

Anita’s brow furrowed. “How so?”

“State agencies are always showing up at the last moment. I thought something like that might happen with us.” Dorothy felt like crying.

Anita leaned forward. “Hey, now. You can’t be this way around the residents. They can’t see you sad. You need to be strong. We all gotta be strong.”

Dorothy nodded.

“Pull yourself together, Mother Hen. Do what you do. Make sure everyone is okay.”

A sad smile creased Dorothy’s face.

“Because I sure as hell can’t pull that off.” Anita crumbled her notice into a ball and tossed it into the wastebasket. “No one would believe me.” She headed for the door. “I might be a little late today.”

Dorothy eyed her. Anita appeared ready for work. In fact, Dorothy had been about to ask if she wanted to start early. “Where are you headed?”

“The Lamplighter.”

“For?”

“What do you think?”

Dorothy stared at her. “You can’t drink before work.”

"What is Fred going to do? Fire me? That would be putting me out of my misery. If you want, you should join me."

Dorothy considered grabbing a drink. She didn't usually, but— Her face tightened.

"What?" Anita asked.

"*Lester.*"

Anita rolled her eyes. "He's going to be butt hurt over this."

"Especially since Fred's delivering his notice personally."

"He's *not.*"

Dorothy nodded. "He seemed to take great delight in the idea."

"The ass."

"You go ahead and have a drink with the man. Sweet talk him a little. He fancies you."

"And tell him what exactly?"

"That residents need him to hang around for the month."

"He doesn't want to close, Dorothy. I think he had the expectation he would be allowed to stay."

She sighed. "Sweet talk him, okay? I'll be over in a bit to break the bad news and let him yell at me."

***

Shortly before noon, Dorothy walked out of the Hope's main entrance and rounded the corner of Main Street to the front of the building where the Lamplighter was located. She could have entered through the building's lobby—the backway into the Lamplighter, but she avoided that way as much as possible. That entry felt seedy while the front door felt official. It was the little things that Dorothy held onto now.

Lester Poole had purchased the bar almost twenty-five years ago and made no modifications to the business. The heyday for the Lamplighter had been during the Nixon administration. That's also when it had its last remodel. Low yellow tables with short-backed, black vinyl chairs were scattered about. The gold shag carpet was worn to the concrete in places of high foot traffic.

The jukebox contained only music from the seventies, and the bar still smelled of stale cigarette smoke, although smoking inside an establishment had been outlawed for more than twenty years.

Anita sat at the bar and sipped a clear-colored drink while Lester cooed to her. He was tall and thin, and he wore a pale blue button-up and dark slacks. His eyes drifted to Dorothy after she entered. His smile melted, and he straightened.

"The devil," Lester said.

"Mind your manners," Anita snapped. "She ain't the devil."

"Then she's his agent."

Anita lifted her drink. "Then so am I. You gonna be rude to me, too?"

Lester's smile returned. "No, Nita, never. Not you."

"Then treat Dottie like you would me."

The bartender's gaze drifted back to Dorothy. "You here to deliver more bad news."

She noticed the two yellow eviction notices on his bar. "Seems you've gotten enough for one day."

"Tresko made a special trip down to see little ol' me." Lester reached over and crumbled one of the notices. "All this time, that motherfucker—"

"Lester," Anita whispered.

"—said I'd have a chance to negotiate a new lease whenever the developers took over. I bet they're gonna bring in one of those fancy beer joints—a *gastropub*." Lester air-quoted the last word. "Hipsters and their fucking craft beers."

"*Lester*," Anita said.

"It's okay," Dorothy said, "He's got every right to be mad. But Lester, I've never handled your lease. I only do the apartments."

He sneered. "Well, anytime I talked with the man, he shined me on with some bullshit about how I was his guy, and he was going to take care of me."

Those words sounded familiar to Dorothy.

"Guess I'm out on the street now."

"Everyone else is losing their home," Dorothy said.

"Yeah? Well, I'm losing my business."

Anita shook her empty drink, which caused the ice cubes to clink together. "Dottie and me are losing our jobs *and* our homes, so we win." She cast a sideways glance to Dorothy. "That doesn't sound like a win, though, does it?"

Lester took the tumbler from Anita. "That true, Dottie? You both out of jobs and on the street?"

"That's right."

The bartender grabbed a bottle of Seagram's and filled Anita's glass. He then put a splash of tonic on top and dropped a fresh lime in. "There you go, doll."

Anita took the drink and sipped deeply.

"Maybe you should ease up," Dorothy said.

The assistant manager pulled the glass from her lips. "What're they gonna do?" she muttered.

From the back bar, Lester shook a cigarette free from a pack of Camels. He stuck it in his mouth and lifted a lighter.

Dottie frowned. “You can’t smoke in here.”

Several patrons turned to look at them.

With the Camel tucked tightly between his lips, Lester motioned toward Anita. “Like the woman said, what’re they gonna do?”

“There are rules to be followed.”

“Says who?” Lester asked. He then ignited his lighter and inhaled deeply.

“The law.”

“Let ’em write me a ticket.” Smoke billowed from the bartender’s mouth as he spoke. “What’s the worst that’s gonna happen? They shut down my bar? I’ll be kicked out before it works its way through the system.”

Dorothy looked around, helpless. “You need to pay your rent.”

Lester inhaled from his cigarette again. This time he held the smoke for a while, then exhaled from the corner of his mouth. “I ain’t paying shit.”

“But you have to.”

“Make me.”

Dorothy glanced at Anita then back to Lester. “You have a lease.”

“Which Tresko refused to extend. Let him hire an attorney to kick me out for non-payment. I’ll get out under the wire. Until then, I’m staying rent-free. Makin’ bank for an emergency nest egg.”

Dorothy stared at Lester. “They won’t allow it.”

“We’ll see about that.”

Anita’s eyelids drooped slightly, and she remained silent.

"If I can give you some advice," Lester said. He pointed the two fingers that held his cigarette. "Get while the getting's good. They're only using you while you serve a purpose." Lester sucked on the cigarette before continuing. "And when you no longer serve a purpose, well, that's when they kick you to the curb."

Anita thunked her glass on the bar two times. "Amen."

"The only person you should have loyalty to," Lester continued, "is you." He looked to Anita. "Both of you. Look out for number one as they say."

"We need to go," Dorothy said, reaching for her assistant manager.

Anita pulled her arm away. "I'm taking a sick day."

"A sick day? You never call in sick."

She slowly nodded her head. "I'm not feelin' so well."

"You were fine an hour ago."

"Well, now I'm not. What are they gonna do?"

Lester chuckled. "Yeah. What are they gonna do?"

***

When the day finally ended, Dorothy was yelled at and cursed more times than she could count. Some of the residents had threatened to sue her, the property management company, and the building's owner. A few of them said they weren't going to pay their rent.

But most did.

In the office's lockbox were fourteen money orders and eight hundred dollars in cash.

She wasn't supposed to take the cash, but she had done it repeatedly over the years without telling Fred. The policy was only to accept cashier's checks or money orders. But Dorothy took cash to make it easy on the residents. Even though it was opposed to corporate policy, that had always been her policy—to take care of *her* residents.

Just like Alma Moore, nine of the residents paid with money orders with uncompleted payee lines.

Dorothy separated the money orders into two piles. Those with the payee identified and those without. There was almost $4,100 in a stack without a payee identified. With the cash added, it was just short of $4,900.

She made out a deposit slip for the properly completed money orders and tucked the money into a deposit bag.

Then Dorothy slipped the pile of improperly filled-out money orders and cash into the receipt book and put it into the office safe.

Only she and Anita had the combination.

***

"Only seventeen hundred was deposited yesterday?" Fred Tresko asked. It was clear he was irritated.

"Yes," Dorothy said into the telephone. "I know."

"Today's the second. Usually, we have about seven grand deposited by now."

"People are upset by the eviction. Many have said they aren't going to pay."

"You *make* them pay," Fred angrily said. "What about the Lamplighter? Lester's our biggest tenant, and he always pays on the first."

"He said he wasn't paying."

Dorothy glanced at the safe. There were more money orders in there now that hadn't been filled out. More cash too.

Fred said, "Lester didn't say any of that bullshit when I saw him."

"He was pretty upset about how you treated him."

"Fuck him. Tell him he has to pay."

"I did, and he said no."

"Tell him again." Even through the phone, she heard Fred pounding on his desk. "He owes us rent."

"What am I going to threaten him with?" Dorothy asked. "He's already being evicted."

Except for Fred's heavy breathing, the phone was silent for several seconds.

"I pay you for results," the property manager said. It was clear that he was trying to control his anger. "I don't care how you do it but get that rent. The Lamplighter's, too."

Dorothy thought about Lester's comment about how when she no longer served a purpose to Fred Tresko, she would be on the street. He was closer to the truth than he knew.

"Are you still there?" Fred asked.

"Yeah."

"Why? You should be out collecting the rent."

Fred hung up before Dorothy could respond.

***

"There're a lot of angry people living in this building now," Earl said.

"I'm one of them," Dorothy said.

They were in the manager's office. Dorothy was filling out a deposit slip for a couple of cashier's checks that had the management company's name on them. Earl stood in front of the maintenance request basket and flipped through the slips of paper that had come in since the previous day.

"How long you staying around?" Earl asked.

"Today?"

"No. Here." Earl pointed at the floor. "Are you staying until they fire you?"

"What other choice do I have? I need the paycheck and the apartment. Besides, I need to take care of the people who live here."

He grunted.

"What?"

"We should quit," Earl said. "All of us. Fuck them before they can fuck us."

"Language, please."

"Sorry, but that don't make what I'm saying not true. We need to hit them where it hurts—the pocketbook. It's the only thing rich people understand. Hit them in the wallet, they pay attention. You can't appeal to their... what's it called?"

"Sense of decency?"

"Right. You can't appeal to their decency 'cause they ain't got none."

"How does our quitting hit them in the wallet?"

"They got to hire someone to get these people out. You think those Vietnamese or Haitians—"

"They're Dominicans. We don't have any Haitian families living with us."

He waved his hand. "Dominicans. Haitians. It's all the same."

"No, they're not."

"They're Cubans with worse food."

"*Earl.*"

"What I'm saying is this. None of those foreign families are going to leave willingly. They like it here. Same thing for the junkies. Those sons of bitches are going to hide in every nook and cranny to avoid hitting the street. They know the score. When the bomb goes off the only thing that will survive will be junkies and cockroaches."

"Earl, the pocketbook?"

"Right. Without you, me, and Anita, what would that bastard Tresko do? He'd be up to his ass in alligators trying to get these people out in time. He'd have to spend a ton of money to hire emergency workers. He'd hate to do that."

Dorothy smirked. "He'd just bring someone over from another property. Fred will have contingency plans." She puffed out her cheeks. "Wished I would have thought ahead. I don't have a dime saved."

Earl tossed the maintenance requests back into the request basket. "Well, don't be surprised if I fail to show up one day."

"You got some money saved up, Earl?"

The maintenance man smiled. "Of course, I do. I'm not as stupid as everyone makes me out to be."

***

By the fifth of the month, Dorothy had deposited nearly $6,000 in the bank. Another $4,000 had been sent directly to the property management office by social service agencies helping out tenants. That was only a portion of the rent that should have been collected by now—that *had* been collected.

Dorothy hid almost $18,000 of cash and unmarked money orders behind a refrigerator in a vacant apartment.

She could no longer leave the money in the safe where Anita might see it or in the office where anyone would find it. And she couldn't bear to take the money to her apartment—not yet at least. Doing that was the final act—a line she knew if she crossed, there would be no turning back from.

But if the money remained inside the Hope, but not in her residence, Dorothy convinced herself she really hadn't done anything wrong.

That afternoon she sat before Fred Tresko to account for the lack of rent collection.

"You're twenty-two thousand outstanding," he said. He leaned forward and glared at her. "When are you bringing that in?"

"You don't know what it's like there," Dorothy said. "It's not a happy place."

"It's never *been* a happy place. Do your job. Get the rent."

"Nobody is worried about getting evicted for not paying."

"Play on their sympathies then. Tell them you can lose your job."

Her mouth fell open. "You'd fire me over this?"

Fred closed his eyes. "Of course not." When he opened his eyes, he looked away. "I just said that as an example, you know, so you could say something to get them on your side. They like you."

Dorothy watched him.

"Do this for me," Fred's eyes closed again, "and I'll give you a bonus. The best bonus you've ever seen." When he opened his eyes, he smiled. "Okay?"

Dorothy looked away. "Okay." She wasn't any better at lying than he was.

***

When she returned to the Hope, Dorothy found two of the men who hadn't paid rent standing in a corner of the lobby. They appeared to be in the middle of an argument. One of the men, Joe, gesticulated wildly while he spoke. The other, Tom, crossed his arms and frowned. His head was cocked to the side as Joe prattled on.

She approached them and noticed their combined aroma from several feet away. They smelled as if they hadn't bathed in days. Both men had the quick, jerky spasms that many drug users develop.

Dorothy waited patiently for either man to notice her so she could interrupt their conversation. Neither glanced her way, though and simply continued with their argument.

"I'm telling you," Joe said, insistently tapping his friend in the chest. "Britney is a fucking genius."

Tom reared back in mock horror. "The fuck is wrong with you? Saying shit like that."

"She's a pure pop powerhouse." Joe flicked the side of his mouth and made three popping sounds. "Tell me she's not. I dare you."

"She's not."

Joe threw his hands in the air. "You can't be serious. Who are you gonna say is better than the Holy Spearit?"

Tom's face scrunched. "Uh. I don't know. How about Taylor Sw—"

Joe slapped Tom.

Dorothy jumped at the sudden violence between the two friends. "Out!" she hollered. "You two out. Right now!"

Surprised to see her standing there, both men turned and said in unison, "What'd we do?"

"Out!" she repeated. She pushed and cajoled the men toward the door. They went unwillingly and made protesting noises until they were outside on the east stairs.

"There's no fighting in the Hope," she said.

Tom faced her with clasped hands. "Dorothy, hey now, I'm sorry. Me and Joe were only talking."

Joe laughed. "Until I slapped the living shit out of you."

Tom hit Joe then.

A donnybrook ensued that tumbled down the steps and onto the sidewalk where Vernon Brown had been enjoying a cigarette. The older man jumped out of the way and angrily flicked his cigarette at the two.

Dorothy pushed the door shut. "Stay out!" she hollered through the window.

She was halfway to her office before realizing she forgot to ask the two men about their rent.

***

Other than Joe and Tom, Dorothy tracked down the other non-payers. Some of them told her in the shortest way possible to do something anatomically impossible. But four of them reluctantly handed her the rent they owed. One was in cash, and three were in money orders—two of those did not have a payee identified.

Dorothy returned to her office and opened the safe. She pulled out the receipt book and completed a receipt for the one resident who had properly completed her money order.

Then she hurried up to the third floor. Checking the hallway to make sure no one saw her at the door, she opened the vacant apartment and entered. She locked the door once inside. Behind the unplugged refrigerator, she found the envelope and pulled it out.

She added the cash to it as well as the two money orders. Then she tallied what was there. There was now over twenty thousand—enough for her to grab it and run. But she hesitated. She'd never stolen anything before. Not only was it against her upbringing. It was against the bible. She didn't dare to do it.

Don't be naïve, she thought. Twenty thousand isn't enough.

Dorothy closed the envelope and tucked it behind the refrigerator.

***

When she stepped into the bar, a waft of smoke billowed out. Some of it smelled like marijuana. While legal in the state, it wasn't permitted to smoke it inside a place like the Lamplighter.

Lester Poole stood behind the bar with a lit cigarette dangling from his mouth.

The door swung closed behind Dorothy as she stalked over to the bartender. "Lester."

Several patrons near them "Oohed" at the same time.

The bar owner removed the cigarette from his mouth then knocked its ash into a glass tray on the bar. "Yes?"

"You and these people—"

"*These* people?"

"—cannot smoke in here."

He stuck the cigarette back in his mouth. "Call the Health Department."

"Excuse me?"

"Let them come and take away my lighter. I'll go buy another."

Several of the patrons snickered.

Dorothy glanced around. "Can we…"

"Can we *what*?"

"Talk in private? Maybe someplace less smoky."

He jerked his head toward the front then turned to yell at the woman in the kitchen. "Chandra! Cover the bar."

Lester walked out the door with Dorothy close on his heels. When they were on the sidewalk, Lester leaned his shoulders against the building. "What's so important you gotta interrupt my business?"

"You need to pay your rent."

He jammed his tongue underneath his upper lip.

"I'm serious, Les."

"It's not happening."

"But you have a lease."

"A month-to-month contract isn't a lease; it's as worthless as a handshake."

"You made a deal."

"A deal? With the landlord, you mean? The lord of this land." He pointed at the sidewalk. "Having a lease makes it sound like me and her are partners, but I'm not her partner—am I? I'm her lackey, her servant, her—"

"Don't say it."

Lester scrunched his nose. "Out of respect, I won't, but you know that's what I am in this situation—making her rich by breaking my back. Scraping by while she lives in some big house somewhere on the hill. The rich get richer. Remember last year when those white boys were knocking out those suits, making all that noise about the unfairness of the one percent? Starting to make some sense now, huh?"

Dorothy watched the passing traffic.

"You ever met her?" he asked.

She looked at Lester. "Mrs. Caldwell?"

"Missus Caldwell." Lester spat. "Even her name sounds rich. Arrogant. Missus Caldwell, would you like some tea? I bet there was a plantation in her family history."

"I've never met her."

"Never met her, yet you're doin' all this dirty work in her name. Puttin' all these people out of their homes, puttin' me out of my business. And in the end, you'll be out of a job, and she'll be richer. You and me, we're the same in her eyes."

A city bus roared by. A wave of hot diesel exhaustion followed it and turned Dorothy's stomach.

Lester pushed off the wall. "You ever consider walkin' away? Just tell Fred Tresko to fuck himself?"

Dorothy shook her head.

He dropped his cigarette to the sidewalk and ground it out with the toe of his shoe. "I'd rather quit my job than help an asshole like Tresko oppress others to make a woman like Missus Caldwell richer." He faced her now, nose-to-nose. Dorothy could smell the cigarette on his breath. "Don't ask me for the rent no more. Got it? I'm never paying another dime for this place."

He turned and opened the door to the Lamplighter. Some funky music escaped the bar along with another plume of smoke.

***

"You've had enough time," Fred Tresko said. "It's time we do this."

Dorothy leaned forward. "But—"

"You were right. I didn't listen. There's nothing to threaten them with anymore. They know it, so we've got to act now."

She was at the Paulsen Center in the office of Sterling Management. Fred had called her over that morning. It was the eighth of the month.

He continued. "But I'm going to move toward evictions on the lot who didn't pay. Lester included. We need to get them out now rather than later. Set an example if you will. Because if we don't, no one will believe we'll carry through with the evictions at the end of the month."

"What about attorney's fees?"

"It's a drop in the bucket for Mrs. Caldwell."

"I mean for the tenants. You'll bill them back."

Fred sniggered. "Of course, I'll bill them back. And they should have thought about that before they withheld their rent. Besides, most of these folks will get out before we actually hire an attorney. Right now, we're only threatening. Lester will be the hard case. He'll probably hang around, but that old bastard will be fun to do some damage to. Maybe ruin his credit."

"When are you sending out the notices?"

Fred handed her a stack of three-day pay-or-quit warnings. "Don't worry about it. Just deliver these today."

Dorothy's hands shook, and she struggled to swallow.

"You okay?" he asked.

"Not really."

"Relax, Dorothy. It has to be done." Fred picked up the receiver of his phone. "They did this. Not us. This is on them. It's time to drop the hammer."

She left his office without another word.

***

Dorothy sat in the manager's office, reading one of the three-day notices she was to hand-deliver. It gave a delinquent resident three days to pay their rent or vacate their apartment. It showed exactly how much rent was due and the late fees that were now tacked on.

Late fees, she thought. Now, the resident who was late would be required to pay an additional charge. Her heart sunk.

The notice she held in her hand belonged to Alma Moore. Her money order was part of the collective pot hidden away behind the refrigerator. Now, reality set in for Dorothy.

Even if she refused to deliver these notices, the end was in sight. Fred would send the registered notices today and the non-paying tenants would receive them tomorrow.

As soon as Alma received that notice—not the one in her hand—the older woman would complain to the management office, and Dorothy would get caught.

Just holding onto a resident's rent for longer than twenty-four hours was cause for discipline, perhaps even termination. Even though the money never left the building, never entered Dorothy's apartment, she had stolen it. She was as guilty as if she'd left the property and gone to Tahiti.

Dorothy was so lost in her thoughts that she didn't notice Earl Ricci enter the office.

"What're those?"

"Three-day notices."

"Serious?"

She nodded and put Alma's notice back on top of the stack.

"Fred's evicting folks who aren't payin' 'cause they're already being evicted?" Earl's voice rose while his face reddened. "What a prick. Someone should take that guy down a peg."

"If he doesn't get them out, the rest won't believe he'll do it at the end of the month." The words she parroted were pure Fred.

Earl slapped the wall. "Well, fuck that. And fuck him."

"*Earl.*"

"No, Dottie. I ain't watchin' my language. If there was ever a time for the F-word, it's now. Fuck this job. I don't need to work for a place like this. I got my integrity." He tapped his chest. "I quit."

He spun to leave and bumped into Anita, who had just entered the office. She fell against the wall. Earl reached for her, but she lifted her hands in surrender.

"I'm okay," she said.

Earl's face softened. "I'm real sorry, Anita. It was an accident."

Anita straightened. "What's going on in here?"

He thumbed over his shoulder. "Ask Dottie. I'm outta here." Earl hurried away then. The hammer hanging from his tool belt slapped against his leg.

When he disappeared around the corner, Anita raised her eyebrows in a questioning manner.

"Earl quit," Dorothy said.

"Over what?"

"Three-days."

Anita canted her head. "Pay or quits? This month?"

"Yeah."

Anita's face scrunched. "Who hasn't paid?" She picked up the top notice. "Alma Moore? But I thought she came in already."

Dorothy couldn't look Anita in the eyes.

"This doesn't make any sense." Anita's voice was soft.

"None of it makes sense," Dorothy said.

"You're right." The paper slid from Anita's hand back to the desk. "I'm going for a drink."

"You've been drinking a lot lately."

"*And?*"

Dorothy shrugged.

"Write me up."

"Why would I do that?"

"Yeah. Why would you?"

Dorothy met her eyes then. "Mind if I join you?"

"You want a morning libation?"

"Seems a good day for one. I'll meet you over there."

Anita eyed the notices before leaving. It seemed as if she wanted to say something, but then she left.

With Anita gone, Dorothy leaned back in her chair, turned her head, and stared at the safe. She thought about collecting the money she had hidden and putting it in there.

Maybe she could tuck it into a corner and pretend that she hadn't seen it. But she'd already told Fred that the tenants hadn't paid. Those that she'd kept the money from were about to get notified the main office never received their payments.

Dorothy started this ball rolling, and now she was about to get crushed by it.

***

When she pulled the door to the Lamplighter open, it was dark inside, and some music she vaguely remembered from her youth played softly.

Anita was at the bar with a clear drink in her hand. Lester Poole was at the opposite end serving another customer. Even though it was still the morning, the place already seemed busy.

When Dorothy sat on a stool, Anita said, "So, I've been thinking."

"About?"

"Those notices."

Dorothy faced her.

Anita sipped her drink. "Some of those tenants are gonna be real upset to find they're being evicted early—especially after they already paid."

"But they haven't," Dorothy said.

"If that's gonna be your story, best stick to it, but you better be more convincing than that." Anita shot her a sideways glance. "I talked with Alma. She told me she paid. How many others in that stack will say the same?"

Dorothy did her best to appear calm.

Lester sauntered over. "Drinking with us today?"

"She ain't stayin'," Anita said.

Dorothy remained silent, but Lester asked, "She ain't?"

"Nope."

"She's sittin' like she is."

"Dottie's got to get back to the office," Anita said. "Ain't that right?"

"Yeah," Dorothy said. "Gotta get back."

Anita continued. "She's got things to straighten out."

Lester's eyes narrowed. "Another time then."

"Another time," Anita agreed.

The bartender walked to the far end of the bar.

Dorothy whispered, "Anita, what did I do to you?"

Anita's face hardened. "You act like a mother hen, but when the chips are down, you're about to do worse to these people than the one who's evicting them. You're not their friend."

Dorothy lowered her head.

"Don't sit there looking all remorseful. I didn't do this. Go clean up your mess unless you want me to handle it for you."

Her head snapped up.

"I can call Fred and tell him what I think is going on. That'll solve the problem."

Dorothy slid off her stool and took an awkward step back. She held on to the edge of the bar to steady herself. As bravely as she could, she said, "Don't bother coming in for the rest of the day."

Anita raised her empty drink and shook it. "I wouldn't think of such a thing."

***

Dorothy sat on the vacant apartment floor and counted the cash and unmarked money orders in the envelope. This was what her integrity was worth.

She put the money into her pocket, went back to her office, and called Fred Tresko. She didn't exactly know what she would say to the man when he answered, but she'd tell the truth.

He answered on the third ring, "Fred Tresko."

"It's Dorothy."

"You get those eviction notices out yet?"

The stack of them still sat on her desk.

"About those."

"Don't tell me you're having second thoughts about doing your job."

"No, no, that's not it."

"Because if you need me to come down there and do it for you, I will." She didn't like his tone. "We don't have time to screw around with these people."

"I'm just running behind, is all."

"Then get them out."

She rubbed the cross around her neck. "Yeah, okay."

He hung up on her.

Dorothy picked up the stack of three-day notices and returned to the vacant apartment on the third floor. Carefully, she hid the envelope behind the refrigerator. She put the yellow warnings inside the fridge then locked up the empty unit.

Then she went to her apartment. She was taking a mental health day.

What was Fred going to do? Fire her?

***

Anita's words had rung in Dorothy's head all night, and she finally decided she couldn't live with a lifetime of guilt. In the morning, she checked into the office shortly before seven. There were no new voice mails and no work orders to review. After making sure Earl Ricci had not returned to work, she hurried back to the vacant apartment. She collected the envelope of undeposited rents along with the undelivered notices.

Upon returning to the manager's office, she pulled the rents from the envelope and tossed them haphazardly into the safe. Then she threw the stack of pay-or-quit notices into the trash can.

She dialed Fred's phone and waited for his voicemail. Dorothy wanted to call him before the office opened so there would be no chance for the man to pick up. When the voicemail eventually started, she waited to leave her message.

"Hi, Fred, it's Dorothy. A couple things. First, I found those missing rent payments. They'd fallen behind the safe. Yeah, so, everybody's caught up. Well, almost everybody. A couple of the boys are still behind, but you know how they are. I'll get after them."

She cringed with how she sounded. Her story was stupid and simple, and it made no sense. Her only hope was that Fred would be happy that the money was found.

"When the banks open later," she continued, "I'll process the payments and deposit them. Okay, that's all I wanted to let you know. I'm going to get something to eat now, and I'll be back in a bit. Have a good morning."

She started to hang up the phone when she said, "Oh, yeah, and Earl quit. He was pretty upset about the three-days. So, we don't have a maintenance man around. Not sure how you want me to handle requests until the end of the month. We can talk about that later."

When she finished, she hung up the phone and stared at it.

The mail usually wouldn't arrive until shortly before noon. At that point, residents who had received the three-day notices in the mail would call her to complain, or they would call the main office to find out why their rent payments hadn't been applied to their accounts. Dorothy would need to get the payments to the bank as soon as possible. That way, when the residents called, she would have a reasonable excuse that it was all just a mix-up.

That sounded plausible. Happy with her plan, Dorothy grabbed her purse and left the office. But first, she wanted some breakfast.

The banks weren't open until nine, anyway.

***

The egg and sausage biscuit was hot when she bit into it. She chewed for a moment before sipping her coffee to wash it down. The brown liquid burned her tongue. She clenched her jaw and tightened her lips. She took a long, breath through her nose.

Why had she tried to steal the money? she wondered. She wasn't that type of person. What made her think she could get away with it, let alone live with herself after doing such a thing? Temptation was a powerful thing. She'd been lucky to break free of it before it ruined her life. She'd seen so many lives destroyed by uncontrolled impulses.

Her body began to shake then the tears started. She had never stolen anything in her life, and she was too old to start.

Anita was right. For years, Dorothy acted as a mother to the Hope residents, and now, when push came to shove, she considered stealing from them. What kind of person did such a thing? She was ashamed of herself.

The tears continued for several minutes until she realized several patrons were watching her. A concerned employee walked over.

"Is everything okay, ma'am?"

She nodded. "I'll be fine. Sorry. Bad morning."

The employee, a young woman with kind eyes, touched her shoulder. "Let me know if you need anything."

Dorothy looked down into her coffee as she absently rubbed the cross hanging around her neck.

***

Outside the restaurant, the morning sun shone on Dorothy. She smiled as it warmed her face. In a moment of self-affirmation, she proclaimed, "I'm not a criminal."

"Why'n the hell not?" a man sitting on the sidewalk asked.

Dorothy stared at him, and he extended a hand.

"Got a dollar?"

She gave him the change from her breakfast order.

As she walked back to the Hope, she figured that she needed to apologize to Anita. She owed it to her friend for helping her see that she had been about to make a mistake. When Dorothy rounded the corner on Madison, she stopped.

Two police cars were parked in front of the building. Dorothy picked up her pace.

As she neared the east entrance, Vernon Brown moved away from the door. "Sorry, Dorothy."

"It's okay," she said and dismissively waved at the cigarette in his hand.

But Vernon didn't seem too concerned about smoking near the Hope. Instead, his eyes were on the front door and what might be occurring inside. She hurried up the stairs and yanked open the door. Two officers stood near her office. Dorothy hurried through the lobby toward them.

"Can I help you?" she asked.

The first officer turned to her. He was a young man with a genial demeanor. His blue nametag read *Sutton.* "Ma'am?"

As the officer stepped aside, Dorothy saw Fred Tresko sitting behind her desk with the door to the safe open. The stack of pay-or-quit notices were now on the corner of her desk.

"Come in, Dorothy. We've been waiting for you."

"What's going on?"

"There's been a theft," Fred said.

"A theft?" Dorothy asked. She looked at the first officer and then to the older officer whose nametag read *McCrea.* They both stared back at her. "Of what?"

"Rent money," Fred said.

"But it's all in there." Dorothy pointed at the safe. "Well, except a couple boys, but I figured we'd talk about those."

The property manager leaned over and swung the safe's door fully open. It was empty inside.

Dorothy inhaled. Where had the carelessly thrown money orders and dollar bills gone?

Fred frowned and shook his head. "It's not your fault, Dorothy."

"It's not?"

He looked from her to the officers. "How were you to know that Earl would do something like this?"

"Earl didn't steal the rent money."

"But he quit, right?"

"Well, yes."

"And you said he was pretty angry over the three-day notices."

"We all were."

"I got a message from a resident last night who said she paid her rent a week ago."

Dorothy suddenly felt light-headed. "The mail already came?"

"We mailed the notices two days ago. I waited for you to hand-deliver them, so they'd get them on the same day."

Fred's eyes searched hers and she did her best to stay calm. Her mouth was dry, and she struggled to swallow.

"Alma Moore," Fred said. "Lady left a heckuva message—a real earful. I figured it must have been a mistake. Then I heard your voicemail. That's why I ran down here right away. I saw the receipts inside but no money. I knew you wouldn't have taken the money without the receipts. That's not how you do things. Anita neither. But maybe Earl, right?"

Dorothy glanced to the two officers who watched her closely.

"What about this Anita?" Officer McCrea asked.

"No, she's in the clear," Fred said. "She called me last night, too."

"Anita?" Dorothy croaked.

"She wanted to talk about the rents, too."

Dorothy swayed slightly. "She did?"

Fred nodded. "Did you know she drank during the day? We probably should talk about that. Liability issues and all."

Dorothy nodded. "What did she say?"

"I don't know. She was so messed up, I told her we would talk today."

"Oh," Dorothy said.

"But after I got your message, I figured she was calling to say the same thing you did. That the money was found. You two must have talked."

"Yeah," Dorothy muttered.

Fred glanced toward the safe. "You didn't take the money, did you, Dorothy?"

"I didn't take it," she blurted. Dorothy fought the urge to look back at the policemen. Instead, she stared at Fred. "The money was in the safe. I promise."

"That's what I figured. So, it must be Earl, right?"

Nothing made sense to Dorothy. Earl didn't have the combination to the safe. Only she and Anita had it. So, maybe Anita took the money while Dorothy was at breakfast and left her holding the bag for the theft. That didn't seem like something she would do, especially after the scolding she gave Dorothy at the Lamplighter.

"So, Earl?" Fred prompted. "Am I right about him or what?"

"I don't know," Dorothy mumbled and lowered her head.

What else could she say with the two policemen standing there? Pointing the finger at Anita would be like pointing the finger at herself.

Officer McCrea said, "Has anything been stolen or not?"

Fred eyed Dorothy. "Why don't you fellas give us a couple minutes until we can figure this whole mess out?"

The policeman thumbed toward the lobby. "We'll be out front. Let us know when you come to a decision."

When the officers left, Dorothy turned back to Fred. She didn't want to tell him about her suspicions regarding Anita. She couldn't believe her friend would steal the money, yet only the two of them had the combination. There was no way Earl could have taken the money.

As Dorothy stared into the open safe, her eyes slanted. She cast a sideways glance to Fred. He watched her with mild curiosity.

"You took the money," she said.

"Me?" he said.

She pointed at the safe. "You have the combination, too. You're the one who gave it to us."

Fred closed his eyes. "I didn't take it."

"You're lying."

"How can you say that?"

She swallowed before saying, "You close your eyes when you lie."

Fred folded his arms over his belly. "I do?"

"Ever since I've known you. Yes, you do."

"And you never told me?"

She shook her head.

"It's a good thing we don't play poker, or you could have taken me for a lot of money."

"I should tell the police it was you."

"Where's your proof?"

Dorothy glared at him.

"Besides, it was you who held it back."

"The money never left the property," Dorothy said, "and I put it back."

"Holding the money and not depositing it shows intent of theft. And the fact is the money isn't here now." Fred pointed at the empty safe. "Two plus two. And since you don't know where the money is…" He widened his eyes and lifted his hands. "Oops. Doesn't matter. That still equals four. Do you know what Anita told me?"

Her face flattened.

"That's right. We talked. She was drunk as a skunk and let loose on you. Phew. Boy, was she mad. Called you a crook."

Dorothy held onto the back of a chair. She felt lightheaded.

"Anita said you stole the missing rent payments. I was planning to confront you this morning, but then you left that voicemail. You must have been all torn up inside, so I ran down here to see the money for myself."

"I knew it," Dorothy whispered.

"I called the police, so I think I have a little better alibi than you. However, feel free to grab those officers and let's tell your side of the story. Then we'll talk to all the residents who paid their rent to you. And we'll talk to Anita, who told me about her suspicions. Then we'll ask the cops what they think."

"But you have the money."

"Again, where's your proof?"

Dorothy's lip trembled.

"All you got to do is play it smart, Dorothy, and I'll give you a thousand dollars. We'll blame it on Earl. Or Anita. Hell, make it Lester's fault, for all I care. You pick. But we won't tell the cops. That'll be another one of our secrets."

She cocked her head. "Why are you doing this?"

"What do you mean why? There's twenty grand at stake, plus the thrill of getting away with it. Why were you doing it?"

"Because I was out of a job."

Fred closed his eyes. "I told you I would take care of you." His eyes popped open. "I did it again, didn't I?"

She nodded.

"Son of a bitch."

Dorothy's gaze drifted over several pictures of her, Anita, and Earl that hung on the walls. The three of them were at various functions held by Sterling Management. They were often standing together with big smiles.

She faced Fred now. "And you won't tell the cops?"

He stood. "It's hard to get away with anything if we tell the truth."

"In that case," she said, "I want half."

He nodded several times. When he finally decided on a course of action, he held out his hand, and Dorothy shook it. Fred Tresko never closed his eyes when he said, “You’ve got a deal, Dorothy Givens.”

She smiled and breathed a sigh of relief.

Did You Like the Book?

If you enjoyed this story, we'd deeply appreciate it if you told your friends and family or left a review at where you got the book.

All writers need feedback on their work—not only to help other readers discover them, but so they know they're delivering the goods.

Also, if there was a particular story you enjoyed in this anthology, take some time to learn about the author behind it and perhaps read more of their work. They are listed on the following pages.

About the Authors

Hector Acosta

Hector Acosta is the Edgar and Anthony award nominated writer and author of the wrestling inspired novella *Hardway*. His short fiction has appeared in *Mystery Tribune*, *Shotgun Honey*, *Thuglit* and others. He currently resides in Texas with his wife, dog, and inexplicably, two cats.

Mark Bergin

Mark Bergin retired from the Alexandria, Virginia Police Department as a Lieutenant in 2014 after 28 years and, in the end, two heart attacks. He was twice named Police Officer of the year for drug and robbery investigations. Prior to police service he was a newspaper reporter in suburban Philadelphia, Pennsylvania, and in Northern Virginia where he earned the Virginia Press Association Award for General News Reporting. A graduate of Boston University, he splits his time between Alexandria and Kitty Hawk, North Carolina with his wife, family, and not-so-new dog. His debut mystery novel *Apprehension* was published in 2019 by Quill. Find more at markberginwriter.com.

Joe Clifford

Joe Clifford is the author of several novels, including *The Shadow People*, *Junkie Love*, and the Jay Porter Thriller Series. You can find out more about him at joeclifford.com.

Colin Conway

Colin Conway is the creator of the 509 Crime Stories, the Cozy Up series, and the co-creator of the Charlie-316 series (written with Frank Zafiro). He served in the U.S. Army and later was an officer for the Spokane Police Department. He lives in Eastern Washington with his girlfriend and a codependent Vizsla that rules their world. Follow his journey at colinconway.com.

Paul J. Garth

Paul J. Garth has been published in *Thuglit*, *Tough*, *Needle: A Magazine of Noir*, *Plots with Guns*, *Crime Factory*, *Rock and a Hard Place*, and several other anthologies and web magazines. He lives and writes in Nebraska, where he lives with his family. An editor at *Rock and a Hard Place* and *Shotgun Honey*, he is at work on his first novel, and can be found online by following @pauljgarth.

Carmen Jaramillo

Carmen Jaramillo is a Minnesota-born, half-Panamanian pulp writer. Her stories about people behaving badly have appeared in *Shotgun Honey*, Noir at the Bar, the *Writer Types* podcast, *¡Pa' Que Tu Lo Sepas!: Latinx Fiction for Puerto Rico*, *A Grifter's Song* season three, and other fine venues. She lives in Chicago and is currently working on a novel.

Dana King

Dana King has two Shamus Award nominations from the Private Eye Writers of America for his Nick Forte series. He also writes the Penns River series of police procedurals. His website is danakingauthor.com.

James L'Etoile

James L'Etoile uses his twenty-nine years behind bars as an influence in his novels, short stories, and screenplays. He is a former associate warden in a maximum-security prison, a hostage negotiator, facility captain, and director of California's state parole system. He is a nationally recognized expert witness on prison and jail operations. He has been nominated for the Silver Falchion for Best Procedural Mystery, and The Bill Crider Award for short fiction. His published novels include: *At What Cost*, *Bury the Past*, and *Little River—The Other Side of Paradise*. Look for *Black Label* in the summer of 2021 from Level Best Books. You can find out more at jamesletoile.com.

Gary Phillips

Son of a mechanic and a librarian, Gary Philips has published various novels, comics, novellas, short stories, worked in TV, and edited or co-edited several anthologies including the Anthony-winning *The Obama Inheritance: Fifteen Stories of Conspiracy Noir*. *Violent Spring*, his debut book more than a quarter century ago, was named in 2020 one of the essential crime novels of Los Angeles. His latest effort is the retro pulp adventure *Matthew Henson and the Ice Temple of Harlem*. Get more info at gdphillips.com.

Matt Phillips

Matt Phillips lives in San Diego. His books include *The Rule of Thirds*, *You Must Have a Death Wish*, *Countdown*, *Know Me from Smoke*, *The Bad Kind of Lucky*, *Accidental Outlaws*, *Three Kinds of Fool*, *Redbone*, and *Bad Luck City*. More info at mattphillipswriter.com.

Tom Pitts

Tom Pitts is a Canadian/American author and screenwriter who received his education on the streets of San Francisco. He remains there, working, writing, and trying to survive. He is the author of *Coldwater*, *101*, *American Static*, *Hustle*, and the novellas *Piggyback* and *Knuckleball*. Find more of him at tompittsauthor.com

Travis Richardson

Travis Richardson is originally from Oklahoma and lives in Los Angeles with his wife and daughter. He has been a finalist and nominee for the Macavity, Anthony, and Derringer short story awards. He has two novellas and his short story collection, *Bloodshot and Bruised*, came out in late 2018. He reviewed Anton Chekhov short stories in the public domain at chekhovshorts.com. Find more at tsrichardson.com.

John Shepphird

John Shepphird is a Shamus Award-winning author, two-time Anthony Award-finalist and writer/director of television films.

Mystery Scene Magazine hails his novel *Bottom Feeders* as "A fast-paced, fun read that explores a part of the movie business that often gets overlooked… from 'Action!' to 'Cut' it's a pleasure to read."

His short fiction has appeared in *Alfred Hitchcock Mystery Magazine*, *Coast to Coast Noir From Sea to Shining Sea* and *Down & Out: The Magazine*.

As director, titles include *Jersey Shore Shark Attack*, *Chupacabra Terror*, *I Saw Mommy Kissing Santa Claus* and *Teenage Bonnie and Klepto Clyde*.

Check out johnshepphird.com.

Holly West

Holly West is the author of the *Mistress of Fortune* historical mystery series. Her debut, Mistress of Fortune, was nominated for the Left Coast Crime Rosebud Award for Best First Novel. Her Anthony Award-nominated short fiction has appeared in numerous anthologies, and she's the editor of *Murder-A-Go-Go's*, an Anthony Award-nominated crime fiction anthology inspired by the music of The Go-Go's. Her novella, *The Money Block*, is out now from Down & Out Books. Visit hollywest.com for more information.

Frank Zafiro

Frank Zafiro was a police officer from 1993 to 2013, retiring as a captain. Frank is the author of over thirty novels, most of them crime fiction, that include the River City series, SpoCompton series, and Stefan Kopriva mysteries. He co-authored the Charlie-316 series with Colin Conway, the Ania trilogy with Jim Wilsky, and the Bricks and Cam Job series with Eric Beetner. In addition to writing, Frank hosts the crime fiction podcast *Wrong Place, Write Crime*. He is an avid hockey fan and a tortured guitarist. He currently lives in Redmond, Oregon. You can keep up with him at frankzafiro.com.

Printed in Great Britain
by Amazon

40420093R00179